BATTLE of THE BANDS

BATTLE OF THE BANDS

EDITED BY
LAUREN GIBALDI
AND
ERIC SMITH

CANDLEWICK PRESS

Compilation copyright © 2021 by Lauren Gibaldi and Eric Smith

"Miss Somewhere" copyright © 2021 by Brittany Cavallaro
"Cecilia (You're Breaking My Heart)" copyright © 2021 by Ashley Poston
"Sidelines" copyright © 2021 by Sarah Nicole Smetana
"Battle of the Exes" copyright © 2021 by Sarvenaz Taghavian
"Love Is a Battlefield" copyright © 2021 by Shaun David Hutchinson
"You Found Me" copyright © 2021 by Ashley Woodfolk
"Adventures in Babysitting" copyright © 2021 by Justin Courtney Pierre
"Peanut Butter Sandwiches" copyright © 2021 by Jasmine Warga
"Reckless Love" copyright © 2021 by Jay Coles
"The Ride" copyright © 2021 by Jenn Marie Thorne
"Three Chords" copyright © 2021 by Eric Smith
"Merch to Do About Nothing" copyright © 2021 by Preeti Chhibber
"All These Friends and Lovers" copyright © 2021 by Katie Cotugno
"A Small Light" copyright © 2021 by Jenny Torres Sanchez
"Set the World on Fire" copyright © 2021 by Lauren Gibaldi
"The Sisterhood of Light and Sound" copyright © 2021 by Jeff Zentner

First edition 2021

Library of Congress Catalog Card Number pending
ISBN 978-1-5362-1433-8

21 22 23 24 25 26 LBM 10 9 8 7 6 5 4 3 2 1

Printed in Melrose Park, IL, USA

This book was typeset in Warnock Pro.

Candlewick Press
99 Dover Street
Somerville, Massachusetts 02144

www.candlewick.com

MIX
From responsible sources
FSC® C103098

To Leila and Maya—
sometimes you have to light your own fireworks.
LG

To Glen Tickle,
who came with me to every ska show in college.
I'm so sorry.
ES

CONTENTS

MISS SOMEWHERE

BRITTANY CAVALLARO

Beckett Scibelli didn't believe in omens. But if she did, she would've bailed out of her family's U-Haul in the middle of I-70 and run screaming along the median all the way back to Peoria, Illinois, and let her family go to New Jersey without her.

The first omen was her snare drum disappearing the morning before they moved. She'd almost had a heart attack when she couldn't find it. Then it reappeared—*hey, presto*—in her parents' empty walk-in closet the minute before they locked up the condo for good. "I don't know, Becks," her dad said while the two of them played furniture Jenga, trying to stuff the drum into the overstuffed truck. "Did leprechauns do it? Real industrious mice? Did you maybe do it in your sleep?"

"Don't listen to him," her mom said, hopping down from the cab. She lifted the bill of her Cardinals cap and wiped the sweat from her brow. "You know your father. When he's distracted, he picks things up and just . . . takes them places."

"It's like I give them a little vacation." Her dad waggled his eyebrows. "I whisk them off on mysterious missions, off into the great unknown . . ."

"Billy." Her mom giggled. "Stop it!"

Her mom thought her dad was hilarious, which was good. Someone had to.

It was Beckett's cue to make a gagging sound, so she did, wiggling the snare bag in next to the one that held her floor tom. Their gigantic coffee table wobbled threateningly over her drum kit, and she shot it a look. "Stay," she told it. Then: "Hailey, when you were packing up the basement . . . are you sure you didn't move my snare?"

Her twin was uncharacteristically quiet, staring down their driveway into the condos across the street like she could see straight through them into the fields beyond. "No," Hailey said, and without another word, she got into the minivan. She'd convinced their parents to let them drive it so she and Beckett could say goodbye to Peoria together, on their own terms. Beckett had sort of imagined them rolling down the windows, yelling *BYE, SUNOCO STATION* and *BYE, STEAK 'N SHAKE* and *BYE-BYE, PHS,* like a pair of giddy overgrown toddlers.

But Hailey didn't talk at all that day, just brooded out the windshield behind her scratched-up Clubmasters while Beckett said goodbye in her head.

The second omen was when their family stopped for the night at a Holiday Inn Express in Zanesville, Ohio. "Zany Zanesville," Beckett said, but Hailey didn't even smile. The parking lot was packed, and so they followed the U-Haul to the mall lot across the street. She turned off the engine and just sat there for a long moment, her hands still clutching the steering wheel.

"You okay, Hay?" Beckett asked. She'd been trying to give her space, but this was pretty dramatic, even for her sister.

Hailey swallowed, looked up at the ceiling. "I *hate* Holiday Inn Express," she said, and slammed her way out of the car.

Beckett took their duffel out of the trunk and followed. "Did Danny text you and I just not see it, or—"

Both girls looked reflexively at the U-Haul. Their parents were still in the cab, looking at something together on their mom's phone.

"Do you think I would be this upset if *Danny* had *texted me*?" Hailey hissed.

"I don't know! Maybe! I mean, if Dad saw you? Or if Danny texted and told you he was happy you were leaving? Or if he texted and told you he had, like, tattooed your name across his forehead—"

Hailey's mouth twitched. "That would make me mad?"

"It wouldn't?" Beckett grinned, dropping the duffel between them on the asphalt. The air shimmered in the early-evening heat. "Your name, three-inch Gothic letters, the *y*, like, curling down into his eyeball—"

"I don't know, loverpants. Three-inch letters? That's commitment."

"Can't get mad about that," Beckett said as kindly as she could, because Hailey was cheering up, and because she knew as well as Hailey did that Danny was a major douchebag who probably started hooking up with Jenna Marten the second the Scibellis pulled out of Peoria.

"I'll be okay," Hailey said, picking up their bag. Their parents were clambering down from the truck, finally, laughing like they always were, the two of them in on some really bad private joke. "I just wish I was as okay as you are. You are *so* okay with all of this, leaving the Sleepyheads behind and everything. How are you okay?"

Beckett grabbed Hailey's hand and squeezed it. "We have our own music. We have Miss Somewhere. We're gonna be okay."

And then they turned toward the road, and there it was, omen number two, with a LEASE SPACE AVAILABLE sign on the door: a faded old husk of a Guitar Center. She could see the shadows where the lettering used to be.

That would've been bad enough, but Hailey dropped her hand and ran toward the door.

"Hay, what are you—?"

She tugged on the handle. "Locked," she said. "Too bad. I would've grabbed it for you."

Just inside the glass, on the other side of the door, a hi-hat cymbal lolled like the head of a horror-movie clown.

"*Shit.*" On instinct, Beckett made the sign of the cross.

"Kiddos, you coming?" their dad yelled from the crosswalk.

"Okay, Mother Teresa," Hailey said, a little spooked. "Let's go get you some minibar M&M's so you can chill the hell out."

Omen number three bided its time. It waited through the rest of their drive to New Jersey until they unpacked most of their boxes into the echoing, giant house their mom got with her new marketing job in Manhattan. Her commute into the city was about an hour, and so that first Monday, their dad dropped her off at the train station, then swung over to deposit Hailey and Beckett at Raritan River High School. It was huge.

"All of Peoria could fit inside there," Beckett said, staring up at it through the window, "and there would probably be room for Springfield, too." Hailey just grinned.

"Call me if you need me," their dad called, too loud, as Beckett snatched her backpack out of the back seat. Kids turned to look. Someone snickered, because of course they did.

At the front office, Beckett and Hailey got their schedules and compared them as they pushed their way through the hall. It was actual pushing: the hallway was wall to wall with people and their bags and their elbows, nothing like PHS back home. Beckett sidestepped a bunch of emo kids and almost brained herself on an open locker door.

"Jesus H. Christ," she said. They pulled up by the locker deck they'd been assigned, and Beckett began twirling her combination lock with shaking fingers. "This is monstrous. I knew it was going to be bad coming in on the third week, but I didn't know how bad. This is *nothing* like PHS—"

Hailey was only half listening. The whole of the Raritan River soccer team was streaming by, chanting what sounded like "GO, KEG, GO."

"That can't be right," Beckett said. "'Keg'?"

"I think they were saying 'Ken,' loverpants."

"Are you sure? What if the school mascot's a keg? What kind of school *is* this, anyway?"

"Beck, what happened to okay? I thought you were okay."

"I left my okay in Zanesville, Ohio," Beckett said, "at the Guitar Center Haunted House." And when she finally yanked her locker open, omen number three came pouring out.

Some idiot had left a Taco Bell bag in the locker over the summer and the bottom of the bag had rotted out because there was a *burrito* in there.

Well. It used to be a burrito. Now it was the rancid, runny memory of a burrito, its rancid, runny juices looking like black mold, running out of the locker.

All over her Zildjian T-shirt.

Beckett yelled something foul, dropped her backpack, and began to yank the shirt off over her head.

5

"Beck"—Hailey sounded like she was laughing (God, if she was *laughing*)—"you can't just strip in the middle of the hallway!"

"Burrito!" Beckett said, trying not to puke. "*Burrito*, Hay!"

"You can't be naked on the first day of school!"

"I am wearing"—*tug*—"a tank top"—*tug*—"underneath!"

But the collar of the shirt was caught around her chin, and she was gagging on the smell of the burrito mung through the cloth. She'd been wearing a bunch of chokers, and her dark hair in two long braids, and her favorite cut-up jeans, and a pair of amazing knock-off Chloé studded boots, and her Zildjian shirt, because she was a drummer, because it was her first day at this awful school and she wanted to look like who she was.

And now the shirt was stuck on her chokers and she was, well, choking.

"*Hailey*," she howled just as the bell rang.

The hall went silent.

When Beckett finally got the shirt up over her head, Hailey was gone. Beckett threw her T-shirt in the trash.

Beckett was not okay through first period physics, which she didn't have with Hailey, or through second period AP English lit, which she did. Hailey tried to grab her before class to apologize. "I'm so sorry. I knew you would be fine and I didn't want to be late and I freaked!"

"You," Beckett said, "laughed at me."

"Well." Hailey had the good sense to look embarrassed. "It was pretty much the worst thing I'd ever seen. You still smell like burrito mung."

"Dammit, Hay—"

"Ladies," the teacher said from inside the classroom. He was frowning down at his iPad. "My attendance roster tells me I have two new Scibellis in this class. Are you my new Scibellis?"

"We are your Scibellis," Hailey said.

"Take us to your leader," Beckett said.

No one laughed. No one even looked at them; they were too busy whispering and looking at one another's phones. With a sigh, the teacher marked something on his iPad. "Take a seat," he said. "You're lucky you've only missed two weeks—we're still talking about *Jane Eyre*. And in the future, Miss . . . Tank Top Scibelli, our dress code doesn't allow for spaghetti straps. I'll let it pass since you're new, but next time, you're headed full speed to the office."

Beckett nodded jerkily and sat down in the closest open seat before he could lecture her any more. Hailey tried to make eye contact, but Beckett took out two pencils and her laptop and forced herself to breathe. She wasn't good at confrontation. She wasn't good at being *bad* at things, or talking to lots of people, or anything this first day was throwing at her.

Back home, Hailey had had four zillion friends, a straight-B average, and a job at the Triple Dip scooping ice cream.

Beckett had had Hailey.

Okay, yes, Beckett had been the drummer for the Sleepyheads, who'd been getting gigs at U of I bars an hour and a half away, but her bandmates were all in college. They had been getting tired of the third degree from the promoter about their Kid Wonder Drummer every time they booked a show, and now that she was finally eighteen and a senior and less of a liability, she'd left the state. It was all moot. Beckett had good grades, even in her honors classes, because, though she wasn't a genius, she knew how to study; she had a lot of patience for practicing, period, so she was really good at the drums. On the weekends, she

7

played a lot of video games with good stories and read thrillers on the sofa. It was a small life, well curated. It didn't need to have a lot in it if the things in it were beautiful.

Because what she *had* was Hailey, and in the fairy-lighted wonderland of their Illinois basement, they had had two guitars and a synth and a drum set. They had had Miss Somewhere.

But as the year went on, Beckett had Hailey less and less.

By the end of the first week, Hailey had joined drama club. By the end of the *third* week, Hailey had quit drama club to start doing sound and production design for the musicals and concerts and performances at RRHS. But she was still friends with all the actors, and then with the band kids, and then with the *orchestra* kids, and soon Beckett sort of didn't know where Hailey had met the girl whose toenails she was painting in the living room. "This is Katrina," Hailey said, dipping her brush back into Beckett's bottle of Essie Ballet Slippers. From the tutus and tiaras and green face makeup on the coffee table, it looked like they were doing prep for Halloween. The next day at school was costume day.

"Hi, Katrina," Beckett said. She scratched her temple with a drumstick; she was on her way down to the basement. "Hailey, not to suck, but I thought we were going to . . . practice tonight? I almost have the chorus worked out for that song I told you about."

"Shit," Hailey said, and looked at Katrina like she was waiting for permission to go. Katrina looked down at her toes. They were half painted.

"Never mind," Beckett said as breezily as she could, and breezed on, breezily, down the basement stairs.

"You can always work on your costume with us!" Hailey yelled after her.

"I'm not going to be an undead ballerina!" Beckett yelled back.

"How did you know we were going to be undead ballerinas?"

"You were an undead ballerina last year!"

"So were you!"

"That's my whole point!" Beckett yelled, and stormed back up to the living room. She made accidental, awkward eye contact with Katrina, who was playing with her bright red hair and trying to look invisible. Then she made awkward eye contact with Hailey, who grimaced, and then she looked at the hardwood floor. It was so much nicer than the carpet in their old house. Beckett hated it.

"We were going to be the twins from *The Shining* this year," she said to her feet. "We decided in May. That's all." And when Hailey didn't say anything else, she went back down to the basement and began pounding out a Rush drum solo, double time, until her palms ached. She'd hung all the twinkle lights, set up Hailey's synth. She'd even found the old My Bloody Valentine and Jesus and Mary Chain posters and taped them to the wall behind Hailey's mic stand.

But Hailey didn't come down to apologize.

Beckett broke a stick and, panting, made a decision. She'd play a game: How long would it take before Hailey noticed she was mad? It was easier to play that game, to play it *hard*, than to deal with the fact that Hailey's life now had nothing to do with her.

Beckett got a job serving breakfast in the cafeteria for the zero-hour students, and so she biked the twenty minutes to school while it was still warm. After school a few days a week, she biked to work at a Chipotle in the strip mall a few blocks from their house. By the time it started snowing in December, she'd put together enough money, when she added in what she'd saved from her last job in Peoria, to buy herself a junky 2003 VW Bug. Sure, it broke down all the time, and yeah, the passenger side window was always rolling down in a thunderstorm, so when she wasn't working or studying or practicing the drums, she was watching YouTube videos about car wiring. Her life. It was scintillating.

"Beckett 'Scintillating' Scibelli," she muttered to herself in the freezing garage, popping the hood of Barry the Bug. Again.

"Sure you're not going to scramble your brains, kid?" her dad asked, poking his head out from the kitchen. Beckett could smell her dad's snickerdoodle cookies cooling on the counter. It was Christmas break. Beckett had pretty much stopped talking to her twin altogether. Not that Hailey had really noticed.

"I don't love you playing with the car so much," he went on, shutting the door behind him. "If you need help, we can throw in some cash for you to take it to the mechanic. That's something we can afford to do now, you know. It's good that we're here in Jersey."

Beckett shrugged. As she leaned over the engine, she stuck her flashlight between her teeth so she didn't have to answer any more questions.

Her dad walked over and gently removed it. "I can hold that," he said before she could protest.

"Thanks," Beckett said, and then just sort of stood there, holding a pair of pliers, looking at nothing, because she knew if she looked at her dad at all she was going to start crying.

"You should talk to Hailey," her dad said after a minute. "I can tell you miss her."

"I'm just really busy," she said, "with work and school and everything."

It was the excuse she'd been building so carefully for the last few months. It sounded like hot garbage out loud.

Her dad heard it, too. He rested a hand on her shoulder. "Hey. Hey, kid, look at me."

Beckett did. Immediately she started crying. "Dammit," she said. He hugged her until her sniffling stopped.

After she washed her hands and her face and bolted three snickerdoodles standing over the sink, Beckett brought a stack of them and a mug of cocoa up to Hailey's bedroom.

"Hay?" she said, half knocking with her shoe.

The door swung open. Her twin had her phone pressed to her ear, and it sort of looked like she was crying. *What?* Hailey mouthed.

Are you actually talking on the phone? Beckett mouthed back, but it was too much to get across silently, so she whispered it.

"Yes," Hailey said, and "No, sorry," into the phone, and before Beckett could say anything else, she grabbed two of the snickerdoodles, lightning fast, and snapped the door shut. Beckett could hear her say, "No, just Beck . . . No, I don't know. Still bad. No, she just . . . doesn't have time for me anymore. And she doesn't seem to think that's a problem."

In the hallway, Beckett looked down at her sock feet. *You abandoned me first,* she thought.

"No. No, I won't. She can apologize to *me*." Hailey's voice faded in and out; she was pacing. "But whatever. Let's talk about something else. I can run sound this weekend if you need me to."

Beckett drank the cocoa in her room, and then screamed, very satisfyingly, into her pillow. And that was that, until February.

She knew it was the saddest senior year of all time. She knew, too, that she was mourning for a whole bunch of things she didn't want to look at too closely. No one from the Sleepyheads, Audrey or Yiyun or Blake, had texted her in months—okay, maybe she hadn't texted them, either, but *still*—and when she asked Gabe, the guy next to her in AP Euro, to pass a pen, he blinked at her like she'd stepped through a rip

11

in space-time, like she was a ghost. When she found herself looking forward to playing euchre with her mom that Friday night, maybe going all out and getting *two* kinds of Doritos, she knew that she needed a self-intervention.

She drove Barry the Bug to Brunswick Square, marched directly into Hot Topic, and bought herself a new Zildjian T-shirt. (On the way out, she got cinnamon pretzel bites.) The next day, she wore it to school.

It was like the key that unlocked everything.

Two dudes she'd never seen before gave her fist bumps in the cafeteria and asked what kind of kit she had. Her AP English lit teacher, Mr. Zagajewski, almost made up for dress-code-shaming her on the first day by saying, "Good morning, Miss Van Halen." And in AP Euro, Gabe kept looking at her sidelong while Mrs. Rasmussen lectured about the revolutions in France in 1848.

Finally, Gabe leaned over and said, "Why'd your parents name you Beckett?"

"Mother's maiden name," she whispered back. "Why'd your parents name you Gabe?" He opened his mouth, and she said, because she couldn't help teasing him, "No. Stop. Because they thought you were an angel?"

He snorted. "It's my uncle's name. He's great, actually. He taught me to play bass."

Mrs. Rasmussen stopped writing on the whiteboard. "Mr. Gould and Miss Scibelli, do you two have a question for the whole class?"

"No," they chorused, and when the bell rang ten minutes later, Gabe trotted to catch up with Beckett at the door.

"You play drums," he said, like it was a revelation. His eyes were very, very blue.

Beckett wished, fervently, that she had brushed her hair that morning. "I do," she said. Something possessed her to add, "I'm really good."

They stopped in the hall, just outside the cafeteria doors, and he looked her full in the face and said, "I bet you are," like they were in an actual, honest-to-God movie. "Do you wanna eat with me and my band? We're talking about what we're going to play for Battle of the Bands this year."

Beckett raised her eyebrows. "Your school has a battle of the bands?"

"It's your school, too. Where have you been," he laughed, "under a rock?"

And she had to admit that yeah, she kind of had been.

Shifter Focus were all really nice, even if Micah blinked at her and said, "Don't you work at Chipotle?"

"I do," she said.

"Rock on," Micah said, and Beckett gave her a weak thumbs-up, like her nights refilling the cilantro rice were punk or something. "Do you like the Police?"

"Oh man." Beckett sighed. "Stewart Copeland. I love Stewart Copeland."

Gabe grinned a little, draping his arm over the back of her chair. "I really like that vibe. Kind of like mathematical reggae? But punk? I mean, to be clear, we're talking about the Police before Sting went all patchouli."

"Are we also talking about your band?"

"Yeah," Gabe said. "It's what Shifter Focus wants to be. And like . . . it could be your band, too, if you wanted." Brenner and Micah nodded along like a pair of bobbleheads with dip-dyed hair. It was actually pretty adorable. Beckett found herself unaccountably blushing. *Why,*

Prince Charming, she thought semi-hysterically, *are you asking me to the ball?*

"I'm in," she said, and Brenner hooted, too loud, and Gabe said, "See, what did I tell you? I found a drummer!"

Beckett felt her megawatt smile dim a bit. It was a truism, she knew, that drummers were the spotted leopards of the band world. An endangered species. (Which made guitarists and bassists like . . . seagulls, maybe, or squirrels.) Drums were expensive, and loud, and the Scibellis were the only family Beckett knew growing up who had encouraged their kid to learn. Her mom had been a drummer in college, after all.

And her dad had played guitar. That's how they'd met. And how Hailey had ended up with her Fender Jazzmaster. She and Beckett started writing songs together the summer they were twelve, noodling around late one night after watching *Stop Making Sense* with their dad. Beckett had had other projects over the years, the Sleepyheads the most serious of them by far, but she'd always thought—

Well, she'd always thought of Miss Somewhere as her band.

And now she had another one. By the end of the week, word had spread, and suddenly she had two. Rock Your Mouth's drummer had graduated the year before and they were desperate. "We're emo," Theo told her, jogging to keep up with her as she power-walked to physics, "but, like, Jimmy Eat World emo, not screamo, though I sort of want to go in that direction—"

Beckett needed another commitment like a hole in the head, but at the next bank of lockers she could see her twin sister staring at her, white-faced, like it was such a surprise to see Beckett talking to *anyone* that she might lie down and die right there. "I'm in," Beckett said, too loud. "When's practice?"

Practice was Tuesday and Sunday mornings. For Rock Your Mouth, at least. She went to Gabe's sister's apartment to practice for Shifter Focus on Wednesdays after school—they were less serious but actually more technically proficient; the math reggae of it all wasn't a lie—and then she started playing with the Marcia, Marcia, Marcias on Fridays when Sindy approached her in March, literal hat in hand. She quit Chipotle but kept her breakfast shifts, got her acceptance letter from Emerson College, and hung a pennant above her bed. When she wasn't in practice, she was out at all-ages shows with Gabe, who *still* hadn't kissed her, even though they talked for hours in her tiny Bug in his driveway when she went to drop him off, and sometimes she went to Denny's with Sophia, the keyboardist from Breakfast of Champions, and they peeled apart straw wrappers and ate baskets of fries and Beckett talked about Gabe and Rock Your Mouth and how she never saw her mom anymore and everything else in the world but Hailey, like it was a hole in her heart that she had plugged with her smallest finger, like if she made one wrong move she might bleed out right there on the cracked plastic of the corner booth in New Brunswick, New Jersey, miles and miles away from home.

But she had friends, she reminded herself. She had a *life*, in a way she never did before. So what if her twin sister spent dinnertime at their house texting under the table and avoiding all eye contact?

One night in late April, after Beckett had tried, tentatively, to ask Hailey if she could help with her English presentation only to be met with a wall of silence, Beckett took herself down to the basement to pound out her frustration on her kit. It was all there—the fairy lights, the Mazzy Star poster from her dad's old dorm room, Hailey's guitar on its stand. Beckett stood for a moment, chewing a little on one of her sticks, and then she grabbed her laptop out of her backpack and plugged it into the speakers and from the depths of her hard drive pulled up

"I Love This One," the first song she and Hailey had ever recorded. The gauzy wail of the guitar, the brushes on the snare, Hailey's vocals way down in the mix. Beckett turned it up louder, and louder, until she knew the song was filling the house, twisting up through the vents, to where her sister was lying in bed, pillow clutched to her chest, staring at the stick-on stars on her ceiling. She thought maybe she wanted the song to make Hailey cry, and then she thought, *No, I don't want that, I want the song to tuck her in, I want it to sing her to sleep*, and then Beckett was sniffling into the back of her hand and she pushed her laptop shut and stared down at her shoes until she was sure Hailey had fallen asleep.

How did she know? They were twins.

Some things you just knew.

Did she imagine it, the next night, Hailey's footsteps outside her bedroom door, middle of the night, that she maybe whispered "I'm sorry" and "How did we get here?" Beckett didn't think so.

When Sophia broke up with their drummer in May, Beckett knew it was just a matter of time before Breakfast of Champions asked her to play with them for Battle of the Bands, and when she did, she said yes. Why not? Well, Hailey *was* working sound (with her new best friends, but still), and every band Beckett said yes to meant another forced conversation with her sister about levels and mics, and it would be awkward and awful and—

And it would be another chance to make things right.

On the night of Battle of the Bands, as she loaded her drums into the minivan, Beckett could see her dad watching from the window, his ball cap hiding his face. He'd be in the audience later to watch the show.

She shut the trunk and then stood there, shifting her weight, worrying her lip, before she sprinted back into the house. Sound check was in twenty minutes. Hailey was already at school; she'd taken Barry the Bug without asking. Beckett found she didn't really mind.

"Forget something?" her dad called as Beckett ran past him into the basement, and when she came back up with her sister's guitar case strapped to her back, he grinned, opening the front door for her with a flourish. "That's my Becks."

"Bye," she said, kissing his cheek. "Wish me luck." And she wasn't sure (okay, she was pretty sure) that as she backed the minivan out of the driveway, she heard her dad holler, "Go get your girl!"

Beckett tugged at the collar of her Zildjian shirt as she drove. Six green lights in a row. It was a good sign.

CECILIA
(YOU'RE BREAKING MY HEART)

ASHLEY POSTON

Cecilia Montgomery was born from rock and roll.

Okay, that's not *exactly* true, but it sounds way better than "She came from the loins of two best friends who were madly in love with each other, one a rock star, the other the owner of a recording studio, and because of this she has been cursed with greatness." Cecilia should be in love with rock and roll. After all, her mom signed and recorded some of the coolest bands of her generation, and her father *played* with them. She has it in her veins. The pulse of the speakers, the squeal of guitar licks, the salty-sweet lyrics are in her blood.

But the sad and honest truth is—

She fucking *hates* rock and roll. She hates most music, actually. She hates how loud it is, so loud she often comes home from her dad's concerts with migraines. She hates the crowds. She hates how everything smells like beer and sweat, even when there isn't any beer in the venue. She hates the years she spent hunkered back in the corner of her mom's recording studio, asking about algebra problems between one track and the next. She hates the tabloid gossip about rock stars. She hates the radio DJs chattering about the latest scoop.

She hates all of it.

So why did she say yes to going to a battle of the bands tonight with Roxy Williams? She can't even begin to understand it. The winner gets studio time with her mom's studio and a record produced by the lead singer of the New Romantics (a.k.a. her dad), so it's definitely the place she wants to go the *least*.

"Do you think I should wear the black top or the green one?" she asks her little sister, Cherie, as she switches between the two in the mirror. They're two years apart, but they couldn't be more different. Cherie is outgoing, stylish, *popular* even. Cecilia is . . . well. She likes NPR and podcasts about the eldritch gods of Appalachia.

"Like it matters," Cherie replies, and then she looks up from reading *IndieTrash* on her phone. "Unless it's a . . . *date*? Is it a date?" She abandons her magazine and sits up on Cecilia's bed. "*Please* say it's a date!"

Cecilia bristles but doesn't say anything.

Her sister rolls her eyes and flops back down onto the bed. "You're hopeless."

Maybe, but that isn't anything new. What Cherie doesn't understand is that being friends with Roxy feels like teetering on the edge of a cliff. Every day she keeps worrying that it'll be the day Roxy realizes that being friends with her isn't worth the hassle.

Though somehow Roxy never does, and Cecilia can't fathom life without her now. She tries to imagine it sometimes, but her heart hurts every time she does because there's just a hole there where Roxy should be.

She tries not to think about it, and she tries not to get angry when people say they're *just* friends. Like it's dismissive. Something that doesn't mean anything, something that can be traded or borrowed or lost and never missed. But Cecilia knows that if she ever lost Roxy, she would feel it so deep in her bones she would be completely and utterly destroyed. Maybe forever.

"Wear something cool, at least," Cherie says as she pushes herself off of Cecilia's bed. "I'm going out with David tonight. If you see me at the Battle, *don't* say hi."

"I won't know you at all," Cecilia promises, because unlike her, Cherie *is* made for rock and roll. She has the whole aesthetic down—the ripped jeans, the long dark hair, the thick black eyeliner, and the walk that could command an entire venue to fall to its knees. As she leaves, their dad approaches from the stairs and scrubs Cherie's head as she passes. She glares as she retreats into her room and closes the door.

Their dad leans against the doorway, arms folded over his chest. His brownish-red hair is run through with gray, as is his beard, and Cecilia tragically inherited that not-red-but-not-brown hair, almost curly, as if a hairstylist had gotten lazy halfway through styling it. He nods his head back toward Cherie. "What was *that* about?"

"Sisterly love," Cecilia replies, and holds up the two shirts. "Black or green?"

"Green."

She wrinkles her nose.

"Or . . . black?"

She turns the two shirts so she can look at them again. She doesn't like that answer, either.

Her dad sighs and comes into her room and puts a hand on her shoulder. She comes up to his chest, barely, because apparently the fates wanted to add insult to injury and make her his polar opposite—a short and boring daughter who doesn't bleed rock and roll. "You'll look great in whatever you choose. Roxy coming to pick you up?"

"Like always."

"Is this a . . . ?"

"A what?" She prickles when he waggles his eyebrows. "A *date*? No—God, no, we're *just friends*—"

Her father holds his hands up in defeat. "Okay, okay, sorry! *Just friends.*"

She looks away, a little embarrassed. How come it sounds different when other people say it? *Just friends,* like it's a barrier and not a blanket? Because being Roxy's friend is amazing. Because Roxy is cool and funny and smart. Being Roxy's friend should be all she should want.

Because Roxy could never possibly feel the same way about her.

Not ever.

"It's okay, Dad. She'll be here in a little bit."

"Fun—she staying the night again?"

"I think so."

Roxy usually stays over on the weekends. They watch silly anime abridged series, and by the time they're tired enough for Roxy to go home, it's already one in the morning and Roxy lives across town. It's only common sense that she stays the night. Roxy borrows some of Cecilia's pajamas, and they curl up in bed, but neither of them falls asleep until the sun begins to rise because they're whispering under the covers, secret jokes and school gossip.

Because that's what friends do.

She casually forgets that sometimes she wakes up with Roxy's face burrowed into her hair.

"All right, well, your mom told me to come up here and remind you that curfew is still midnight, and if you're going to be any later—"

"Call you, I know."

He nods, and he can't keep himself from smiling. "I'm so excited you're going, you know? I remember my first battle of the bands like it was yesterday. First time I ever smoked a joint, or whatever you kids call it these days. Puffing the dragon? Toking the weed? Inhaling the h—"

"*Stooooop,*" Cecilia begs of him, and he laughs at her pain.

"Fine, fine. What band are you going to see?"

"Erm, just a band."

"Well, obviously. Which band?"

She winces as she says, "Rock Your Mouth."

His eyebrows jump up in surprise. "*. . . Huh.* That sure is a name."

"One of Roxy's friends picked it out," she quickly adds. "I think she has a crush on him."

There's an unreadable look in Dad's eyes, but then he sighs and scrubs her head. "Just do me a favor, okay? Have a little fun tonight."

"Ha, yeah. Fun."

"You never know! Tonight might surprise you."

Easy for him to say. He was born to defy everything—expectations, careers, love itself. When he had to choose between marrying the love of his life or his career, he chose both. He defied everyone who said he was ruining his career when he wrote a whole album dedicated to her, and now, sixteen years later, those songs are still on the radio.

Too bad Cecilia hates those songs.

Like, not *hate*-hates them, but whenever they come on the radio, she turns to a different station. Her entire life has been chock-full of music and concerts and recording studios and backstage passes and world tours—she should love it as much as her younger sister does. She should embrace it. She should revel in it.

But being known as Roman Montgomery's eldest daughter your entire life would wear on you, too.

After he's gone, she turns back to her mirror, still unable to decide on which shirt, and finally she just drops both and stares at her reflection with the shirt she has on—an I AM AN AVENGER T-shirt with the OG Avenger, Sasuke, on the front. Does she really want the worst night of her life to be in a *Naruto* T-shirt and ripped jeans?

Why not, honestly.

Her mom is humming "Killer Queen" when Cecilia finally comes downstairs. The smell of pancakes for dinner suffocates the air. Not just any kind of pancakes, though, but her mom's specialty: chocolate murder pancakes. Grandpa taught the recipe to her, and his father before that, going far back into the Devine family line until . . . well, the invention of pancake mix, probably.

She turns to Cecilia and asks, "You're wearing *that* to the Battle of the Bands?"

Cecilia looks down at her wardrobe. "Sasuke gives me strength."

"Then let my chocolate murder give you energy," her mom adds and sets a plate on the counter. Cecilia takes one of the smaller brown chocolate pancakes, slides up to the counter, and nibbles on it. The bar stools have the perfect line of sight out the front dining room windows to the driveway. Cecilia waits anxiously for Roxy's motorbike to pull up. Usually she can hear it before she sees it, but Mom isn't a very good singer and she isn't quitting "Killer Queen" anytime soon.

In fact, Dad decides to sing right along with her.

"Oh, Roman! You're so off-key." Mom laughs.

"Only to be in tune with you, junebug," he replies.

Ugh, disgusting.

Cecilia is saved from her parents' blissfully happy marriage by the roar of Roxy's beat-up motorbike as it pulls into the driveway. Thank *God*. She grabs her tiny backpack—full of fandom pins and sparkly key chains—and heads for the front door.

"Make good choices!" her mother calls after her.

"Don't do anything I wouldn't do!" her father adds.

Which doesn't really rule out a whole hell of a lot, but it's the thought that counts, Cecilia supposes, as she slips out the front door and down the front walk to the driveway, where Roxy is waiting with a helmet. She's in her concert best, as always—a glittery rose-pink skirt with bike shorts underneath and a crop top under her riding leathers. Cecilia mounts herself onto the back of the bike.

"You going to hold on this time, Ceci?" Roxy teases.

Cecilia hesitates.

"You'll feel safer."

Of course she would. That's obvious. But as she wraps her arms around Roxy's middle—her fingers brushing against the warm skin of Roxy's stomach exposed by her crop top, her heart jumping into her throat—she wonders if this might be more dangerous after all.

The line wraps around the outside of Raritan River High School. Cecilia wrings her hands, glancing up at the ticket booth, wondering what's taking them so long to let people inside. It's sweltering in the afternoon sun. She can feel herself sweating through her Sasuke T-shirt. She tries to remember if she put deodorant on, but she's been such a ball of nerves today that she's thankful to remember her own name right now.

"Calm your tits, it's not like we won't get in together," Roxy says to alleviate her anxiety. She rocks back and forth on her platform Doc

Martens, so instead of just being *slightly* taller than Cecilia, she's astronomically taller.

We look like a joke together, Cecilia thinks. Maybe she shouldn't have worn her *Naruto* T-shirt. Maybe she should've combed her hair, or put on that green top, or maybe—

"My tits *are* calm, but can't the guy go *any* faster?" Cecilia complains, to stop all of the anxious thoughts racing in her head. She glances toward the parking lot, where a group of kids look like they're about to get into some trouble. Cecilia doesn't want to be a part of any of that. Thankfully, the line moves and they squeeze into the auditorium's lobby, where it's at least a little cooler, inching closer to the ticket booth. Cecilia looks past the line to the booth. "Yeah, the guy is definitely asleep. Or half dead. Maybe both?"

Roxy laughs. "What's the hurry? Do you have somewhere else to be?"

"N-no! Of course not."

She's afraid that someone else might tap Roxy on the shoulder and let her in on the joke—that they look like the strangest duo. Like a nonfiction book shelved in the fantasy section, Cecilia just doesn't fit where Roxy exists so perfectly.

"I just . . . I want us to get a good spot! Maybe you can see Theo early," she adds, because Theo is the reason they're there, after all. They've never talked about it, but she sees the way Roxy always looks at him in trigonometry. It's like she can't take her eyes off of him.

Roxy's eyebrows jump up. "Theo? I mean, sure, I guess . . . Oh, hey, we're up next." She nods her head toward the ticket booth and begins to reach for her wallet when Cecilia takes out two tickets from her purse and presents them to the guy.

"Perks of my mom sponsoring the Battle," Cecilia says by way of explanation.

"Nice! Thank you." Roxy grins as the ticket guy tears the tickets in half and gives them the stubs back. They meander through the crowd into the high school auditorium, quiet for a minute, and then Roxy says, twirling a lock of her rose-gold hair, "Thank you for coming with me, by the way, Ceci. I know you hate this kind of thing."

Cecilia shrugs. "It might not be that bad."

"Yeah, or you might hate it."

"Probably," she agrees, "but at least I'll get Dad off my back. You know he's always like, 'You should carpe way more diem!'" She tries to mock his deep voice, then shrugs. "Now he'll have to pester me some other way."

Roxy looks away. "Ah. So I'm a means of getting your dad off your back."

"Well, the company's not bad, either."

Roxy grins and elbows her in the side. "Gee, thanks."

Cecilia forces a smile, but what she wants to do is say the company isn't bad—the company is perfect, and she really couldn't care less about getting her dad off her back. She's here for one reason, and one reason only:

To be a good friend.

And good friends go to concerts where their friend's crush is playing, even if the thought of it twists some strange, deep part inside of them, because that's what friends do.

When they *finally* make it into the venue, Cecilia sees enough people from her school that she wants to crawl into the bathroom, lock the door, and not come out for the entirety of the show. The acoustics in this place are going to be terrible—the walls are cement, and the speakers look . . . *ancient*, to be polite—but at least there isn't a bar or any nonsense like that. And the curtains almost match the color of the old ones. The drama club had to buy new ones after the old ones caught fire during a particularly rousing production of *The Phantom of the Opera*.

Onstage, the manager and some of the stagehands are setting up for the first act already, plugging in the instruments and making sure everything is in place. Cecilia's familiar with that dance—she's seen stage managers and stagehands set up and break down her father's sets for years.

"The stage manager looks particularly frazzled," she notes quietly.

Roxy glances back at her. "You say something?"

"Nah—where are we going?" she asks as Roxy begins to make her way through the thickening crowd toward a corner of the venue. "Our seats are the other way."

"To find a drink," Roxy replies, gesturing over to a cluster of girls in the front left corner. One of them has overly large cowboy boots on, complemented by a frilly sundress. "I think Aimee snuck in some mini-bottles in her cowboy boots."

"Ah, so *that* explains it. I didn't think she was the yeehaw type."

"You'd be surprised what you don't know about people."

"I think I know most people," she replies, and Roxy grins as if there is a secret tucked into her mouth. Cecilia's heart quickens. *No, calm down*, she tells herself. *You're reading too much into this. It was nothing. It is nothing.*

They pass a few merch booths set up on the sides of the auditorium selling T-shirts, and she stops at one manned by a boy with wadded-up tissue in his ears, though the music hasn't even started yet. Not a great sign.

Roxy says offhandedly, browsing the wares on the table, "You just think the worst of everyone."

"And is that such a bad thing?"

Roxy picks up one of the demos. In addition to loving motorbikes, the smell of an oil change, and bodice-ripping Regency novels, Roxy also loves new music. She and Cecilia's dad get along so well, Cecilia sometimes thinks that maybe *Roxy* should've been her dad's daughter instead. The first time Roxy came over to the house, she and Roman bonded over the complete discography of Motion City Soundtrack. Since then, they've swapped music recs and mixtapes and burned CDs.

"Ooh," Roxy says as she reads the back of the album cover. She points to one of the songs. "'Written in the Stars,' such a good title. I hope they play it."

"Probably will," Cecilia replies, and points toward the girl in the cowboy boots with her group of friends. "That's Aimee, right?"

Roxy looks to where she points. "That definitely is." She digs a ten-dollar bill out of her bra and hands it to the merch dealer before she dives off after Aimee and her yeehaw minibar boot collection, leaving Cecilia alone at the edge of the crowd.

Not that she minds it. She likes being alone. And crowds aren't *that* bad—she actually likes submerging herself in a sea of people. She feels anonymous then. Concerts, on the other hand, are different. Cecilia hates them because they're loud and crowded and smelly, but the main reason she hates them is because—

"You're Roman's daughter, aren't you?" is how a guy in a band T-shirt and ripped jeans greets her. A guy she definitely doesn't know. She doesn't think he even goes to this school.

This is why she hates concerts. She tries to look invisible, but she's been on the cover of too many tabloids with her family to ever go anywhere unnoticed.

"Sorry, you've got the wrong person," she lies, not even looking up from her phone. *Go away*, she chants. *Go away.*

He does the opposite. He doubles down. One of his friends says, "C'mon, man," but the guy is either high or drunk or he doesn't care about being rude as fuck. "No, I know I saw you in the audience at the MTV Music Awards last year when your dad got that lifetime achievement award."

Cecilia glances around for Roxy, but she has successfully disappeared. She said she was just going to get a drink—but Cecilia didn't realize that entailed an expedition to the other side of the universe. With a sigh, she finally looks at the stranger and says, "Yeah, you caught me. Roman Montgomery's my dad."

"Oh, *fuck* yeah! Your parents have a ton of connections. Mateo, let's give her our demo," he adds to his friend, who begins to fish something out of his bag. "We can bypass this whole stupid competition. Trust me, we're better than all these other wannabes."

And here we are, Cecilia thinks, *the same old song and dance.* "I'm sorry, but I don't—"

"C'mon, just help a few guys out? You get it," he adds. "Music's hard. It'd be bomb if your dad could help."

"He doesn't really do that sort of thing."

"Then how about your mom—"

"Dude, asswipe, she said *no*," Roxy cuts in, stepping between Cecilia and the guys. She glowers at them. "So get lost, yeah?"

They step back, debating whether to pursue their dangerous endeavor, but they decide against it. Roxy is good for that. At first glance, she doesn't look dangerous—her nails glitter and most of her shirts have patterns of fruits or cute bears screaming, "THE HEAT DEATH OF THE UNIVERSE IS COMING!"—but her glares can cut straight to the bone. Cecilia had been on the receiving end of one of them before.

She never wants to be again.

As they meander away, Roxy rolls her eyes and hands Cecilia one of the two Cokes in her hand—Coke that smells strongly of bourbon, so she must've tracked Aimee down. Cecilia sips slowly. "I leave you for a few minutes and you find trouble. What am I going to do with you?"

"Protect me like the damsel in distress I am?"

"Alas, my lot in life." Roxy sighs, but she smiles as she says it.

Cecilia quickly glances away. A blush begins to eat at her cheeks, but at that exact moment, the lights flicker—and then dim. The show is starting.

Now all she needs to do is survive the music.

"C'mon," Roxy says, taking her hand. Roxy's hand is warm and dry, and a shiver curls down Cecilia's spine. It must be the bourbon. She can see Roxy smiling in the dim neon lights of the stage. "Let's get closer!"

Which means getting the closest possible seat. Which means she'll be sitting elbow-to-elbow with some stranger, suffocating in auditorium seats that are too small for her gigantic ball of anxiety, and that seems like a terrible idea to Cecilia. Or it would, if Roxy weren't smiling so wide, and if the neon lights weren't catching her rose-gold hair in highlights of purple and red, and if Cecilia's heart weren't so traitorous.

But it is, and as Roxy folds their fingers together, and her heart skips like a pebble over a pond, she lets Roxy pull her down the aisle to the first row.

And she doesn't mind.

* * *

"I think Theo's band is on first," Cecilia says, angling the program toward the neon lights to try to read the print. "I usually hate concerts, but this isn't too bad so far. I mean, I could do without all of the people, but . . ."

Roxy laughs. "The music hasn't even *started* yet."

"Thank God. Since Theo's first, maybe we can leave after and—"

"Oh no, you're with me for the entire ride. Start to finish."

Cecilia groans. "Roxy . . ."

Roxy bumps her hip against Cecilia's and says softly, only for the two of them, "And I wouldn't want to be here with anyone else."

Cecilia's heart slams against her rib cage, and she quickly looks away. "Obviously, because we're best friends," she adds, because there's not another reason, or if there *is*, she isn't sure she's brave enough to hear it. It's bad enough that they are here to see *Theo Debruin*. "Besides—"

But before she can say anything else, the lights flicker. The crowd erupts into cheers. The auditorium lights dim. The emcee—Mr. Bolivar, the music teacher—walks out with a microphone, the stage lights shining on his bald head. He's a tall Black man in a polo shirt and khakis, best known for his award-winning music instruction and his terrible dad jokes. "Welcome to the Battle of the Bands! I hope you're ready to have a rockin' good time! But before we start . . ."

"Oh no," Roxy mutters, "he's going to tell a joke."

"Oh *no*," Cecilia groans.

"What is Beethoven's favorite fruit?" He waits for a moment, then another, but the auditorium is silent. Roxy shakes her head, muttering under her breath about why she quit band. Mr. Bolivar takes a deep breath before he sings, *"BA-NA-NA-NAAAAAAA!"*

Cecilia laughs. She can't help it. The joke is terrible. Roxy elbows her in the side and hisses, "Don't support his dad jokes!"

Too late.

Mr. Bolivar says, "Thank you, thank you. First up is a group who met in Mrs. Sanchez's seventh grade science class and bonded over frog dissection. Please give a warm welcome to . . . *ROCK YOUR MOOOUUUUTH!*"

The lights dim again, and then Rock Your Mouth's Theo Debruin jogs onstage with his bandmates. He winks at Cecilia and Roxy in the front row.

Cecilia's mouth falls open. "Wow, he's really wearing suspenders and no shirt, isn't he?" she says, a little concerned at the sight of his nipples. Roxy almost spews her drink everywhere. His acid-blond hair is pushed back, red Fender guitar slung over his shoulder, and he strikes the Captain Morgan pose on one of the ancient speakers (which the stage manager probably doesn't appreciate) and winks down at the crowd.

"I think the first row was a massive mistake," Roxy adds, wiping her mouth. "He's really committing, isn't he?"

"I guess it's . . . kinda cool?"

"You think so?"

In the flaring stage lights, she can barely see Roxy's face. Is she grinning in the way she does when she's making a joke? No, it doesn't look like she's grinning at all. ". . . Don't you?"

"*Theo?*" She sounds incredulous. "He's a dumbass."

Has Cecilia read this wrong? No, it's not possible.

"You keep looking at him in trig," she shouts above the din of the crowd. "You can't take your eyes off him!"

"I keep looking at Theo because he keeps looking at *you*."

Oh.

But why would Roxy care about that? Unless . . .

Oh—*oh!*

And Cecilia never noticed because she kept looking at Roxy.

Onstage, Theo takes the microphone and screams, "Hellooooo, student body!" And most of the crowd, sitting a little too close to one another and a little shell-shocked by the nipples-out lead singer, cheer in that awkward way you cheer for things you don't really understand but support anyway. "We're Rock Your Mouth and we're happy to be here!"

Roxy quickly looks away from Cecilia. "I thought you knew?"

I knew?

"I mean, how can you not, right?" Roxy goes on, curling her hair around her finger nervously. "Everyone always comments about it. And, like, I know you always correct them and tell them we're just friends, and I get it."

Oh no, Roxy is babbling. She only babbles when she's flustered, and she's hardly ever flustered. Cecilia stares at her because her mind has shut down. Cecilia.exe is no longer working. Because she never expected the impossible.

Because the impossible doesn't happen to Cecilia Montgomery.

"Listen," her best friend goes on, turning back to the stage, "just forget about it, okay? Please, Ceci," she adds softly, begging.

And just like that, the moment is passing them by. The moment Cecilia never thought she would have.

It's the kind of moment that happens in the blink of an eye, a cloud passing over the sun, shade and then gone, and she doesn't *want* the moment gone. Cecilia wants to live in this moment. She wants to scramble the letters in *just friends* and rearrange them into a new phrase, a new title, a new possibility. They are so different: polar opposites. Cecilia is a forgotten nonfiction novel, and Roxy is a book full of wonder and magic and adventure, and they never should have been shelved together, but . . . but . . .

33

Roxy is just the kind of story Cecilia wants to get lost in. She wants to burrow into her pages because that is the only place where she has ever felt understood and okay. No, better than okay. When she's with Roxy, she feels like she is home.

Because the truth is—

The silly, horrible, wonderful truth is—

"Roxy," she says, her mouth dry, "I like—"

"*YOU!*" Theo and his loud band shout from the stage. The lights flare. Theo does a somewhat wanting guitar squeal, and this close to the stage, it sounds even worse.

Roxy's eyebrows furrow. She shakes her head. "I can't hear you!" she shouts over the drums.

So Cecilia shouts louder, "I do, too! I was never looking at Theo! I like—"

"*YOU!*" Theo howls again. Honest to fucking God, are there *any other lyrics* to this song? He puts his mouth on the microphone and screams into it with the rage of a thousand scrawny demons, "*YOU! YOU! YOU ARE HELL! I CAN'T STAND YOU. OUR TONGUES DANCE BUT OUR HATRED IS ETERNAL—!*"

Ah, there they are.

"*I LIKE YOU, TOO!*" she screams, but it doesn't matter how loud she is, she isn't loud enough.

If words can't carry across the distance of a few inches, then she'll carry herself instead. And so there in the front row of Raritan River High School's too-crowded auditorium she takes Roxy's face in her hands and presses their lips together. Roxy tastes like cherry cola and cheap cowboy-boot bourbon, soft and sharp, a myriad of opposites that make up Roxy Williams.

Rock Your Mouth is screaming about tongues dancing, but they have missed the mark entirely. It's not rage and hate and poison. It's soft and sweet and true.

The world feels like it has stopped. Gone silent. As if it's holding its breath as two best friends come up for air, and Roxy breathes against her mouth, "Me too."

Me too.

Cecilia doesn't realize she needed to hear those words until that moment. "How long?"

"Years," her best friend replies, pushing Cecilia's not-quite-red, not-quite-brown hair out of her face. They are so close to each other, the rest of the world looks like a kaleidoscope of colors and music, jumping and raving to a song neither of them has any interest in. "I gave you *so* many signs. You've just been too hardheaded to see them."

She . . . *has*? Though now that Cecilia thinks about it—the gentle touches on her arm; the glances at her from across the room; the way they wake up on weekend mornings, tangled in each other and the bed-sheets, always circling each other like two satellites in orbit, drawing closer and closer. Even earlier tonight, that secret tucked into the side of Roxy's smile as she said, "You'd be surprised what you don't know about people," their fingers folded together.

Oh.

In the breath between one kiss and the next, she can hear a love song—not of the Rock Your Mouth variety, but one made of her heart beating so fast, drumming against her rib cage, so happy and full it wants to burst. A love song to the tempo of Roxy's laughter, as tempting as the grin she feels curling across her mouth as she kisses her again.

Cecilia Montgomery hates love songs.

But I love the sound of us, she thinks, and kisses Roxy again.

SIDELINES

SARAH NICOLE SMETANA

I stood outside the back door of Parker's garage, ear pressed to the paint-slick wood, and listened to the muffled sound of something miraculous.

Music. *Our* music. The very same songs we'd written together inside that room. Except now they were no longer ragged or empty, off tempo, beat thin. For the first time since Colin, our drummer, left for college in Oregon, the Greatest Place sounded extraordinary.

The only thing missing was me.

Heart beating staccato, I threw open the door, a wild grin blossoming on my face. Over the past few months, we'd been auditioning drummers—which was quickly followed by rejecting drummers, and then arguing about where else we could possibly look for one, having seemingly exhausted all possibilities within the greater New Brunswick area. But here was someone new. As good as Colin, or even better. I felt buoyant with anticipation. All the nerves in my body began to hum.

And then I saw him, and every part of me deflated.

"Mina, hey," Diego said, fingers halting the dull metal strings of his bass. He waited, no doubt hoping Parker would jump in. But I could tell by the nervous sway of his body, the crest of sweat beading above his lip, that he'd been assigned the role of news breaker. "You, uh . . . you know Jeremy."

Diego motioned toward the sparkly red drum kit in Colin's old spot by the window. And behind it, sitting smug on his throne, was my ex-boyfriend.

"Yeah," I managed, voice catching in my throat. "I think I remember."

What else I remembered: the text message he sent me, out of the blue, breaking it off. And the next day, when he was making out with Leslie Mendoza three lockers down from mine. They walked right past me, his hand in her back pocket, his nose nestled in her hair. I cried all through the lunch period.

I knew Diego and Parker remembered, too.

"The thing I don't understand," I continued, addressing the room but keeping my eyes on Jeremy, hoping my anger burned a hole straight through him, "is what he's doing here."

Parker gave Jeremy an apologetic glance before corralling Diego and me into a corner. "Just hear us out for a second, okay?" he began, voice low. He placed one hand over his guitar strings to control the feedback. "We ran into him last week at Guitar Center, and it came up that we needed a drummer, so we just thought, what the hell, let's see. If it's awful, no big deal. But Mina." He gripped my shoulder, pulling me closer. In his eyes, I caught the sparkle of awe. "He picked up our songs in an hour. *All* of them."

I scoffed. "So what? He's still an asshole." I shook off Parker's hand and plucked my guitar from its case, then strapped its turquoise body

37

across my chest like armor. "He'll ditch us the second he thinks he's found something better."

Parker crossed his arms. "Look, it sucks that he dumped you sophomore year—"

"And we absolutely respect your opinion in this process," Diego interjected, shooting Parker a warning glare, "but he's the best drummer we've seen."

"By *far*," Parker stressed.

"And we can't play in the Battle without a drummer."

"We're playing," I snapped. "We have to. We need that recording session."

Diego nodded, the left side of his mouth rising. "Exactly."

I cringed. The trap had been obvious, yet I'd plunged right into it. "There has to be someone else," I tried.

"Name one," challenged Parker.

My fingers scaled the neck of my guitar as I mentally scrolled through the last few auditions. There was that kid Douglas, a freshman, who'd never actually played with a band before and kept stopping in the middle of songs and then apologizing until it looked like he might cry. Nate from a neighboring high school, whose technique was sloppy and frayed. A girl named Jessica who beat her snare ragged, as though she were picturing her irritating and invasive little brother. She wasn't so bad, I thought. All we had to do was stay on her good side—and definitely never go in her bedroom without permission.

"What if we just try it this afternoon," Diego offered, attempting to bring us all back to common ground. "See how it goes from there."

I racked my brain one last time for a way out of this, any other drummer we could possibly use, but I already knew all the decent ones were taken. Even that quiet new girl, Beckett, had been snatched up by several other bands before we could get to her, the rumor of her existence spreading as if she were a shiny, time-keeping unicorn.

Our options were dwindling. So was our time.

With a heavy sigh, I gave in. "But if I'm still uncomfortable with this after the show, we look for someone else."

"Deal," they agreed in unison.

The three of us turned back around to find Jeremy standing in front of his kit, idly twirling one of his sticks between his knuckles. He flashed that same lazy grin I remembered falling for, and something smoldered in my stomach. That was two years ago, right before he graduated. It felt like a lifetime had passed, and yet somehow, standing across from him, the wound was still oozing.

"No hard feelings, right?" he said, stretching out his free hand.

The only hard feeling, I thought, *is going to be my fist against your face.*

"Let's just play," I said, walking past him.

As I stepped up to the mic stand, I prayed to the gods of rock and roll (*Are you there, Joan? It's me, Mina*) that Jeremy would blow it. That something about me or our history would screw up his beat, set his internal metronome askew. I wanted the satisfaction of affecting him, however slightly.

But when we finally began practicing, I understood. There was no deal, no compromise, no audition. Before I had even set foot in the garage that day, Jeremy was already in.

A spark of betrayal lit in my chest, but I tramped it to cinders. If we wanted to win, we needed him.

* * *

The Greatest Place had played the Battle of the Bands three times before.

The first year we were terrible—all power chords and simple beats, lyrics that rhymed too perfectly and were sung with a savage strain. It was punk, but not on purpose, which is undeniably the worst kind. Luckily, though, by sophomore year we'd mellowed out a bit and found Colin. By junior year, we'd finally developed an authentic sound.

And this year, we were seniors. We were ready, and we were *good*. But more than that, we were acutely aware of the ways our world was changing. The tight-woven days at Raritan River High School were unraveling too rapidly, the end of the thread drawing near. College acceptances would be coming soon, and though we hardly spoke of it, I felt a shared worry wrap around us. Last year, when Colin moved, it was like an earthquake that shook our core. Since then, so little seemed truly stable.

So that fall, Diego, Parker, and I had decided to complete our applications together. We applied to all the same schools, or—in the case of Ivy Leagues that only Diego, with his APs and nearly perfect SAT scores, had a shot at—at least the same cities. Splayed on the floor of my bedroom, we'd pored over the catalogs, the options, dreaming up plans for each state.

"If we go to LA," I said, "we could totally play at the Troubadour."

"And if we move into New York City, we could play the Bowery Ballroom," Parker said.

"Terminal Five," I added.

"Madison Square Garden."

For a moment, we were quiet, all gazing at our respective laptops, minds dewy with possibility. Then we erupted in laughter.

"And if we end up in Boston . . ." I began, because *of course* Diego had to apply to Harvard. "What's in Boston?" I finished.

Parker tousled Diego's hair and said, "If our super-genius gets into Harvard, then I guess we'll find out."

At that, Diego sprang on him and I yelped, clambering up onto my bed as they crashed around the carpet, play-fighting. It was in moments like these that I could see how far we'd come together. Those awkward fourteen-year-olds were still in us, still dreaming, still sure of so little except each other. We'd named our band the Greatest Place because that's what we'd found through our music: somewhere we could be our truest selves. Somewhere we belonged.

When the wrestling match was over, our laughter exhausted, and our laptops once again perched on our thighs, Diego asked, "But what happens if we all get into different colleges? Just hypothetically, I mean. Like if I get into Harvard, but you get into Hunter, and Mina gets into San Francisco State?"

A charged silence sat between us, growing tense and tumultuous, like feedback from an amp.

In the end, no one attempted to answer.

But if we won, the logic went, it would prove to everyone (ourselves, our parents—even Mr. Grover, my precalculus teacher, who once said I could really make something of myself if I cared as much about school as I did about the silly poems I'd been caught writing) that our passion wasn't just a passing whim, something to be shed like a reptile's outgrown skin. If we got the recording time, if we finally made a real EP, our future as a band would stretch open. Not even college could break us apart.

Jeremy, however, was another obstacle entirely.

And before you ask: no, this wasn't about my *feelings*. I wasn't still pining, or still scorned, or any of that other crap they feed us on TV. In fact, the truth was far simpler.

I was jealous of him.

Jeremy had an obvious, innate talent that I didn't. His confidence radiated like a furnace while I sat shivering, always worried I'd be branded a fraud. It would have been a lot easier if he sucked. Just a little. Just sometimes. Not the night of the show, of course, but during practice, when he started getting too cocky, I wished he would forget a transition. I wanted to see his arms knot over his sticks. But every day, he only grew more comfortable in that spot by the window, and I hated it. I hated when he started suggesting tweaks to our songs. I hated it even more when those tweaks made them stronger. And most of all, I hated that Parker and Diego grew so obviously enamored of him, like light-starved moths drunk on his glow. Before my eyes, the Greatest Place was transforming into the Jeremy Show, and I felt powerless to pull myself from the fringes.

This became fully apparent two weeks before the competition, when I arrived at practice to find them much the way they'd been that first day: already settled in, jolted through with energy. Except this time, I didn't recognize the song they were playing. I snuck in the side door, camouflaging myself against the wall of gray egg-carton foam, and stood there until all three of them ended on one practiced, drawn-out note.

When the sound faded, I launched my voice between them. "Is that a new song or something?" They all startled, as if they'd forgotten why they were gathered in the first place. "It sounded pretty clean."

"We're just jamming," Jeremy said, punctuating the words with that unconcerned twirl of his drumstick. It reminded me of a magic trick, some sleight of hand. "Waiting for you."

I picked up my guitar and turned on my amp, struck a few swift chords. Part of me wanted to jump in, abandon the tension clenching my stomach, and recalibrate our band's alignment with me back in the center. But I'd never felt comfortable jamming. Even just that word, the lighthearted spontaneity it suggested, filled me with an anxious thrum. I refused to let Jeremy glimpse me at my weakest—flummoxed over key changes, the scales I'd never managed to memorize. So I shrugged the notion aside.

"Only two weeks left until the show," I reminded them, voice casual. I stepped up to my mic stand, adjusted the height up, and then down, and then right back to where it had been initially. "Probably shouldn't be working on anything new right now, anyway, if we want to make sure Jeremy nails our set."

It was a futile jab, but I needed to remind him of his place here. I needed him to remember: this was my band first.

"I think I'll manage," Jeremy said, and then began to show off with a quick, intricate fill. I rolled my eyes, unimpressed.

When practice was over, though, I decided to ask about what I'd heard, because I knew that if I didn't, I'd worry the thought over in my mind until it was smooth and irrefutable. I waited until a rare moment when Jeremy went to the bathroom, and I had Parker and Diego alone.

"Have you guys been practicing without me?" I asked.

"What? No. Jeez. We were just waiting for you," Parker insisted, parroting what Jeremy said earlier. He looked to Diego for affirmation, and Diego nodded. "What'd you expect us to do? Twiddle our thumbs in silence?"

There was a laugh behind his question, but something else, too.

Something dark, glittering. I only allowed myself to glimpse it for a second.

That day, I'd arrived exactly on time.

But if we won, the logic went, shifting and refining, it wouldn't just mean that the Greatest Place was good enough to make it. It would mean that *I* was good enough—not an imposter, a failure, unworthy—and that had to bring my best friends back to me.

So as the days whittled down and the Battle grew near, I made sure we all worked harder, practiced longer. We perfected our set until it felt like a precise science—until I felt certain that not even Safe & Sound stood a chance.

Then, with one day to go, something strange happened. We got sloppier.

Parker began picking the wrong notes during his solos. Diego kept forgetting when he was supposed to speed up and when to pause. I grew hyperaware of their mistakes and started making my own, mixing up bridges, overreaching for notes. And after our third time bungling "On the Edge of Something New," which was arguably our best and, under normal circumstances, most well-executed song, I threw up my arms in frustration.

"All right, stop, stop." I waited for the rest of the guys to halt their instruments. "What's going on today? We've played this song perfectly a thousand times, and yet all of a sudden, none of us can manage to get it right. Your lead is all over the place. Your bass line is slow. And you—" I turned to Jeremy, wanting to blame him for something, but his beats were flawless. Mechanical, yes. Unenthusiastic even. But nothing I could confidently criticize. "Just put some effort into it," I managed.

"We're exhausted," Parker moaned.

"And hungry," Jeremy said. "Let's go get a pizza or something."

"Maybe we *should* call it a night," Diego offered.

I crossed my arms. The sharp, metallic scent of our sweat hung heavy in the air, so thick I could taste it. "The show is tomorrow."

"Yeah, we know," Parker scoffed. "You've only said it a hundred times."

"*Do* you know, though? Because sometimes it feels like you've forgotten."

He leveled his gaze at me, eyes narrowing. Tension shivered between us as he mumbled, "I'm not the only one who's forgotten some things."

"Guys, chill out. I really think we all just need a break," Diego said. "We've been working really hard. After a good sleep, we can come at it fresh and ready tomorrow. We know this."

He was right. It was probably dark outside by now, and my body was depleted, aching for rest. But even as I considered stopping, I had a vision—not of the show but of after, in the studio, the rest of the guys having knocked out their parts in single takes while I kept screwing up, stopping, frazzled, having to start over. I remembered Douglas, that freshman we'd auditioned, and felt a pang of regret for having judged him so harshly, because I knew how he must have felt.

I also refused to become him.

"No." I shook my head. "Not until we nail this song. All of us."

The guys groaned, their resentment grating through my chest. When had I become the bad guy? They had to know I was doing this for them. For us. After we won, I told myself, everything would be better.

I turned back around, placed my mouth directly above the microphone. My voice reverberated through the curtain of humid air when I said, "Again."

* * *

The night of the Battle, we arrived early for sound check, then split off until the show. The guys wanted to grab some food, but I could never eat anything before a gig, let alone a giant, greasy cheeseburger. I was too torn up with nerves already. Everything depended on our performance tonight, and as the singer, so much of that pressure rested on me. So I decided to take a break and go home. We agreed to meet back up at five thirty.

And then it was five thirty-five. Five forty. I hunched against the far wall of the theater's backstage area and shot off another text to Parker and Diego: *Where are you guys??* I stared at the string of unanswered texts until my screen clicked off, then shoved my phone back in my pocket. Around me, the room buzzed with excitement. Lilly, the stage manager, rushed from group to group, checking off bands, getting the lineup in order. A guy with a ukulele wove his way through the crowd, strumming some summery song that didn't make sense, and every few seconds, my eyes caught the pop of a camera's flash as Raven, the show's designated photographer, snapped pictures. But really, the only other person standing alone was Steven, the kid who'd transferred here at the start of the year. As far as I could tell, he didn't have many friends. I considered striding up to him, saying something light and witty, just so neither one of us had to handle the frenzy alone. My feet stayed rooted to the scuffed wood floor.

"The Greatest Place, there you are," Lilly announced, suddenly in front of me. She made a mark on her clipboard. "To confirm, you're playing second, right after Rock Your Mouth. That should be at approximately six seventeen, but if we're adding in an extra few minutes for potential technical difficulties, then it will most likely be at six nineteen. Either way, I'll need you on your mark by six ten."

"Six ten," I echoed, only half listening to what she said. I worried my lucky guitar pick between my fingers, rubbing the worn-down impression of what used to say *The Greatest Place Is Here*. Diego had ordered them before our very first show: the Battle of the Bands three years ago.

"Mina," Lilly said, drawing out the sound of my name. She stared at me, concern plain on her face. "Where's the rest of your band?"

I slid my phone out of my pocket. Still no answer.

"They went out for food, but they should be back any second," I said to Lilly. Simultaneously, I typed: *We need to be ready at 6:10. Are you almost here???*

She tapped her pen against her clipboard. "*Please* find them. As soon as possible. We're on a really tight schedule tonight."

"Yeah, okay. I'll go look."

"And then come right back," she stressed.

I knew that Parker and Diego would never be late to a show—especially not one this important—but in my chest, I felt a low rumble of fear. *What if something happened to them?* I thought as I snaked through the throng of kids backstage and out into the hallway. I curved past our lockers, the bathrooms, the crowded corridor in front of the ticket booth, but couldn't find them anywhere. What if they'd gotten into an accident? What if they were hurt?

Mind reeling, I rushed through the front doors and out into the parking lot. Overhead, the sun was setting, lighting the sky in a blaze of pink and tangerine. I scanned the rows of cars and was relieved to see Jeremy's beat-up green Explorer. The relief dissipated when I spotted the three of them lingering around a group of other people I didn't know.

"Guys, what the hell?" I called, frustration billowing behind me as I strode toward them. "Do none of you have your phones? You were supposed to meet me backstage twenty minutes ago."

Jeremy mumbled something to the group. A laugh ruffled through them.

"We're here," said Parker, breaking off to meet me. "Chill out, Mom." He rattled around the ice in the bottom of his soda cup, then slurped up the little bit of liquid remaining.

Diego glanced at his phone. "I guess we got distracted. But we don't go on until six seventeen or something, right? We've still got time."

"That's not the point," I said through gritted teeth. "We need to be professional. Lilly wants us backstage."

Jeremy cocked a smile. "Come on, Mina. It's just a high school battle of the bands."

Parker chuckled in agreement and shook his cup again. Diego didn't say anything, but I saw his mouth twist, some set of emotions warring within him.

"You guys don't really believe that," I said. It was a statement, not a question. Nobody responded. A few moments of strained silence stretched between us until somewhere behind me, one of the auditorium's back doors must have opened, and a crunch of distortion spilled into the parking lot.

The show was about to start.

Lilly was going to be pissed.

"The studio time," I reminded them. "Our EP. This is everything we've been working toward."

"Tell her," Parker said.

"Not now," Diego answered.

"Tell me what?" I asked.

"Nothing. Never mind. We can talk about it later."

"What?" I demanded.

Diego frowned, lips flattening into a thin line. Parker watched him. Jeremy scratched at the chipped wood of his drumstick.

"I got into Princeton," Diego said.

Out of all the things I imagined he might say, I hadn't expected this. *Princeton*—a place Parker and I hadn't applied because we never would have gotten in. And we didn't apply anywhere else in New Jersey, either. Staying in our home state was never part of the plan.

"You didn't tell us you were applying to Princeton," I said, fully aware that this was not the right response.

Diego toed some loose gravel, nailed his eyes there. "It was kind of a last-minute thing. And I only found out a week ago."

"I'm happy for you." Recovering, I slapped on what I hoped was a breezy smile. "It's not what we were expecting, but we can totally make it work. Princeton isn't that far from New York. If Parker and I both get into schools in the city—"

Diego looked up then, but not at me. His eyes found Parker.

"There's something else," I said, reading it on their faces.

I watched as Jeremy shoved his twitching hands into his pockets. Next to him, Parker sighed, as though already exhausted by our conversation. "Diego's going to Princeton. I want to go to the University of Washington. And you? You're always talking about the English program at San Francisco State. That author you really like teaches there, right?"

"But—" I shook my head. My thoughts were swimming. "What about everything we've been through? Everything we planned? We all agreed, the band comes first."

"How do you expect us to be a band if we're scattered across the country like that?"

49

"The Postal Service did it," I said, referencing an old electro-indie band I'd found through my Spotify Discover Weekly playlist some time ago, and who'd famously recorded their hit album by sending tracks back and forth in the mail. I'd turned Parker and Diego on to them, too, enormously proud to have found the album first—prouder still when they instantly loved it as much as I did.

But none of that love, that collective *spark* we'd felt listening to their poppy beats seep through my speakers, was present now. Instead, Parker looked at me sadly. "We're not the Postal Service, Mina."

"Well, yeah, of course not. We can't just copy them. And obviously, email would be way easier than—"

"I mean," Parker interrupted, "that we've been talking. And we just want to have fun for the rest of the year."

Out past the parking lot, brakes hissed. A horn blared. I waited, heart plummeting, for the shattering sound of a crash that didn't happen. "What are you talking about?"

Jeremy angled his body away from us. "Maybe I should leave," he mumbled.

"No," Parker and I both snapped.

Jeremy stiffened, then sank back into his stance. I should have delighted in how uncomfortable he appeared—finally, I had an effect on him!—but all I felt was sick.

"What I'm saying," Parker went on, "is that we don't want to do this anymore. At some point you got way too serious, and our band stopped being fun. *You* stopped being fun."

I turned to Diego, desperate for some other explanation, but he still wouldn't look at me. "It hasn't been fun for a while," he said to the ground.

The worst part of that moment was the fact that I couldn't argue.

It hadn't been fun for me lately, either. But that was only a temporary symptom—a necessary sacrifice for a much greater goal. They had to have known that. The Greatest Place meant everything to me. It *was* everything. Wasn't it everything to them?

Around me, the parking lot tilted. I was standing still, simultaneously careening, and realization slammed into me like a fist: the extra practices, the "jam" sessions. The way the mood always seemed to shift as soon as I entered the room. It all made sense now.

A laugh clawed its way out of my mouth, and my eyes turned hot, burning. "So let me get this straight," I said, voice sharp as a blade. "You're breaking up with me. For him."

Diego: "It's not like that."

Parker: "We didn't want it to go down like this."

Diego: "We were going to tell you after the show."

Don't cry, I demanded. *Don't cry, don't cry, don't cry.* But in my head, as I worked the pieces together, the worst betrayal was just beginning to unfurl.

This year, we could have won. I truly believed that. And though I wanted to leave now, to turn away before I allowed them to see me crumbling into a million pieces, I couldn't. I needed to know.

"So what would have happened if we had won? The EP, the recording session . . . what would have happened to them?"

Three sets of eyes stayed averted, their collective pity the only answer I needed.

They would have taken the studio time without me.

Beneath the dim lights of backstage, I hunted through the clutter of empty bags and guitar cases, but I couldn't see anything, let alone the small black purse holding my car keys. Why the fuck did it have to be so dark back here? My eyes blurred with tears. I could hardly breathe. Applause thundered through the auditorium, and I thought it might crack me wide open. It wasn't just the fact that my band broke up on the most important night of the year, either. In a handful of minutes, my whole life had imploded. Suddenly, I didn't know where I'd sit at lunch. I didn't know what I would do after school, or on weekends. I didn't know if my only real friendships would overcome this, or if, in a few months, we'd simply move to separate quadrants of the country. And there, on top of it all: I didn't know how to be in any other band. I didn't know if anyone else would even want me.

The sound of power chords pealed through the speakers, followed by a raw, rasping voice. I sank into the detritus of everyone's instruments and realized I'd never been so completely alone.

"Mina, thank God," Lilly said, appearing above me. "I've been looking for you everywhere. Rock Your Mouth just went on. You're up next."

I brushed the backs of my hands against my cheeks, but it was useless. I was clearly crying. She had clearly seen.

She knelt down. "Hey, what's going on?"

"We're not playing," I said.

Her lips parted in a tiny oval. "What do you mean? You play every year."

How many times, in the coming days, would I stumble into this same conversation? What could I possibly say? I thought about the guitar pick in my pocket, about how luck was a figment of my imagination. About how maybe best friends were, too.

"I'm—I'm really sorry, okay? I need to go." And then I was up, out the door, barreling into the harsh glare of the hallway, searching for somewhere to wait out the show. I rounded a corner. Another band, giddy with anticipation of their set, strode toward me. I spotted Sindy, with her shock of pink hair, from physics class, and spun around again, hoping she didn't see me.

But in my rush to avoid her, I rammed my shoulder into someone else.

"Shit. Sorry." I reached out, trying to steady the girl across from me as my vision slowly focused. She looked vaguely familiar: thick, dark hair curling around her shoulders and worn-out Chuck Taylors. I recalled seeing her around school, or maybe at a show. Not onstage, though; in my memories, her face was cast in shadows.

"I'm sorry," I said again. "Are you okay?"

"Yeah. Yeah, I'm fine." Her gaze shifted, disoriented, around the hallway before settling on me, and then it instantly sharpened. "Are *you* okay?"

Maybe it was because she was a stranger to me, or because the answer was obvious, or because I'd been pretending in so many ways for so long that I simply couldn't anymore. Whatever the reason, I slumped back against the row of lockers and said, "No. I'm really, really not."

For a moment, we stood in silence. I could feel her watching me. Waiting. But when I didn't elaborate, she spoke again. "You know, if we're being completely honest here, I'm not really okay, either."

She leaned into the space next to me. Her expression, I saw now, was eager yet nervous, as though she'd been standing on the precipice of something monumental before I smacked her out of it. "I think I have stage fright," she continued, "except it's not, like, sweet little butterflies fluttering around in my stomach." Her fingers danced through the air before hardening into tight, violent fists. "Instead, it feels like my insides are being ravaged by a horde of hysterical hummingbirds. No, a horde of hysterical *blood-hungry* hummingbirds. Hysterical blood-hungry hummingbirds *with a personal vendetta.*" Finally, her hands relaxed and fell to her sides. "As you can probably tell, I've never done this before."

I pushed away the disturbing image of carnivorous hummingbirds and asked, "Done what?"

"Played. In front of people."

A small smile lifted the corner of my mouth. "In the interest of complete honesty," I said, "it *is* pretty terrifying. I want to throw up every single time I do it."

"Oh. Well." The girl crossed her arms, as though unable to stay still. "Check mark on that one."

"But," I added, "once you're out there . . ." I dragged down a deep breath and closed my eyes, conjuring the feeling. The blaze of spotlights on my skin. The sway of an almost invisible crowd. That moment, in the center of every song, when I forgot, even if only for an instant, whatever insecurities usually encompassed me, and there was no worthy or unworthy, no expectations, no frauds. Nothing but the music, and the music was everything.

I opened my eyes to a water-stained ceiling tile. I said, "It's the greatest feeling in the world."

Next to me, I heard a relieved sigh. "I figured it might feel something like that, once the nausea part was out of the way."

"You're going to be great," I told her. "Promise."

"And what about you? What time do you go on?"

"I don't," I said.

Confusion creased a line between her eyebrows. "But I saw your band on the lineup."

"You know my band?" I asked.

She shrugged. "I know all the bands. My ex is in Raging Mice, and I . . ." She trailed off, began chewing the edge of her thumbnail, and suddenly, I remembered exactly where I'd seen her. At Bean and Ballad, parked with a notebook in the back corner behind the merch table, seeming somehow both purposeful and distracted. I'd assumed she was one of those dutiful girlfriends who supported her boyfriend's music even though she didn't personally care for it and had brought along the weekend's homework to complete while he was busy backstage. Now, though, the memory shifted, details carving new pathways in my brain. I zoomed in on her worn composition book, the disintegrating spine sealed lovingly with colorful washi tape. The way she tapped her pen against her cheekbone in what I had thought, even then, was deliberately 3/4 time. I had almost asked her about it, but then she started writing again and the lights dimmed for someone's set and I figured the beat was my own projection, something I'd imagined.

But I hadn't. Of course I hadn't.

"Let's just say I went to a lot of shows over the past year," she finished.

"Meaning you got stuck in the back watching everyone else perform when really you should have been up there all along?"

Her mouth quirked up. "I suppose you could say that."

"Well, good for you. Seriously. Some people don't have the courage to get up there, and sitting on the sidelines really freaking sucks."

"It does, doesn't it?" she agreed through a laugh. Then: "I'm Amina, by the way."

"Mina," I said. "We've got so much in common, even our names sound alike."

"Guess that means we're destined to be friends."

Her head fell back against the locker, and as the echo of our voices faded, I could hear it again—the sound from the theater. It was faint, like a memory, and a jolt rushed straight to my heart. Any second now, the band onstage would finish, and the Greatest Place wouldn't be there to follow. I wondered where the guys were, what they were thinking, if a scrim of sadness had settled over them or if they felt weightless, being free of me.

"My band broke up," I blurted. The words were heavy, like lead in my mouth. "And the finality of it, knowing that we're never going to play another show . . . That I might never . . ." The back of my throat tightened. I could feel Amina watching me, but I kept my eyes trained on the row of lockers opposite us. In the bottom corner of number 127, someone had scratched the word *loser*, and I stared until the word blurred to nothing. "We were supposed to go on, like, *now*," I finished.

"So why don't you?" she said.

"What, just me and my one amped guitar?"

She nodded.

I coughed out a laugh. "No way. It would sound empty and ridiculous."

"I don't think it would sound ridiculous at all."

I cut my eyes to her, trying to gauge whether she was serious.

"I've heard your songs, Mina, and they're great. The lyrics especially. Take 'On the Edge of Something New.' It's this super catchy, upbeat, fast anthem about diving wildly into the excitement of the unknown, but it's also imbued with so much sadness, so much loss and fear and uncertainty. It's almost a song of mourning, when you really think about it."

Naturally, I had thought about it. I'd written that song shortly before Colin left, while trying to work through a hurricane of emotions I hadn't figured out how to name. It was about how every feeling lived alongside its very opposite. It was about learning, for the first time, that bright new beginnings only existed because something else had to end.

But no one else had ever mentioned the subtext. I don't think Parker or Diego even noticed it.

"You really caught all that just from hearing my song a few times?"

She nodded, a glimmer of pride on her face. "I pay attention to that kind of stuff."

Right then, I felt pummeled by the unfairness of not having known Amina before tonight—the cruelty of a universe that would allow us to walk the same hallways, and stake out the same shows, without ever speaking a word. It was another mourning, a gain and a loss all at once.

"Look, I love the way a full band sounds," Amina said. "The pounding of drums, the way a bass line can snake into your heartbeat until you're not sure what's you and what's the music. But some songs . . ." She paused, eyes focused across the hallway. I wondered if she saw the word *loser*, too. Either way, she shook her head and turned back to me. "Some songs don't need all that. Some songs are actually more powerful when they're simple, and stripped bare."

"But there's a difference between raw simplicity and emptiness," I argued.

"Your songs aren't empty, Mina," she shot back. "And because I know you're probably thinking it, neither are you."

From the theater came an explosion of cheers. This was it. This was our time, our set. The moment that was supposed to define our future.

But there was no *our* anymore. There was only me.

"All I'm saying," Amina went on, "is that maybe that hollowness and the threat of background silence intruding on every note—all those things you're afraid of—maybe they're exactly what your songs need right now. Maybe they're the *only* things you need, because they're the only things that are true."

Her words ricocheted through my mind alongside a thousand

worries. That I'd sound terrible. That my fingers would freeze, refusing to find the right chords. That my voice would split like a frayed wire, and without any other instruments to hide it, the sound would echo in the auditorium with such force that for the rest of the year, the Raritan River High student body would ask me how my late-stage puberty was going.

Or, maybe, all the heartbreak and despair would seep into my sound, the emotions amplified by the candor of my one small voice, my one weepy guitar.

Amina placed a hand on my arm, drawing me back to the moment. Our fears may have been separate, I realized, but in the end, they weren't so different.

Winning was no longer the point. I just wanted my voice to be heard.

"We both deserve more than the sidelines," she said. "Now *go*."

I wrapped her in the tightest hug I could manage, spilling a song of gratitude into her hair.

"And if I don't find you again before your set, good luck! You're going to be amazing, I know it," I said, then raced down the hallway, straight to the edge of the stage, where I found Lilly peeking around the curtain with a wince on her face. Out in the spotlight, Mr. Bolivar, the school's music teacher and the Battle's annual emcee, was chuckling to himself and saying, "Here's another one for you. What do you call a bear with no teeth? Anyone? Anyone?"

"A music teacher!" someone yelled.

"Don't quit your day job!" called another.

Lilly sighed and pressed her palm against her face. I tapped her on the shoulder.

"Put me on," I said.

Her expression twisted from confused to hopeful to disappointed. "I'm sorry, but I can't. There are only a few minutes left, and anyway, you didn't sign up as a solo act. The rules clearly state—"

"So disqualify me," I said. "I don't care if I win, I just need to go out there. Come on, Lilly, please. One song."

As her gaze shifted from my face to the stage, I could practically see her brain working. Which would be worse: leaving Mr. Bolivar out there to tell terrible dad jokes for another few brutal minutes, or breaking the rules and letting me go on alone? Her eyes darted to the side, pausing on something—someone—past my shoulder. And just like that, her expression unfolded.

"One song," she repeated, reaching for her headset. Then, with a quick glance back at me, she added, "Make sure it's a good one."

While Lilly spoke instructions into her mic, I dashed across backstage. I still had no idea where my purse was, but I found my battered guitar case quickly, yanked my Stratocaster from its bed. Heart clattering, I threw the strap over my shoulder, checked the tuning, and ran with my small amp back to the curtain just as Mr. Bolivar said, "Looks like our next act is making a late appearance after all." He gestured toward where I stood in the wings. "Let's give a big Narwhal welcome to Mina Wright!"

Beyond the beam of the spotlight, the stage bled into the vast darkness of the auditorium. It looked infinite, the applause crashing like the swell of waves. I thought about Amina, and everyone on the sidelines, and the boys who always seemed so much bigger than us, who never worried that they weren't enough.

Then I stepped forward to greet them.

BATTLE OF THE EXES

SARVENAZ TAGHAVIAN

"Let's take it from the top," I say, frowning at the orchestra room's cluster of black metal music stands, which are bearing witness to our one last, desperately needed rehearsal. For inanimate objects, they sure feel judgy.

"Again?" Gwen asks, an incredulous tone creeping into her normally soft-spoken voice.

"We're still not totally in sync," I reply, and then look to Charlotte and Vivienne for backup. I can hear raucous whistles and applause coming from the auditorium just down the hall. Another band must have just finished their set, and from the sound of it, they're stiff competition.

"We're not even the Backstreet Boys," Charlotte says, and then gives herself a ba-dum-cha on her drum set. Gwen giggles. "Thank you, thank you. I'll be here all day. Or, at least, for the next forty-five minutes."

I give her a *Can we get serious for a minute, please?* look, and Charlotte clears her throat. "We should rehearse it again," she says loyally.

My eyes silently thank her and then cut over to Gwen, who, as Charlotte and Vivienne both know, is the reason we're not sounding in rhythm. Though that's not entirely Gwen's fault. When the rest of the band has been rehearsing together since middle school and one member has just joined a week ago, one can expect a few growing pains. Besides, I have to keep reminding myself, Gwen is doing *us* a favor. She's the only one who attends Raritan River High, which is the sole reason we're allowed to compete in its Battle of the Bands at all—far and away our biggest gig to date, with a chance to win a real recording session to boot. When Charlotte found out about the contest, she asked Gwen—her friend from church—if she'd consider playing with us on a lark. She was surprised that Gwen said yes right away, though I was less so. Charlotte, with her quick sense of humor, has a way of attracting a legion of fans; come to think of it, so does Vivienne and her effortless cool. I might be the weak point of the Grants in terms of natural charm, but I like to think I make up for it by writing most of our original songs and living up to the archetype of aloof bassist.

I like Gwen. I really do. What I don't like, quite honestly, is having keys in our band at all. We tried it once before and it didn't work then . . . and I'm pretty sure it isn't working now. Maybe it's not even the keys themselves, more that Charlotte, Vivienne, and I are such a tight three-piece. I think the Grants are meant to be a three-piece. I mean, even the name we chose for ourselves: it's short for the Immigrants. And even though Gwen is Chinese-American, like Charlotte, she's third-generation, and doesn't quite share in the bond that was forged between three tiny children from the scattered corners of China, Haiti, and Iran back in first grade ESL classes.

Gwen doesn't look totally convinced that we need to rehearse again, but she still dutifully places her hands on the keys in preparation for the opening chord.

Which she doesn't get to play because the door to the music room opens and a girl with blue dreadlocks and a camera comes walking in.

"Hi, Raven," Gwen says.

"Hey, guys. Don't mind me. I have to take some photos for the school paper. Just carry on and pretend I'm not here." She points her camera at us and snaps a photo. I decide to do exactly as she says and ignore her, mainly because we don't have time for socializing.

"Ready?" I ostensibly ask the whole band, but I'm looking at Gwen. She nods.

Except we're interrupted again by a bang from one of the windows. A kid outside has apparently just accidentally swung his case into the window frame. A bass comes tumbling out of it, but he manages to catch it right before it hits the ground.

Christ. At this rate, it'll be time for our set before we acceptably get through even *one* of the numbers.

Finally, Charlotte bangs her sticks together, counting us off, and we launch into the song I wrote last week. Vivienne sings, with her long braids swinging:

> *"You say you're leaving and you wait for me to fall apart*
> *You're feeling big thinking you took a dump on my heart*
> *Two years older and you think that you're so smart*
> *But the headlines scream, 'Who Do You Think You Are?'"*

And then the chorus, which we're all supposed to harmonize on.

"Heart shitter!
You're so full of it
Heart shitter!
Go on and quit
Heart shitter!
Don't need no babysitter
Heart shitter!
Damn, that sweet was bitter"

This time I pinpoint what the problem is: the chorus doesn't sound right with four-part harmonies. I'm trying to think about how to gently ask Gwen if she'd mind not singing at all when there's another bang, this time on the door of the music room. It swings open and there's a teacher standing there.

"Mr. Bolivar!" Gwen says, the first to stop playing, though we all quickly follow suit. Raven snaps one last photo and ducks out the open door.

"Gwen," the teacher says, and then looks at us, clearly trying to figure out who on earth we might be. "Ladies . . ."

Vivienne walks over to him, already tying her hair back in conjunction with her patented Let's Charm an Adult™ smile. "Mr. Bolivar," she says, "Gwen has told us amazing things about your music department here. Thank you *so* much for letting us perform at your Battle of the Bands."

Mr. Bolivar blinks. "I . . . Did I?"

"You made the rule that only one member of the band has to attend the school in order to play, right?" Charlotte chimes in sweetly.

"Oh," Mr. Bolivar says, eyeing Gwen. "Yes, I guess those are technically the rules."

There's silence for a second, and Vivienne and Charlotte both look to me. Right, my turn to suck up. "So here we are" is what I come up with. Charlotte shakes her head affectionately. I mean, she should know better than to throw it over to me when attempting subterfuge. "Your feelings are written all over your face," Baba says to me over FaceTime whenever he's able to get to my uncle's house in Tehran to tap into his Internet.

Mr. Bolivar takes in my dark, cropped hair, Joan Jett T-shirt, and black jeans that are more holes than pants now. My hair is purple, too, but it doesn't really show unless we're under stage lights. It looks killer under them, which is usually the only time I care about how I look, and only since it's part and parcel of how we sound, how we come across, how we perform our music.

"Right, well, welcome," Mr. Bolivar says, not sounding quite convinced of what he's saying. "But I sincerely hope what I just heard is not one of the songs you're going to be performing at the contest."

"Why not?" I ask, feeling immediately defensive. I wrote the whole song in a frenzied two-hour session about fifteen minutes after Mateo sent me an Instagram DM dumping me. *I really like you, Mitra, but I think this is too hard with us being at different schools. I hope you keep writing music, though. You have so much potential.* ♥

If art is all about conveying your deepest, rawest emotions to an audience and making them feel that way, too, then I think "Heart Shitter" is some of my best work.

Mr. Bolivar looks at me as if I've sprouted a second head. "This is a school-sanctioned event, Ms. . . . ?"

"Pars," I say. "Mitra."

"Ms. Pars," he finishes. "There is no profanity at a school-sanctioned event."

"Oh," I say, my face falling. I hadn't thought of that. Why hadn't I thought of that?

I look around at my bandmates, who each look equally dumbfounded.

"Of course, Mr. Bolivar," Gwen says to him with a nervous smile. "We'll adjust it."

"Great," he says as a tiny brunette girl with a headset comes into the room. I've seen her roaming around backstage. I think she's the stage manager.

"Are you guys the Grants?" she asks, out of breath.

"We are," Charlotte says.

"You need to be on deck backstage. You're on in five."

"Sure, Lilly," Gwen says as she follows her and Mr. Bolivar out the door.

I hang back, staring at my real bandmates in horror. "We can't perform the song?" I ask.

"We can do 'One Way or Another,'" Charlotte offers. "Or 'Bad Reputation.'"

"Does Gwen know those?" Vivienne asks.

But that's hardly the point. "Our first song is already a cover. I don't want to do another one," I say, even if it would be a cover of one of the two greatest songs ever written.

"Can you . . . I don't know, just change the words of the chorus?" Charlotte asks. "*Heart . . . crapper*? Or something?"

No, I can't just change the words of the chorus, I want to scream. There are multiple internal rhymes to consider.

But what other option do we have?

"Guys, seriously!" Lilly has come back, and she looks immensely stressed out. "You have to go NOW."

"Yeah, okay," I mumble. "We'll do that."

Lilly leads us through the unfamiliar school into a door that opens up to the auditorium's backstage area. I'm looking down, trying to make sure I don't trip over the wires that snake beneath our feet, when my peripheral vision catches sight of something up on the stage, a different kind of snake altogether. One that's tattooed on an arm that, up until last week, I'd grab on to at will, sometimes even absentmindedly tracing the inked scales while we sat on my basement floor in songwriting sessions together.

Mateo.

What the hell is he doing here?

"What the hell is *he* doing here?" I then voice, and Charlotte, Vivienne, and Gwen turn their heads to where I'm gesturing. Charlotte's and Vivienne's mouths drop open.

"Uh. Looks like he's playing," Vivienne says.

And he is. At the Battle of the Bands *I* told him about. Is. This. For. Real?!

"But he's in college," Charlotte says, plucking the words straight from my mind. "Why is he playing at a high school battle of the bands?"

Gwen squints, looking at the trio that's gathered on the stage. "The other two guys go to my school," she offers. "Maybe he's playing as a favor to them?"

Except, as the applause dies down for their first song, Mateo is the one going up to the microphone. Mateo's the lead singer. More like they're playing as a favor to him.

"This is a new song," he says, and then his guitar bursts forth with a searing power chord progression that I recognize because it's what he'd been working on during our final writing sesh. The lyrics, however, I don't recognize.

"We were young, but you were younger
Your first taste of tongue made me a wonder
Your moony eyes, the pedestal you built
I can't disguise it gave me a thrill
But it got old as we got older
And I got bored being a placeholder
A cutout, an icon, an object of awe
Nobody tells you it's lonely as a god."

"Holy Karen Carpenter," Charlotte says. "Is this . . . is this about you?" She turns to me. "And did he just refer to himself AS A GOD?!"

I can't respond, but it turns out I don't need to because then comes the chorus.

"You were all about me, me, me, me, me . . . Mitra.
There was too much of me, me, me, me in you . . . Mitra."

"I. Will. Kill. Him." Vivienne throws off her guitar and hands it to Charlotte before storming to the edge of the stage—a move that would, under normal circumstances, shock me since Vivienne is the most naturally chill of the three of us.

"What is she doing?" Lilly hisses, her eyes wide in fear.

Gwen runs after Vivienne and takes her arm, holding her back, and after a split second, Charlotte does, too, taking the other arm.

"Let go of me," Vivienne says, her typically patient, low voice going up at least an octave.

"You can't just walk out onstage in the middle of their performance!" Gwen says, exactly at the same time as Charlotte says, "I will gladly go out there and murder him with you . . . as long as that's what Mitra wants."

Charlotte and Vivienne both look back at me.

I am frozen, clutching my bass like it's the only thing that's stopping me from melting into the floor and draining away in a pool of mortification. Am I dying? I feel like I may be dying because if that thing they say about your life flashing before your eyes is true, then that is exactly what's happening.

Or maybe not my *whole* life, but the last five months—the parts with Mateo in them.

Scene 1: Meeting him outside one of the local townie bars in Huntington Village. His drummer arms (because of course he's a multi-instrumentalist) and tattoos are on full display because he's wearing a *goddamn vintage Blondie T-shirt*. Honestly, it was like a freakin' screenwriter had written him just for me.

Scene 2: He asks about our band, tells me about his band, Chump, flirts with me, gets my number.

Scenes 3–47: A montage of all of our songwriting sessions, him giving me pointers, me giving him pointers, us making out in between.

Except . . . did he ever take any of my pointers? Or did he start kissing me almost as soon as I started to talk? My imaginary film reel comes to an abrupt halt.

And then I remember that final DM.

I never knew what was worse: the word "potential" or his belief that everything would be cool because he ended the whole thing with a *mothereffin' heart emoji.*

"He thinks . . ." My voice is shaking. Charlotte and Vivienne immediately come back to my side, ready to burst into action the second I burst into tears. "He thinks . . . he was my *icon*?!"

A fat drop leaks from the corner of my eye, and it is 100 percent not of sadness but of pure, unadulterated rage. And my friends know it.

"He's a tool," Vivienne says.

"Grade-A prick," Charlotte chimes in. "Do you want me to 'accidentally' poke him in the eye with my drumstick? Because I will."

Gwen looks back and forth between Mateo and me and says, "So . . . uh, I take it that's your ex-boyfriend?"

"About to be her dead ex-boyfriend," Vivienne mutters.

Gwen stares wide-eyed at Mateo, hears him sing one more rousing round of "Mitras," and then looks back at me. "What a fucking bastard."

I burst out with a loud guffaw. I have never heard prim and proper Gwen curse in my life.

"So what's the consensus?" Vivienne asks. "We all storm out there right now?"

And suddenly I'm calm. Because I know exactly what to do. It's almost like last-week me had prepared for this very moment.

"Nope," I say. "We're going to wait until they're done. And then we're going to perform 'Heart Shitter' first. Exactly as I wrote it." I look at Vivienne and Charlotte, who each give me a firm nod.

Gwen, on the other hand, looks frightened. "But . . . Mr. Bolivar," she whispers.

"Gwen, don't sing. That way you can say you had no idea we were going to use the original lyrics." Now I can save some face *and* our harmonies. "Is that okay?"

Gwen hesitates for only a moment, but then gives one more look over at Mateo and all his snake imagery and nods bravely. "Okay."

"Thanks, everyone!" Mateo says onstage. "Once again, we're Chump 2.0!"

Latest version of the same jerk, I think, finally realizing what a perfect band name he'd chosen for himself.

Charlotte hands Vivienne her guitar back and goes and picks up her drumsticks. Vivienne takes her hair tie out. We're standing as one united front when Chump 2.0 leave the stage to enthusiastic applause. The other two guys are ahead of Mateo and stroll by us, without a clue as to who we are. Mateo gives one last wave to the audience, grinning, and not watching where he's going until he almost runs smack into me.

"Sorry . . ." he starts, before realizing who he's talking to. His face goes pale for a second, but he recovers quickly. Makes sense, considering he's a god and all. "Hey," he says.

I just smile at him, a big, fat unnerving smile. I see the color leave his cheeks again. Suddenly he's looking less rock star and more gangly teenage boy. Because that's what college freshmen are, I realize. "Um. Good luck out there," he mumbles.

I wink at him, the smile never leaving my face. "You should stay and listen."

He rushes past me, not even daring to look into Charlotte's and Vivienne's faces.

"You're on," Lilly says.

"Ready, ladies?" I ask the band.

"Like Debbie," says Charlotte.

"Like Chrissie," says Vivienne.

"Like Gwen," says Gwen with a giggle.

"Like Joan," I finish off our litany of trailblazing female lead singers. And then we're on the stage.

As soon as we get into our places, I go close to the microphone and say, "This is a new song."

And then we're off. And we sound amazing.

We get through the first verse and then the chorus hits. The audience goes crazy as soon as we spit out the first *"Heart shitter!"* It's a universal feeling of triumph, hearing a curse ring out through the sound system of a high school auditorium; after all, there is usually no profanity at a school-sanctioned event. I even see the one student judge laugh and immediately sit up a little straighter, like he's suddenly paying more attention to us.

I grin with every *"Heart shitter!"* we get out. By the third one, I notice the stage lights pulsing in time with them. I squint up into the lighting and sound booth and smirk conspiratorially at the three girls I see through the window.

Vivienne even gets to sing the second verse.

"There was a flutter, but I mistook it for love
It's gutter water, everything I thought it was
I see it clearly now that you took off the gloves
You're just a scorched-earth anthem to get rich off"

We get out one last *"Heart shitter!"* before our mics and amps go out. I look to the side of the stage and see a fuming Mr. Bolivar holding a plug in his hand. The audience boos loudly. Up in the lighting booth, the girls are frantically checking their equipment.

All I can do is turn to Vivienne and Charlotte and give them a huge smile. We brush hands in inconspicuous low-fives, trying to look con-trite as we filter off the stage, mostly for Gwen's sake.

But deep down, I know we all know. Whether we got to finish the song or not, that was our best performance yet. We don't even need the rowdy applause that's following us and the chants of "Let them play!" to realize it. Or even the next band, currently being introduced as Breakfast of Champions, who stick their own hands out for high-fives before they take the stage.

As Mr. Bolivar stalks over to us, I see a snake-adorned elbow slipping away through the backstage door.

I guess now there's a little bit of "me, me, me, me, me . . . Mitra" in him. I hope it stays like a pebble in his shoe.

I mean, even gods wear shoes, right?

LOVE IS A BATTLEFIELD

SHAUN DAVID HUTCHINSON

Leon brushes my hair out of my eyes before he kisses me, and even then I can feel his hands slowly reaching around my back to tuck in the tail of my shirt, which is hanging out because I'd gotten dressed in a hurry.

"What're you doing?" I say, pushing him back a little. "You know we can't be seen together."

"That's what I like about you, Dane." Leon taps his finger against his temple. "You're always looking out for me."

I'm looking out for myself, because if I get caught sucking face with the lead singer from Breakfast of Champions, Mr. Khatri is going to skin me alive and leave my bones in the discount-cassettes bin in the store. Besides, I'm not so much looking out for Leon as looking *at* him. I really do enjoy looking at him. He's a gymnast in his spare time, which makes me feel like the laziest sixteen-year-old human on the planet seeing as all I do in *my* free time is sleep and eat and slay monsters— the digital kind.

"You're definitely voting for us, right?" Leon asks.

"It depends on how good the other bands are."

Leon grins knowingly and winks. "Got it." He tucks my hair behind my ears and straightens my collar.

"I'm serious," I tell him. "I have to vote for the best band. I can't vote for Breakfast of Champions just because you look good in your underwear." He does. Don't ask how I know.

But Leon just winks again. "Totally understand. The *best* band."

Breakfast of Champions call themselves postindustrial absurdist electronic punk pop.

Yeah, I don't know what it is, either, but they're loud at it.

I disentangle myself from Leon and peek down the other hallway. It's still a couple of hours until the Battle of the Bands begins, but a few of the other bands are already showing up, and I saw Lilly Altman, who's stage-managing the show with an iron fist, stomping around earlier, too.

"I should get going," I say. "I'm meeting Abbie before the show."

Leon backs away and eyes me up and down. "Do you think you'll have time to go home and change?"

"What's wrong with what I'm wearing?" Jeans, plaid button-down. I thought I looked good when I left the house this morning.

"Nothing," Leon says. "I guess it's all right."

"Anyway," I say. "Text you later?"

"Definitely. We can celebrate me winning." And then Leon's gone, and I'm not sure if I'm glad or not.

My phone buzzes. It's Abbie telling me she's going to be late, which is typical. I usually just assume she's going to be fifteen minutes later than she says she'll be. It saves me from being annoyed all the time. I should get out of here anyway, though. I only dropped by because Lilly wants to go over how Mr. Bolivar is going to introduce the judges. Total waste of time.

I head out to the back of the auditorium, and the second I hit the sunshine, I'm pinned to a wall and someone is grabbing my ass and kissing my neck. It takes a second to realize it's Sindy, one of the lead singers of the Marcia, Marcia, Marcias, a rhythm and blues pop fusion band that draws their inspiration from Amy Winehouse, Tina Turner, and Janelle Monáe, or so Sindy is always saying. I don't hear it. Leon's drummer, Beckett, is also the drummer for the Marcia, Marcia, Marcias, which is kind of weird. Sindy's not worried about it, but if she finds out about us, or about me and Leon, I am so screwed.

"Whoa," I say, scrambling out from under Sindy and looking around to make sure no one saw us. "What're you doing?"

Sindy's curvy, with short, punky pink hair and a tattoo that says *Sure, Jan* on her arm that she stole her older sister's ID to get. Her mom kind of lost her mind when she saw it, but that only made it more punk rock.

"Sound check," she says. "This is the time slot that overbearing stage manager Linda gave me."

"Lilly."

"Sure." Sindy bumps me with her hip and runs a hand down my arm. "So, who do you think's gonna win tonight?"

I grit my teeth. "No clue," I say, "seeing as I haven't seen anyone play yet."

"You've seen *me* play."

"Not here."

Sindy slaps my arm. She probably thought it was playful, but there's no way it's not going to leave a mark. "You don't really think any of these poseurs are gonna be better than the Marcia, Marcia, Marcias, do you?"

75

"I . . ."

Sindy kisses my cheek and whispers, "You don't have to answer. I already know." Then she smacks my ass—hard—and struts inside.

I look straight up at the cloudless sky and say, "Why the hell is this happening to me?"

I don't give a shit about music. I can't tell Fiona Apple from Princess Fiona, I'm still not convinced ska is an actual musical category and not a prank that got out of hand, and my favorite beetle is Jaime Reyes. And yet I'm a judge for the Raritan River Battle of the Bands who's also kind of dating the lead singers of two of the bands in the contest, both of whom have assumed, without any encouragement from me, that I'm going to be the deciding vote that awards them the win. Even if I do vote for one of them, there's no guarantee the other judges will.

I didn't even want the job at Atomic Records. I went in to get an album for my older sister, Ruby. She's the music snob, not me. For her birthday, I figured I'd do something thoughtful and buy her a copy of Prince's *Purple Rain* to replace the one she'd given to her boyfriend the day he left for college. She immediately regretted the decision when he texted her the following day to tell her he couldn't do a long-distance relationship, sorry, but thanks for the record.

Anyway, I went into the store, found the album, took it up to the counter, and there was the most beautiful boy I'd ever seen. He was working this preppy punk look with bleached-blond hair and a nose ring, and he smiled at me, and basically my brain melted because all I could do was stand there and stare and drool.

"You like Prince?" he asked. His name was Liam because of course it was.

"Love him." And then I desperately tried to remember every single thing I'd ever heard Ruby mention about Prince, and I regurgitated it back to Liam like I was being quizzed.

Liam nodded appreciatively. "You know a lot about Prince."

"I know a lot about a lot," I said, because talking is hard when your brain is the consistency of warm yogurt. "Music especially."

Liam pointed at a sign on the counter. "You should apply for a job."

And I did. Right there on the spot. My mom had been bugging me to join a club or play a sport or get a job or something so that I wasn't sitting around the house wasting my life on video games. The next day, I interviewed with the store's owner, Mr. Khatri, a virtual encyclopedia of music, and got the job. I spent my nights dreaming of what it would be like to work with Liam. We'd talk about music, he'd fall totally in love with me, I'd take him to prom, and we'd have some beautiful happily-ever-after. It was fate, and it was going to be amazing.

I showed up for my first day of work, and Mr. Khatri was there to train me. I asked him when Liam worked. I'd been pestering Ruby about the difference between hard rock and heavy metal, whether the Ramones were better than the Violent Femmes, and if she thought Blondie still rocked so that I could impress Liam. I was impatient for my fairy tale to begin.

"Liam doesn't work here anymore," Mr. Khatri said.

"Wait, what?"

"He quit to go to culinary school." Mr. Khatri seemed to think I should have known that. "Whose job did you think you were interviewing for?" He laughed. "I've already got Rodney and DeeDee. How many of you kids do you think I can afford to hire?" He cackled through the rest of my training. I didn't find it nearly as funny.

*   *   *

"I'll tell you why this is happening to you," Abbie says. I don't really want to know, but there's no stopping her once she gets going. Besides, I'm not going to leave. The chairs in Bean and Ballad are the best part of the quiet coffee shop. They're like sitting on clouds. "It's because you don't value yourself, Dane. The second someone shows even the slightest bit of interest in you, you become the person you think they want you to be."

"That's *so* not true."

"When you dated Luke Schweitzer in seventh grade, you were all about building model cars even though you'd never built a model car in your entire life before that point."

I sip my hot chocolate, which I really only ordered for the whipped cream. Bean and Ballad is kind of a hole-in-the-wall, but the baristas don't give me dirty looks for camping out and playing video games on the days my mom forces me to "leave the house and get some sun on my pasty face." There also isn't anyone around to overhear my conversation with Abbie, thankfully. "I enjoyed building those cars with Luke."

"Did you enjoy learning how to cha-cha with Lauren Whittaker? Or the countless hours you spent picking up garbage on the side of the road with what's-his-name? The one who was obsessed with saving the planet one plastic straw at a time."

"Sanjay," I say.

"Right." Abbie pauses for a moment. "He was really cute. What happened to him?"

"His parents moved to Texas or something."

Abbie grimaces. "Yikes. But at least there's a lot of trash there." Abbie is my best friend. She is the smartest person I know, able to talk with the same authority about royal family gossip and quantum physics. She is also beautiful and athletic, and I'm pretty sure there's nothing she can't do. It's intimidating and often annoying. Not quite as annoying as how she's almost always right, but pretty close.

"Did you have a point?" I ask. "Or were you just going to insult me all afternoon?"

Abbie's double-fisting drinks. A medium cup of something caffeinated in one hand and a massive bottle of water in the other. She takes hydration seriously, though don't mention it unless you're prepared for her TED Talk about it. She's got slides on her phone.

"My point," she says, "is that maybe you shouldn't be dating anyone at all."

I roll my eyes. "You're supposed to be helping me decide between Leon and Sindy. 'Neither' isn't a valid response."

"It should be," Abbie says. "What do you think is going to happen when they find out about each other?"

"We never said we were exclusive." It hasn't come up with Leon because he's so self-absorbed that he probably assumes I couldn't possibly want to be with anyone other than him, and Sindy's too punk rock to talk about labels and commitment.

"You're a walking cliché!"

"Am not."

Abbie's shaking her head, giving me the same look my mom gives me four times a year when she gets my report card. "I don't know why they call boys like you dogs. Dogs are sweet and faithful, and you are neither of those things."

"Hey!"

"They should call you bunnies—"

"Because I like carrots and have good teeth?"

"Yeah," Abbie says, rolling her eyes. "That's totally why."

I don't think Abbie's being fair. It's not like I'm having sex with either of them. Or with anyone. Yet. I'm pretty sure I'd like to have it with someone at some point—maybe—but it's not at the top of my list of priorities. Honestly, sometimes I'm not sure it ever will be.

"Are you going to help me or not?" I ask. "Sindy or Leon?"

Abbie sighs as if I have asked her to provide the answer to the meaning of life through the power of interpretive dance, and she has grudgingly agreed to oblige. "Tell me one thing you like about each of them."

"Leon is . . . prompt."

"Prompt?" Abbie asks. "Is that a dig at me? Because I told you I was going to be late."

"He's got nice fingernails."

"Wow, Dane, you are really selling this guy to me. I mean, prompt *and* he has nice fingernails? Where can I get a piece like him?"

I set down my hot chocolate. "Are you going to take this seriously or not?"

"Not if those are going to be your actual answers."

I scrub my face with my hands and growl loudly enough that people at the other tables look over. "Okay, fine," I say. "Sometimes, when I watch his band play, and he's singing, he looks right at me and I feel like I'm the only person in the room."

"Sometimes you are," Abbie says, but I ignore her. Though she's also not wrong.

"Leon has this way of making me feel special."

"You *are* special."

"But with him, I feel it," I say.

Abbie types something into her phone, and I hope it's not my answer because if she's actually writing it down, I might scream. "Now do Sindy."

80

"Sindy makes me feel alive." A smile finds its way onto my lips as I recall the last time we went out. "It's like I'm sleepwalking through my life until I'm with her, and then I'm wide awake."

"Now," Abbie says. "What do you hate about them?"

"Pretty much everything else."

Abbie puts her phone away and looks me in the eye, trying on a maternal kind of stare that I don't much care for. "What do *you* want?"

"Truthfully?" I say. "Someone who wouldn't mind playing video games with me. Someone who wants to be my player two."

Mr. Khatri handed me the flyer and said, "I have better things to do. You go."

Judging the Battle of the Bands had been Liam's idea, and he'd signed Mr. Khatri up to be a sponsor and a judge. People are into vinyl again, but most of the kids I know listen to music on their phones. You can't fit a record player in your pocket. The Battle of the Bands was a chance to get some exposure for the store.

"I don't know anything about judging a music competition," I said.

Mr. Khatri was busy rearranging the shelves again. Grunge, he claimed, was making a comeback, and he wanted to make sure it was closer to the front. Nobody wanted grunge to come back—I'd tried Nirvana, L7, Dinosaur Jr., and 7 Year Bitch just to make sure I wasn't missing anything; I wasn't—but I kept my mouth shut out of a sense of self-preservation. Mr. Khatri's musical tastes were vast. One day he might be listening to Nipsey Hussle, the next Carly Simon or Rihanna or Marvin Gaye or the Commoners. And mocking his music would result in a history lesson that could cure an insomniac.

"You sit and listen to the bands play, you pick the one you like best, the end. Don't overthink it."

"What if I don't like any of them?"

Mr. Khatri shrugged. "Then vote for the band that is dressed the best, or pick the one with the name you think is funniest. I don't know. That's why you're judging and not me."

"Way to support the local scene, Mr. K."

"I'm hosting the winning band's release party," he said. "Do you want to plan that, or do you want to spend an evening sitting on your butt listening to music?" Mr. Khatri flashed me a wry smile.

I couldn't even organize my bookshelves, so the idea of having to organize an entire gig was the stuff of nightmares. "Fine," I said. "You win."

And that's how I wound up judging the competition. The bands, who had probably spent a lot of hours rehearsing, deserved a judge who was a David Bowie–loving super-nerd who could spend hours talking about deep cuts from obscure bands. Instead, they got me, and the last album I listened to from beginning to end was *Dance Dance!* by the Wiggles when I got stuck watching the Alberts' toddler because there was some emergency involving a hammer and a thumb and I was the only one around. Mr. Albert gave me fifty bucks, so it wasn't a total waste.

Anyway, how the hell am I supposed to choose between sixteen bands when I can't choose between two?

"Wow," I say to Melissa Nuvel, the judge sitting on my left. "They sure do like to scream."

"I don't know." She picks up her sheet listing the band names and the order they're playing in. "They're not so bad."

Wrong. Rock Your Mouth is the first band, and I'm already bored. Melissa Nuvel is the lead singer of a local New Jersey band called

You Try Smiling that had stumbled onto fifteen minutes of fame when one of their songs appeared on the soundtrack for a popular movie I'd never seen. Mr. Khatri told me she'd been riding the popularity of that song for a decade and that she'd pretty much show up to the opening of a bag of Doritos these days, but that we were lucky to have her.

"The local music scene is an important part of every community." Melissa is still talking, but I'm barely listening. "And I'm happy I can come out here and support these kids."

Happy? Is she serious? I resist the temptation to list everything that would be less painful than listening to sixteen bands "play" their "music." Anyway, Melissa's not so bad. I've got Vice Principal Pulley on my other side. Picture your dad. Now picture your dad with sleeves of tattoos. Now picture your dad, with his tattoo sleeves, also wearing those weird poly-cotton-blend shorts that male PE teachers frequently wear. The ones that are both a little too tight and a little too short. Now picture your tattoo-covered, indecent-shorts-wearing dad banging his head along to the screams of a band called Rock Your Mouth while taking notes with his left hand and throwing devil horns with his right.

Whatever image you're now holding in your mind, Pulley is so much worse. And the thing that makes it sad is that he practically begged to be here. As I look away, I catch the eye of a guy with brown hair and glasses who's standing near the wall. He motions at Mr. Pulley with his chin and rolls his eyes. I smile, glad that I'm not the only one here to bear witness to Mr. Pulley's shameless enthusiasm for a high school rock band, and then shift my attention away so that I don't become some random weirdo staring at him in a story he tells his friends later.

At the far end of the table is Claudia Ramirez. She's a lifestyle guru, whatever that is, with a few hundred thousand followers on YouTube and Instagram. I introduced myself to her earlier, but all she said to me was "Venti, two-pump sugar-free vanilla, oat milk, one-hundred-sixty-two-degree latte. Quickly." I don't know who ended up making a Starbucks run, but it wasn't me.

After Rock Your Mouth finishes—and I'm so grateful they're done—Mr. Bolivar comes out and starts telling jokes like he's at an open mic night at a comedy club, only the jokes are terrible. "I thought the Greatest Place was up next," I whisper to Melissa. She answers with a shrug.

Mr. Pulley starts laughing on my other side and says, "A gummy bear! That's hilarious."

Something has clearly gone wrong. Maybe the Greatest Place didn't show or the band members developed a sudden case of food poisoning. Just when I think Mr. Bolivar can't embarrass himself more, he finds depths of humiliation that I didn't know existed. I'm about to say a prayer for him to develop an immediate case of laryngitis when he finally says, "Let's give a big Narwhal welcome to Mina Wright!" Instead of a band playing two songs, we get one song from a girl with a guitar.

Melissa smiles and bobs her head along to the music. Mina is definitely better than Mr. Bolivar.

After Mina, the Marcia Marcia Marcias take the stage, and I do my best not to make eye contact with Sindy when she steps up to the mic. Sindy announces the name of their first song: "Nobody Nose." It's great that the band has a thing, but Sindy is seriously obsessed with the Bradys, and I'm not sure it's entirely healthy. The truth is that they're not bad—the way Xiomara harmonizes with Sindy, Maya on bass looking like she's in her own little world, and Beckett keeping perfect time on the drums. If all their songs weren't focused on a fifty-year-old TV sitcom, they might have stood a chance at winning.

I try to pay attention to the set, to do the job I'm here to do, but

I can't stop thinking about the question Abbie asked: Why do I like Sindy? The thing is, going out with Sindy was an accident.

I was waiting in line at the theater to get into the latest Star Wars movie. I was supposed to be meeting Wesley Cho. We'd been dating for a month, and he'd asked me to wait in line since he had a debate tournament that afternoon and knew he wouldn't get there in time to score a ticket. About ten minutes before they opened the door, I got a series of texts from Wes.

WES: *Hey, I'm not gonna make it.*
WES: *I'm at the theater in Hadley with my D&D group.*
WES: *Also, I think we should break up.*
WES: *Sorry, dude.*

"You have got to be kidding me." Did I mention that it was freezing out and my balls were two little hailstones stuck to the side of my leg?

"Problem?"

This girl, who I hadn't noticed before, was standing by me. She had pink hair and a million earrings, and I had no idea where she'd come from. But she was there and I needed to vent.

"Yeah. This guy I was seeing just bailed on me, and then dumped me with 'Sorry, dude.' Who the hell does that?"

"Ouch."

"I mean, I've been standing out here for *five hours.* I already bought the tickets, and I don't even like Star Wars."

The girl elbowed me in the ribs. "Maybe don't say that too loud in this crowd." She glanced meaningfully at the Wookiee to our left, who was glaring at me.

"Fair point."

"I'm Sindy."

"Dane."

The doors finally opened and the line began shuffling inside.

"So you're not a fan," Sindy said, "but you're still going to see the movie?"

I shrugged. "I mean, I'm already here, and I paid for the tickets."

Without warning, Sindy snapped her fingers. "I knew I recognized you. You work at Atomic Records, right? You're judging the Battle of the Bands in a couple of months."

"That's me," I said.

"Right on. How'd you luck into that gig?"

I wasn't sure she'd believe me if I told her it was an accident predicated upon another accident. My whole life seemed to be one accident after another.

We got through the door and I bought some popcorn and candy and a drink, and it wasn't until I got to my seat and Sindy sat beside me that I realized she hadn't had a ticket. That she'd let the guy who'd scanned the tickets on my phone think we were together.

Sindy reached her hand into my popcorn during the previews just as I was reaching *my* hand in, and her fingers drew buttery lines across my palm. By the middle of the movie, her tongue was in my mouth, and by the end of the movie, I think we were common-law married in some states. Either way, that's how that happened.

Vice Principal Pulley elbows me in the ribs. "Do you think this is goth or emo?" he asks.

The band is Chump 2.0, and I wasn't paying attention when they introduced themselves, so I don't know what the song they're singing is called, but I think it's about a girl named Mitra. Maybe. The lead singer's kind of cute, if you're into college guys who act like they're still in high school. I'm not, but I'm sure there are people who are.

"I honestly don't know the difference," I said.

Pulley rubs his chin like he's putting a lot of thought into it. "I think goths love darkness."

"Don't emos?"

"Yes," he says. "But I think they pretend like they don't."

"If you say so." My stomach is starting to hurt because Leon's band is up soon. Sindy expects me to vote for her band and Leon expects me to vote for his. I could always vote for neither so I don't have to pick a side. That would be the least painful option. Of course, I'm still going to have to choose between Sindy and Leon since I can't keep dating both of them forever. If they don't find out about each other, Beckett might find out and tell them. I'm surprised she hasn't already.

My anxiety cranks up to a hundred when Chump 2.0 finishes their set and is followed by the Grants. I don't recognize their singer, but I recognize Gwen on keyboards. We had earth science together. Or was it algebra? The lead singer steps up to the mic and says, "This is a new song."

"That's Mitra," Melissa says. "The girl Chump 2.0 sang about."

"How do you even know that?" I ask, but before she can reply, the Grants leap into the song. It's all right, I guess. I'm about to zone out when Mitra yells *"Heart shitter!"* into the mic. It catches me off guard and snaps me out of my reverie.

"No, ma'am," Pulley says on my other side, sounding offended, though I'm not sure what he's going to do about it. The audience is cheering—everyone is into the song. Besides, who hasn't had their heart shit on—or shit out; the lyrics weren't clear—before? I've never understood why people get so bent out of shape about a little profanity.

The Grants could probably fake-murder someone onstage and no one would care, but scream *"Heart shitter"* once, and the adults in the room lose their minds.

At the start of the second chorus, Mr. Bolivar pulls the plug, cutting off the mics and amps. Behind me, people are booing. I kind of want to give the Grants my vote for their display of sheer nerve. Maybe I will.

Mr. Bolivar manages to quiet the crowd as Breakfast of Champions take the stage. Leon is basically sex personified, and he knows it. For him, it's less about the music than it is about the fame. He wants to be seen and adored. The irony is that Leon's actually got potential. If he put a tenth of the effort into practicing the music that he puts into deciding what to wear, he could be amazing.

"Yeah, we're Breakfast of Champions. Open up and say ahhhhhhhh!"

Leon launches into his first song without even saying what it is, and while I recognize some of the parts where he screams, I can't remember the title. I wish I'd brought earplugs. At least he's pretty to look at. The funny thing is that I really didn't like him when I first met him, and I definitely didn't want to go out with him.

I was at a party a couple of weeks after I'd met Sindy. We weren't really anything yet. Sometimes we texted, and sometimes she showed up at the store right before closing and told me we were going out. I didn't really have much say in the matter. That night she was playing a gig with the band, and Abbie had convinced me to meet her at a party. I nearly bailed at the last minute—parties aren't my thing—but my mom was so happy that I wouldn't be spending my Friday night in my room that I couldn't bear to disappoint her.

"You're allowed to drink if there's alcohol there," my mom said as I was leaving. "But no driving. And no driving with anyone else who's been drinking."

"No one's going to be drinking, Mom." Everyone was going to be drinking.

"If you do need a ride, call me no matter what time it is."

"There's no way I'm calling my mom to pick me up from a party."

"You don't have to tell them I'm your mother," she said. "Tell them I'm an Uber driver. I don't mind."

My mom's the worst. But also the best.

So I went to the party. I don't even know whose party it was, but everyone from Raritan River High was there. I'd hoped to get some Abbie time so I could tell her what was going on with Sindy, but she was destroying some kids from the National Honor Society in a game of drunk Trivial Pursuit, and I didn't want to ruin her night. I wound up outside on the patio sitting with some stoners around the firepit. I don't smoke, but stoners always have the best snacks. This time they had s'mores.

And then in walked Leon in cutoff shorts that exposed his pale, hairy legs, showing off his lip piercing to anyone and everyone who'd look at it.

"Yeah," I said. "That's infected."

"How the hell do you know?" he asked.

I leaned forward to get a better look. "Because it's red and crusty, and unless you've had collagen injected into your lip on one side only, it's super swollen."

Leon touched the ring going through his lip and tried to hide his wince. "Yeah, well, you've got chocolate on your face."

"Do I?" I wiped my mouth with my sleeve, and it came away with a big glob of chocolate, which I licked off. "You should really go back to the place that pierced it for you and get a refund."

"Joke's on you," Leon said. "I did it myself."

"Of course you did." I got up and headed inside, hoping Abbie was done, but she still had one pie wedge to go to win. The sports category, which was always my downfall. I had thought I'd left Leon outside, but when I turned around, he and his infected lip were right there.

"You think I should take it out?" he asked.

"Only if you want to keep the lip."

Leon's eyes darted left and right. "Can you . . . ?"

"Can I what?"

"Help?"

"You pierced it yourself," I said, "but you can't take it out?"

Leon whined, "It hurts!" low enough so that no one but me could hear him.

"Fine. I need to use the bathroom anyway."

We wound up in a boy's bedroom that had an adjoining bathroom. There were pictures of the boy all over, but I still had no clue whose house I was in. I spied his video game setup, and was trying to work out a way to ditch Leon so I could play, but he dragged me into the bathroom.

"Sit." I pointed to the toilet while I washed my hands in scalding water with antibacterial soap, as much for my protection as his.

"I'm in a band," Leon said, unprompted. "Breakfast of Champions."

When I turned back around, Leon had stripped off his shirt and was sitting in just his shorts on the toilet. I'd only seen muscles like that in superhero movies. "Jesus Christ," I said.

Most people would've been a little embarrassed or awkward, but Leon, and I swear this is true, flexed. His chest rippled. "I'm also a gymnast," he said.

Look, it's a good thing I was about to pull a scabby, pus-covered ring from Leon's infected lip because my disgust at that was all that kept me from turning into a walking hard-on.

"Why is your shirt even off to begin with?"

Leon shrugged. "In case this gets messy."

I don't know what he was expecting to come out of his lip, but I wanted to get the whole thing over with. For someone with muscles like Leon's, he sure did whimper a lot when I was taking the ring out and cleaning it up with some warm soapy water. I searched the cabinets but couldn't find any ointment, so I told him what to buy and then pushed him out of the bathroom so I could pee.

When I'd finished using the restroom and washing my hands multiple times, I opened the door and Leon threw a bunch of clothes at me. "Strip and put these on."

I held out the clothes—some jeans ripped at the knees and a couple of black T-shirts. "Why?"

"Because you look like you're trying to spread the good word of our Lord and Savior, and I can't be seen hanging out with you looking like that." Leon shrugged sympathetically. "I have a reputation."

Seriously, I had *no* intention of changing clothes—I liked what I was wearing, for starters—but before I knew what was happening, Leon had me standing in my boxers trying on different clothes from a stranger's closet. After making me change like ten times, he spent another ten minutes styling my hair. With someone else's brush. In my mind, I kept saying, *Hey, maybe this isn't cool with whoever this room belongs to*, but those words never quite made it out of my mouth.

When Leon was done, we stood side by side in front of the mirror, and I realized he'd dressed me up like him.

"You are so fucking cute," he said. "How come I've never seen you around before?"

"No clue. I go to school, and I work at Atomic Records."

Leon's eyes lit up, and I knew he'd made the connection. "So then you *have* heard of my band before." He wagged his finger at me. "Look at you trying to pretend you hadn't."

"I really—"

Leon pushed me against the wall and went in to kiss me, but I ducked out of his arms and said, "Infected lip. Kissing bad."

Judging by the look on his face, Leon had never been rejected before, and he looked so sad about it. So I added, "It would probably really hurt," which seemed to make him feel better.

Instead, he reached into my pocket, grabbed my phone, made me unlock it, put in his number, and then texted himself so he would have mine.

"Come on," he said. "Let's go back downstairs." Which we did. Where he introduced me as his boyfriend. The stoners I'd been sitting with didn't even recognize me.

My phone vibrates, and I dig it out of my pocket. It's a text, but I don't recognize the number. I open the message, and it just says, *Matcha smoothie bowl with coconut milk, spinach, kiwi, mango, and bee pollen, and two squares of vegan dark chocolate with kale and chia seeds.*

"What the hell?" I mumble. I glance around, and Claudia leans forward, looks at me, raises her eyebrows, and motions at me to hurry up. Did she seriously text me her dinner order? How the hell did she get my number?

This is ridiculous. I don't even know what I'm doing here. I'm not qualified to be a judge. If I'm being honest, all of the bands that have played so far sounded the same to me. They deserve to be judged by someone who actually appreciates the hard work they've put into their music, not by someone whose favorite song is the original *Tetris* theme. Besides, even if Sindy and Leon have no chance of winning, they're each still going to expect *me* to vote for them, and the thought of having to choose makes me sick to my stomach. I don't want to choose between them. I'm not sure I want to choose either of them.

As Mr. Bolivar announces the next band, I Want Your P.S., my chest tightens. I need some air. I have to get out of here. I turn to Melissa Nuvel and whisper, "Yeah, um, diarrhea." I point at my stomach and then sneak out from behind the table and run.

Once outside, I shut my eyes, inhale deeply, then scream in frustration at the top of my lungs. When I look around, there are a couple of guys watching me, looking a little sketchy. Whatever. I don't care. I also don't know what to do. Maybe I should tell Vice Principal Pulley that I have a family emergency and need to leave. That would spare me from having to choose between Sindy and Leon. It would also piss off Mr. Khatri, but he'd get over it. It's probably time for me to put in my notice anyway. There are tons of people who'd jump at the chance to work in a music store. One of them should have the job. I never wanted it in the first place. Just considering quitting feels like a weight lifting off of me.

"What do you think you're doing?" Leon's voice cuts through the quiet in my mind. I open my eyes and find he's not alone.

"You're not leaving yet, are you?" Sindy is standing with Leon. Both of them are staring at me expectantly.

"Uh . . ."

Leon moves toward me, his hand already raised like he's going to fix my hair, and I back away.

Wait. Leon and Sindy are hanging out together, which means they've probably talked. But then why aren't they pissed off at me? Why aren't they yelling? "Do you know about each other?"

Leon and Sindy share a smile. "Only since just a few minutes ago,"

Sindy says. "We ran into each other and I let it slip that my boyfriend was a judge—"

"And I thought she meant Mr. Pulley at first," Leon says with a laugh that makes it impossible for me to tell whether he's joking.

"Ew, never," Sindy says. "Anyway, we worked out you were dating both of us, which you and I are going to talk about later." I have a sinking feeling Sindy's idea of talking is not going to involve any actual talking.

"*I'm* not into sharing," Leon says. "But I assumed you'd be ending it with Sindy when you voted for me. Which you can't do if you leave."

Sindy rolls her eyes. "And I told Leon there's no way in hell you'd ever vote for the watered-down punk-lite crap he plays over the Marcia, Marcia, Marcias. Also, I'm way hotter than he is."

"In your dreams," Leon says.

They literally start arguing over which of them is prettier, and I can't even. Their voices are like bees buzzing in my brain. Neither of them even cares about me. They only want my vote. Maybe that's the only thing they ever wanted from me. The realization should make me feel like my heart got shit on—or out; I'm still not sure—but instead I smile because I know what to do.

"I'm not leaving," I say. "I'm also not voting for either of your bands. Your music sucks."

For maybe the first time since I met them, Sindy and Leon are speechless, and I take off before that changes. I sneak back inside, hoping to get to my seat between sets, but Mr. Bolivar is already saying, "Welcome, Safe & Sound," so I hang out near the wall to avoid distracting them.

Safe & Sound is a girl with a guitar and a guy with a keyboard. They start to sing, harmonizing in a way that gives me goose bumps. It's beautiful and so warm and real. The way she sings about being in love with two people hurts to listen to, yet I can't stop.

I want to be angry at Sindy and Leon for using me, but I don't think I cared about them any more than they cared about me. Being with each of them was easy in a way because they made the decisions I was too scared to make for myself. I want love like in this song. I want to find someone who makes having my heart shit on (or out) feel worth it. I'm just not sure I ever will. What I am sure of is that I have to stop being who others want me to be. I have to be myself whether others like me or not.

When Safe & Sound is done, I really do have to run to the restroom, so I race out and go. On my way back, I hear familiar music playing. I need to return to the auditorium so I can hear the rest of the bands, though I think I know who I'm going to vote for, but I take a moment to hunt down the source of the song. I find a guy sitting on a bench with a Switch cradled between his knees. Chestnut hair with a long nose and black glasses. I've seen him before, but I can't place where.

He looks up. Catches me spying on him. "You're staring," he says. "Again."

That's where I know him. "You were watching the show earlier."

"I was watching Pulley watch the show," he says. "Far more entertaining."

He's not wrong about that. "I'm Dane. Are you playing *Breath of the Wild*?"

He nods. "Alex. Waiting for my brother. Mateo from Chump 2.0."

"What's the deal with him and all the songs about the singer from the Grants?"

"Mateo's . . . got issues." Alex pauses. "You like *Breath of the Wild*?"

"It's only my second favorite game ever."

95

He eyes me appraisingly. "What's your first favorite game?"

"*Link's Awakening*, obviously."

"Obviously," Alex says. He slides a Joy-Con off the side and holds it out to me. "I've got *Luigi's Mansion*. Wanna be my Gooigi?"

I reach eagerly for the controller but stop before taking it. "I'm judging," I say. "It'd be a super dick move to bail."

Alex nods and slips the controller back into place. "It's cool."

"I really do want to play. It's just—"

"You're judging," he says. "I get it." He motions toward the doors. "You should get in there." He turns his attention to the screen.

"How about after the show?" I ask. "I know this great coffee shop."

Alex glances up again cautiously. "Seriously?"

I nod.

"Then, yeah! Definitely." He's beaming, which makes me grin like a fool.

I could never get Sindy or Leon to play games with me. Sindy thinks they're a waste of time, and Leon refuses to play anything he isn't immediately good at because he can't bear to lose.

"I'll meet you out here when this is over, okay?"

Alex flashes me a bright, toothy smile. "It's a date."

"One thing, though," I say. "I get to be Luigi. You can be *my* player two."

You Found Me

ASHLEY WOODFOLK

I'm late.

I am always late, but somehow Rod still seems surprised (and a little pissed) when I come barreling into the empty auditorium.

I sprint down the center aisle, all frazzled and full of apologies, indigo locs trailing behind me, guitar case banging into my jegging-clad legs. "Sorry, sorry, sorry," I whisper, because Rod is singing, and his voice (much like his face) is heaven.

Rodney Lockhart is tall and dark-skinned like his dad, charming and loud like his mom. He has his thick black hair woven into ten even cornrows, but everything else about him is all out of sorts. His knee is a little ashy where it peeks through his dark, ripped jeans. His T-shirt is wrinkled, and the drawstring in his black hoodie is pulled long on one side and unraveling. His shoelaces are untied.

"Uh-oh," I mutter, because I've known Rod since we both brought homemade donuts to our church's bake sale when we were eleven (what are the chances?), and he always dresses exactly the way he feels.

"You good?" I ask once I reach the front row.

His nimble brown fingers don't stop moving across the surface of his keyboard. He keeps holding the note he's singing while giving me a death stare, and the sound makes my bones ache in a good way, almost as much as the stare makes me nervous.

"I'm fine," he lies, finishing the song and walking over to sit at the edge of the stage. "But you're late again and you know we only have the auditorium for an hour. We're seniors, Raven. This is our last Battle of the Bands. If we have any chance of winning this, you have to be all in. Are you?"

I nod, trying not to think about a few months ago when I called him crying and told him I was dropping out of our two-person band. It was the second time I'd quit.

"Did you finish the song?" he says next.

He's talking about the song he found me working on without him. He walked in on me singing the first verse of an original he'd never heard, and because our band, Safe & Sound, had only just gotten back together, I thought he'd freak out. But he didn't. He said the song had potential and told me to finish it and promised we could perform it at Battle of the Bands.

I'm not happy with what I've written so far, but I reach into my pocket and pull out my phone to show him.

Rod reads and reads and doesn't say a word.

"Ugh. I know, I know. It's bad right?"

"No, Raven," Rod says. He's smiling with half his mouth now. "This is really, *really* good. How does it go again?"

I hum the melody, and seconds later he's singing all the words that I wrote, and it never gets old hearing him transform typed letters on a phone into the loveliest sounds. I fit my voice around his, hoping that the sound of us together will fix what still feels broken about this song, when he looks at me. His dark eyes are full of something I can't name, and it makes my heart beat a little harder. And *this* is exactly why I quit the band in the first place. But then Rod's lovable but intense parental units told him they didn't want him playing "in his little band" with anyone but me, a "good girl from a church-going family," and just like that, I got sucked right back in despite what being alone with him does to my heart.

Rod stops singing. "Damn, girl. I don't know how you don't see how good you are."

I swallow hard and look away from him, because I can't hold his gaze when he looks at me like that. It reminds me too much of when we're singing the last note of a song we both love, of how long we've been friends, and of the first time I realized I wanted to be more. I'm about to change the subject, to ask his opinion about how to fix the hook, when someone pushes open the door of the auditorium. The squeak echoes like a record scratch.

"Rave! Rod! I thought you two might be in here!"

Kima Ito flips her long black curls like she doesn't know the scent of her hair is deadly, like she doesn't know that it smells like clove and sunshine. I can't smell that hair (or anything sweet or spiced for most of fall and winter) without remembering . . . *things.*

"Hey, Kima," I say, surprised. "I thought you had to work on the paper all afternoon."

"I do. I am," she starts, "but did you see that Safe & Sound got featured on the *IndieTrash* homepage today?"

"Seriously?" Rod asks. He's all excited, and I start to feel that way, too, until I look at Kima's face.

"Wait, why do you look pissed? This is a good thing, isn't it?" I ask.

IndieTrash is a local music blog, like *Rolling Stone* meets SoundCloud but specifically for New Brunswick, New Jersey. Everyone who's anyone in music around here uploads their songs with the hope that they might be featured, reviewed, or that, if they get enough listens, their band's events will be picked up and listed in the website's epic gigs and concerts calendar.

Kima pulls up the site and hands her phone over to show us. Rod reads the post aloud.

"'Safe & Sound are giving us major Leon Bridges meets the Civil Wars vibes. It's flavor we never knew we wanted in indie music.'"

I see his eyes move over the words a second time before Rod says, "'Flavor'?"

"I know. Low-key racist, right?" Kima asks.

"Damn," I say. "'Leon Bridges meets the Civil Wars' is the only way I want us to be described for the rest of forever, but then they went and ruined it."

Kima shakes her head, then crosses her arms. "Right? I might have sent a strongly worded email."

"Aww, Keem," I say. I want to wrap my arm around her hip and pull her into a hug, but I worry it would overwhelm me. I do the opposite, taking a step closer to the stage instead.

Kima wants to be a music writer. The secret goal she told me she doesn't allow herself to think too hard about is becoming the editor in chief of *Pitchfork*. Or even more secret: starting something new that's just as good, if not better. *IndieTrash* is the best place around here to start if you want to end up on staff at a big-time music publication. Kima's been working her butt off all year to get an internship there after graduation. For her to risk all that just because of one problematic post? Against my better judgment, I reach out and squeeze her soft hand.

I feel what I'm always trying not to feel when the three of us are together: a little crushy, a lot blushy. Having feelings for your best friend is always complicated, but especially so when you're in a band together and you're only days away from performing in a competition that could change everything. (Rod wants to record, wants to tour, wants to be famous, and winning the Battle could be the first step toward making our band into something real.) When you also kinda love your *other* best friend, and when those best friends happen to be dating each other? All bets are off.

"I'll just . . ." Rod says, taking out his own phone. He writes a quick thread, subtweeting the crap out of them, and it makes me love him more than I already do.

I retweet the whole thing immediately, adding a reply that reads, "More like IndieGarbageFire" with a GIF of a dumpster engulfed in flames that makes Rod and Kima laugh.

"Speaking of *IndieTrash*," Kima says, "I need your help." She's looking at me, but it's Rod who answers.

"Kima, babe. Can it wait? We're in the middle of rehearsing," he says, pulling me up onstage with him. "Raven wrote this great song, but it's not quite right and—"

"What do you need?" I ask her. I'm halfway back down the stage steps before I can stop myself. Because as much as Kima's clove-scented hair makes my heart ache, something about the girl pulls at me like a magnet.

"Photos. Simone got the flu, and there's no one else I can count on to take good action shots the night of the show for the paper," Kima says. Simone is the staff photographer for the school paper. Kima's been the editor since she epically ousted Perry Franz by popular vote last semester even though Kima was the new girl.

"But you know I'm performing," I say, looking back at Rod.

"I know, but you guys are only playing for like ten minutes, right? Just take a few pics before you go on and after. I'll take care of everything else."

Rod throws his hands in the air because he knows he can't stop either of us from doing whatever we decide.

"The Battle issue of the paper could be my big break, Rave. It could get me in the door at *IndieTrash*."

"You still want to work there, even after what they posted this morning?" Rod asks her from behind me.

"That's even more of a reason they need someone like her, Rod," I say. "If they had some smart, creative 'flavor' on staff, maybe stuff like that wouldn't slip through the cracks."

"Exactly," Kima says. "See? Rave just gets it." I love that she calls me Rave instead of Raven. It makes me feel like a party instead of a girl.

Kima flips her hair, and since my eyes are still turned in Rod's direction, I only know because that spicy scent of hers wafts over everything.

And with a single, shallow inhale, I'm back at the show where we met this summer.

Boys Behaving Badly was playing, and me and my sister showed up a little late to the show. We didn't want to see the opener, who we'd heard were *awful*, but once BBB came on, we were screaming our heads off nonstop. Black girls at shows like that one stand out, especially in our small college town in the middle of Jersey. So the second I saw Kima and she saw me and my sister, we locked eyes and an unexplainable understanding passed between us.

You like this music, too, our eyes seemed to say. And before I could process what was happening, she was right beside us. Three brown-skinned girls screaming at the top of our lungs. One smelling of seasonal baked goods.

She spent the rest of the show next to me like we'd come together, and we got closer and closer as the hour got later and later. Between songs, she told me that she was half Japanese, that she was "into" my indigo hair, that she was from California and hated almost everything about Jersey except the music scene. I thought I was going to pass out when she touched my mouth and then smeared my lipstick onto her own lips while asking me the name of the purplish color I—we—were wearing. I told her I loved her dimple piercings and asked where she'd gotten her denim shirt. But I was definitely "into" more than just her outfit.

When my sister went to the bathroom, "You Found Me," my favorite BBB song, came on, and when I told Kima it was *my* song, she insisted we push our way closer to the stage. We did, and as the chorus ramped up, we locked eyes, and kissing was basically inevitable.

She was the only thing between me and the lead singer of Boys Behaving Badly, and we were surrounded on all sides by people singing: *"You found me when no one else could. You saw me when no one else would."* And that's how I felt as her soft lips covered mine: lost and then found. Invisible but suddenly seen so clearly. We made out until the song ended, and then we joined the rest of the crowd, screaming for more.

Then she disappeared. I couldn't find her anywhere after the show, anywhere online, anywhere at all. I'd never kissed a girl before, and I wondered if liking it meant something about who I thought was, or who I'd always been. Just as quickly I decided I didn't care.

I wanted to kiss her again. But I didn't even know her name.

I told Rod about her, the girl at the concert, and by the end of

August we'd started referring to her as #GhostHottie. By September I'd convinced myself I'd dreamed her and refocused my energy on the band, and Rod. Which was when I started to notice him: his (normally) clean-cut style, his smooth brown skin, the unique quality of his voice. I started to *like*-like him. But he was too busy texting with some mystery girl he'd met at Atomic Records, the store where he worked, to notice.

When school started, she reappeared like magic. She was just sitting there when I walked into homeroom, like I hadn't spent a solid three weeks scouring the world for her and coming up empty.

"Hey," she'd said. "You found me."

"Holy shit," I said, and she laughed. I knew she meant the song, and that she had no clue how hard I'd been looking for her, but it felt like a sign. Then at lunch, right before I was about to tell Rod that I'd found #GhostHottie, he walked into the cafeteria holding Kima's hand.

"Um," I said, frowning.

"This is who I've been texting with for the last three weeks," Rod said, grinning. "Kima, meet my best friend, Raven."

"Hi," Kima said. I said hi back. And without really talking about it, we decided it would be better for everyone to never tell Rod about Boys Behaving Badly.

They're in love with each other. I'm in love with them both. Which is why I've quit this band twice since they started going out.

And now here we are.

"I'll do it," I say to Kima, who claps and lets out an adorable "Yay!"

When she grins, the studs in her pierced cheeks sparkle like lights in the city skyline. She hugs me, and then kisses Rodney, and I don't know when I'll learn to stop catching feelings for people I can't have.

I look at Rod and his eyes are still turned to me, his lips ready to sing my song.

I take a deep breath, and all I smell is that intoxicating spice.

It feels a little like I'm drowning.

I head to Kima's house after I finish rehearsing with Rod. I begged him to come, too, because the only thing worse than how overwhelming it is to be with both of them is the way it feels when I'm alone with *one* of them.

But he had to get home, and I had to come here, and I'm going to have to keep it together.

"So here's what I'm thinking," Kima says, sliding a glass of lemonade to me across her kitchen counter.

She shows me a list of all the bands performing in the Battle in the order they'll go on. "You take the highlighted ones, which should give you plenty of time before and after your set for sound check and breakdown with Rod. And I'll do the rest. It'll be easy," she says, lifting her dark eyes from the paper to my face. I ignore her impossibly long lashes.

"This looks doable," I say. I pick up the paper and run my finger down the list. "What if more bands get added in the next couple days?" I ask, because people always crash the lineup late. "Will the add-ons be mine or yours?"

"You think Rod is pissed?" Kima says instead of answering my question.

"About you asking me for help?" I ask.

She nods.

"Oh, maybe a little. He just always takes music-related stuff so seriously," I tell her. "And he thinks this will change his parents' minds about music being a viable career choice. But, you know, only if we win."

"Maybe," she agrees. "But I also think he's jealous."

"Jealous?" I ask. "Of what?"

Kima pulls down a bag of chips from the cabinet beside her fridge and plops it between us. "The music stuff has always been *your* thing. Like your thing with *him*. I think he's jealous you'll be spending time with me, too—that he won't have you all to himself for the night."

I laugh and shake my head. "No way," I say at the same time as she says, "I see the way he looks at you, Rave."

I swallow hard. We are always trying to balance all the things between us.

Me and her. Her and him. Him and me.

"Music is our thing for now," I say, because we're all seniors and everything about this year seems impermanent. Time seems insubstantial and hard to hold on to. So many things are about to change.

Kima breaks a chip in half. "Are you . . . really thinking about going solo?"

"What?"

"Rod thinks you're going to leave the band again . . . that you're working on songs without him because you want to go solo and that this time you won't come back."

"Is that why his clothes are a wreck this week? He thinks I'm going to leave Safe & Sound for good?"

"Maybe?" she says. She chomps down hard on her chip.

I take a swig of lemonade. "Okay, look. I don't want to go solo. It's just getting harder and harder to . . ." *Pretend I don't love you both.* "It doesn't matter. It's senior year. It's our last Battle of the Bands. Who knows what's going to happen? And anyway," I add, looking back up at her, "it was really more your idea than mine for me to write that song."

Kima laughs. "Was not. I just said, as good as you and Rodney are together, you could really shine on your own. Rave, you're so good. Not just at singing. It's your writing, too." She licks her lips and leans closer to me. *"How can a heart be split in two? Half loves him and half loves you?* I know you wrote that, not Rod."

I can smell her hair. I bite my lip and look away.

"Do you ever think about the Boys Behaving Badly show?" Kima asks next, and I almost fall out of my chair. When I look back at her, she's leaning against the counter. Her cheeks are resting on her fists, and her fat black curls are pooling in front of her elbows.

"What?" I say.

"The concert this past summer. The one where we met. I know you know what I'm talking about. Do you ever think about it?"

I notice I'm still holding the band list. I put the paper down.

"Um. Yeah. Sometimes." *All the time.*

"Me too," Kima says. "Every time I hear 'You Found Me.'"

She's staring at me like something's on my face, which is to say she's looking very hard in my direction. Without warning she reaches out and dips her finger into the hollow of my throat where the charm of my necklace sits (a tiny guitar on a thin silver chain that Rod got me last year for my birthday), and the heat of her finger there, on that delicate part of me, makes me pull out my phone just for somewhere to look, for something to do with my hands so my fingers don't betray me and float up to touch her back.

"It doesn't matter," I mutter. "How good of a writer I am, I mean. I can't go solo."

Kima pulls her hand away.

"I couldn't do that to him," I continue, shaking my head and maybe talking about more than just music. "I wouldn't be able to bear it."

＊　＊　＊

We fix the hook.

We're in Rod's spotless bedroom, and the neatness of the room just throws his messy clothes into sharper focus. I'm staring sidelong at the droopy beanie Rod's got pulled down over his hair when Mr. Lockhart pokes his head into the room. "Keep this door open, son. Raven, hon, how are you?"

"I'm good, Mr. Lockhart. Real good." I tuck a few of my dreadlocks behind my ear and strum my guitar a little. It doesn't matter how many times Rod tells his parents we're just friends (he's been saying it for five years now); they still pop in to check on us whenever I'm over. Maybe they can feel all the things we never say.

"And then, I think you should sing this part of the line on your own. I won't come in until here, right before the chorus, okay?" Rod says, ignoring his father's presence.

"Mm-hmm," I say, looking now at Rod's untucked shirt, his baggy sweatpants. Whatever is going on with him is getting worse, not better.

"Rod, you sure you're good?" I ask him after his dad leaves. He doesn't answer. "I'm not going to quit, so if that's what you're worried about, you don't have to be."

He frowns. "That's not what I'm worried about," he says, and just keeps playing around with the ending of the song. I put my guitar down and tug on the pocket of his pants so he'll turn toward me, and when I notice that his shoes—all-white Chuck Taylors—are scuffed in a half dozen spots, I unplug his keyboard.

"Hey!" he whines. "The Battle is in less than twenty-four hours, Raven. We don't have time for this."

"Hey, guys." It's Mrs. Lockhart this time. "How's it going in here?"

"We're fine, Mom," Rod says. "Raven's just being annoying. As usual."

I smile sweetly, and Mrs. Lockhart shakes her head. "You two," she says before walking back down the hall.

I wrap the keyboard cord around my wrist and put my arm behind my back. "Less than twenty-four hours, huh? Then you better hurry up and tell me what's going on with you. Your shoes. Are *scuffed*."

Rod looks down like he doesn't know what I'm talking about. Then his eyes widen, and he licks his thumb and tries to wipe away the marks on the rubber toe and sole.

"Okay, fine. But you can't say a word."

"Rodney. Who on earth would I tell your secrets to? You and Kima are the only humans I tolerate."

He presses his lips together.

"Oh. This is about . . . Kima?"

"Yeah. I . . . I think I have to break up with her. And I don't want to."

My heart pounds. My head aches. A dozen possibilities flutter through my mind at once. Does he know about this summer and how I feel about Kima? Is he going to say he loves me, too? I don't know if I'm nervous, excited, or scared. "Why do you think you have to break up with her?"

"I got into the San Francisco Conservatory of Music," he whispers.

"Oh my God," I say. Everything else I was thinking about falls away. I grip his shoulders as a slow smile spreads over his face. "OH MY GOD!" I shout. "RODNEY LOCKHART, WHY DIDN'T YOU TELL ME THIS SOONER??"

"Because I'm kinda devastated?" he says. His eyes get a little watery.

"But Kima is from San Francisco. Her whole family is still there, and she goes back all the time. You don't have to break up with her."

"She's from there, but she wants to be here. Well, in New York. And I mean, what kind of real future could we have anyway? She wants to write, so she needs to be here. I want to make music, so I need to be there. It's what makes sense. But she's not the only reason I'm devastated."

He looks at me in that way of his. And I know he'll miss me because we've been best friends for the last seven years, nearly half our lives. But I'll miss him because we're maybe a little more than that, too.

I've known I'd be staying right here and going to Rutgers since I got in early action, and I can't believe I'll still be in this town without him. Some small part of me wants to leave the band again, right now, before Rod leaves me.

"Don't you do it," Rod says, reading my mind. "I know what you're thinking and I'll kick your ass if you do it, Raven."

Somehow I manage to swallow my sadness. This is what he wants, and I've only ever wanted him to be happy. I smile.

"Oh, Rod," I say. I reach out and wrap him in the tightest hug. "You're going to go. You're going to shine. And it's going to be fucking magic."

"Leave room for the Lord," I hear Mrs. Lockhart say. She can see us from the laundry room. I laugh and let him go, and my stomach aches.

"But what about Safe & Sound? What about *us*?" he asks me.

I look around my best friend's bedroom, and I know the peeling blue paint, concert posters, and nosy parents right outside will always feel like home. "We'll sing our hearts out tomorrow and record as much as we can over the summer. We'll live on as the duo who gave *IndieTrash* flavor they didn't know they wanted."

There are tears in his eyes, but he's laughing. And even though I'm smiling, too, all I can think about is Kima.

* * *

It's Battle of the Bands day, and I'm running late again. I had to go home between school and the concert because I forgot my camera, and then, while I was tuning my guitar, my E string broke. I've already missed two of the bands I was supposed to photograph for Kima, so she's gonna be pissed. I park, jump out of my car, and rush into the building. The whole school is buzzing. It's giving me life.

I head straight to the auditorium, and it is packed. Kids from all over Jersey are here to see the Battle. There are scene kids and emo kids, goth kids and metal kids, and a ton of kids like me and Rod and Kima, who don't quite fit into a box. The great thing about concerts is that once the music starts, it doesn't matter what you're wearing or who anyone thinks you are. All that matters is the noise.

I pull out my camera and start taking a bunch of shots of the Marcia, Marcia, Marcias, the band onstage. Kima gave me a lanyard with a badge that reads PRESS in big red letters, so luckily I don't have to shove my way to the front. I hang out just below the lead singer, then move to the left to get some shots of the girl drummer. I'm kind of obsessed with her. I snap one of the guitarists midair, a photo that I pray will win Kima's forgiveness for the bands I've missed.

Before long, it's time for me to head backstage. I still haven't seen Kima, which is surprising. The press-pass area wasn't crowded, so unless she's taking behind-the-scenes photos in the green rooms or shots from the middle of the crowd, I should have spotted her by now. I glance around one more time before going to find Rodney.

"Kima is #GhostHottie?" is the first thing Rodney says when I push my way into the green room.

"I'm sorry, what?" I whisper it, partially because I'm out of breath from running up the stairs with my guitar and all my camera gear and partially because *what*. Three other bands are in the green room with us, which equates to roughly a baker's dozen people total sharing a very small space.

"Raven, what the hell. How could you keep that from me this whole time?"

I swallow and rub my face. I grab his hand and pull him out into the hall and I am freaking out.

"Kima told you?"

Rod nods.

"When?"

"Last night."

I lean against the wall and slide down until I'm sitting. Rod crosses his arms and leans against the wall opposite me. A kid with a ukulele walks between us. "She said I'd been acting weird all week and that she knew something was up with me. Then she asked if I was cheating on her. With you."

"I'm sorry," I say again. *"What?"*

"So, I couldn't let her think I'd do that to her, you know?"

"Obviously," I mutter. I was still trying to catch my breath.

"So I said that Safe & Sound was breaking up. I was still trying to avoid telling her that I was breaking up with her. I wanted to do it after Battle of the Bands because I was stressed and she was stressed and everything was a mess."

"So you said the band was breaking up?"

"Yeah. But then she asked if it was your idea. And I said yes because you've quit the band so many times before."

"Hey, only twice."

Two people dressed in all black run between us carrying a dozen drumsticks between them.

"Whatever. She got upset and said it was all her fault because of something she'd said to you. Then she told me about Boys Behaving Badly."

"Shit," I say.

"Yeah," he says. Then he screws his face up, and it looks like something's hurting him. "Why didn't *you* tell me?"

I clear my throat. I hear the crowd roaring from the auditorium, and the concrete floor is cold against my thighs. "You both seemed so happy together. I didn't want to ruin it."

Rod shakes his head. "There's always been something between *us*, Raven. I just wish I'd known there was something between you and her, too." He kneels in front of me and touches my hair. I close my eyes. "Has it been awful?" he asks. "Hanging out with us all year?"

"It wasn't awful," I say, and it's true. "Sometimes my heart hurt a little. But you guys are my best friends. What was I supposed to do?"

"I just wish I'd known," Rod said. "Everything would have been different."

"Everything?" I ask. Rod looks at a bit of wall over my head. His hand is still in my hair. I wrap my fingers around his wrist and hold so tightly I can feel his leather bracelets leaving imprints on my palms. I think about relationships and *three*lationships and a dozen other possible, impossible things.

"I told her about San Francisco and broke up with her last night. She hasn't been answering any of my calls or texts since."

"Really? Where is she? Is she okay?" I ask.

"No clue. I looked everywhere. I haven't seen her all day."

I pull out my phone and text her: *Where are you?*

Bubbles appear and disappear and appear and disappear.

"Come on, come on, come on," I whisper.

"Let's go back to the green room and go over the set list," Rod says,

113

and I suddenly notice that he's put together today in a way he hasn't been for a while. Clean dark jeans, a white T-shirt with a red X across the front, a leather jacket, and spotless red Chucks. Even though everything's a mess, he must feel better. "We go on soon and we'll look for Kima after."

We find a quiet corner of the room to try to put a bit of space between ourselves and the other bands. I tune my guitar, and Rod reads over the lyrics we added to the hook of my new song. We'll be good. Great even. We're ready, but I can't stop thinking about Kima.

"We're singing 'Memories' and 'Until Next Time,' right?" I'm talking to Rod, but I keep looking at my phone. Still nothing.

I tie my indigo hair up in a black headwrap and chug a bottle of water. I fold down the collar of Rod's jacket and pick a bit of lint out of his hair. We line up in the wings and I pull out my phone. But before I can text Kima again, we hear our band name boom through the mic.

"Welcome, Safe & Sound!"

The stage lights are warm and bright and I'm instantly sweaty, even though all I'm wearing is a thin maxi dress. Rod steps out right behind me. He's grinning and everybody screams. I think about him saying, *Everything would have been different*, and the thousands of things that could mean. I remember Kima asking, *Do you ever think about the Boys Behaving Badly show?* And I want to know where she is.

I try not to think about how hot I am, or the fact that I still haven't heard back from her. Rod is leaving to go to school thousands of miles away, and I try not to think about that, either, but the truth of how much I'll miss him makes my throat ache. Instead, I focus on the music: the guitar in my hands, the words on my lips. We start with a song we wrote together, and we'll end with one I wrote all on my own.

Our voices twist and tangle with the din of the crowd and the instruments we're playing, and we sound strong and right and real, the way we always do: a little like Leon Bridges meets the Civil Wars, like indie folk and neo soul all in one, like a song you've heard before but made new with something more.

Maybe it *is* flavor.

Near the end of the first song I see her. She's right up against the stage, and her curls are pulled up in a high ponytail that cascades down either side of her face. She's holding a camera, and it's pointed right at me.

I keep singing, feeling close to tears. And when I get to the line about my heart being divided, I try to tell her with my eyes and my voice that these words, this line, this whole song, is about the three of us.

"How can a heart be split in two?" I sing. *"Half loves him and half loves you. And in the end who will decide the outcome of this gorgeous divide?"*

She lowers her camera. She pulls out her phone, and I see her typing something but I just keep singing. I imagine the bubbles on my screen like they're inside me and I let them fill me up. As I finish the song, I feel my phone vibrate in my pocket. A text that I can't check until the end of our set. The length of a lifetime.

"Oh my God," I say to Rod. We're holding hands and bowing, and we're still holding hands as we walk offstage. "Oh my God!" I scream. I climb Rod like a tree, wrapping my legs around his hips and my arms around his neck, and my sweat rubs all over him but I don't care and he doesn't, either.

"Holy shit," he says. "That was *sick*."

"You were perfect," someone says from somewhere behind us. I hop down from where I'd attached myself to Rod because I smell clove. Even if I didn't recognize her voice, I'd know it was Kima.

Rod and I look at her, then we look at each other, and then Kima rushes over and wraps her arms around us like she hasn't seen us in years.

"You guys were fucking magic!" she says. And we laugh and hug her back, squeezing so tightly that nothing can come between us, not colleges on separate coasts, not messy, heart-splitting love, not secrets, and not even what we used to be or the infinite possibilities of what we might become now.

I have to go take more photos, and Kima has to go get a different lens for her camera, and Rod has to go to the bathroom, so a minute later, we all part ways.

Once I'm back on the floor, I grab a seat near the front, and being shoulder to shoulder with everyone else makes the music feel more real. Before I pull out my camera, I take out my phone.

I have one text message. It's from Kima.

It says, *Hi. You found me.*

ADVENTURES IN BABYSITTING

JUSTIN COURTNEY PIERRE

I was running late. I mean, technically I was still early. Shannon said to be there by four, which meant she wouldn't be there until four thirty, and I always like to be early just in case, and it was four fifteen when I pulled into the school parking lot, among the chaos of all the bands already loading all their gear into the auditorium. I was hoping to sneak back behind the gym without anyone spotting me, not like anyone really notices me anyway.

I parked as far away from the madness as I could and walked around the edge of the entire parking lot, attempting to will myself invisible. I arrived at the back door of the gym at precisely four twenty and sat down next to a dumpster and waited. Shannon showed up at exactly four thirty with two of the worst human tools I had ever met. They were in my algebra class and made the most nonsensical comments all the time. Identical, unoriginal dude bros. Hot and shredded as fuck, but still . . .

"'Sup." One of them nodded at me.

"Is that a sentence?" I couldn't help myself.

"KC!" Shannon exclaimed. We hugged. She introduced me. "This is KC, my oldest and bestest friend in the entire known universe. KC, this is David and this is Eliot. They work at Dellwood. We met on the course." I wasn't surprised they didn't recognize me. I was already nervous to begin with, but now I was entering a whole new level of nervousness.

It's happening.

Soon it will happen.

Holy shit.

"We stopped at Arby's. You want some?" Shannon opened a bag and took out a half-eaten sandwich. One of the guys stuffed his hand into the bag and pulled out some fries.

"No. Never. How can you eat that shit? It's garbage."

"Suit yourself." She began to inhale her leftovers. Definitely high. I mean, who eats Arby's on purpose?

"Are you the guy with the acid?" one of the bros asked me. Shannon shook her head.

"No. That's KC. She's a virgin." I shot Shannon a look. "No, like, she's never done it before." *Jesus, Shannon.* "The guy who's bringing it is gonna be here any minute. KC doesn't *do* drugs."

"I just . . . you know, never got around to it." I have no idea why I was trying to impress them.

Suddenly there was a loud bang just around the corner. I froze. One of the guys walked toward the noise and yelled, "Hey, are you the acid man?"

"No, I'm the life of the party," shouted Micah. I'd recognize his deep voice anywhere. He sounded like a radio DJ. He played bass in Shifter

Focus. He came into view carrying his bass in one hand and his case in another. "Case keeps bustin' open. Hope I didn't fuck up the action."

We all waited in awkward silence for a bit, nobody looking at one another. It felt like hours, but it was probably only a couple of minutes. Then the top of the dumpster swung open and out crawled Lucy. Nobody flinched. She did stuff like that.

"What's the date today?" She frantically patted each of her pockets in search of something.

"I think it's the fifth," I said.

Finding what she was looking for—a hair tie—she quickly whipped her wild head of curls into a top bun that resembled an abstract ice sculpture. "Mmmm . . . Mmmm . . ." she continued. "And the month. What month is it?"

"May?" I was suddenly unsure myself. She had a way of making you second-guess everything you knew to be true.

"Oh, thank Christ!" She bent over and let out an exclamation of air. "Whooooo!"

Nobody asked. We'd long learned nothing good ever came from asking Lucy anything.

"Are *you* the acid guy?"

"Curb it, Eliot!" Shannon shouted.

"I'm Eliot," the other guy said.

"Curb it, David," she corrected.

Lucy began inspecting each of us, her right eye twitching. "Y'all wanna get inside?" Without waiting for an answer, Lucy grabbed the door handle and pulled it open. She ripped a bit of duct tape off the lock, put it in her pocket, and waved us in. The inside of the gym was typical. The school prided itself on sportsball, and they had clearly dropped a bundle on this joint. I can't lie: walking out onto the court, I felt a combination of excitement and sadness. I imagined all the people over the years who had stood there playing to bored parents, siblings, students, and faculty. All with the same sad dream of "making it" one day. I hadn't heard of a single person from our school ever going on to do anything even remotely notable. But being there, looking out into the darkness, I suddenly wanted the same ridiculous dream. Not a sports dream. Something else. Something to hope for, to cling to.

Lucy made her way toward the far end of the gym and turned on the lights. They were the slow kind that took a while to fully commit to lighting up. Now I could make out the seats and the shape of the room. Both sides of bleachers were fully extended, as a game of some sort must've been played relatively recently. The Dellwood twins immediately started up the bleachers. Micah was trying to tune his bass by placing his ear on his instrument while plucking the strings. Shannon sat in the center of the court eating Arby's.

"Hey, you! Beauty queen!" Lucy shouted.

I looked around. "Me?"

"Yeah, you. Come help me check these locks."

I made my way across the court to where the main doors open into the school.

"Let me in if it locks me out," Lucy said, and went out.

The doors clicked shut. She tried to open them. No dice. I let her back in.

"Only way anyone's getting in here is if they have a key."

Just then the door we initially came in through opened and a shadowy figure entered.

"How the fuck?" Lucy muttered.

"James!" Shannon exclaimed. She got up from the floor and hugged him. "Hey, everybody, James is here!"

Lucy and I made our way to the door. James looked about our age, dressed in all black from head to toe, and was wearing a stocking cap. It was hard to make out the shape of him. He was drowning in his clothes. His face stared straight ahead, but his eyes moved all around the room as if studying it . . . or something. He walked to the middle of the court, his footsteps echoing in the vast room.

"I come bearing gifts," he calmly said as he reached into a messenger bag and pulled out a large white canister of dental floss. Everyone gathered in front of him, intrigued.

"Are you the acid man?" David or Eliot said. Shannon elbowed him in the ribs.

"I don't know how to answer that," James began, his eyes looking at each of us in turn as he spoke. "If I say yes, then that's who I'll be from now on and I'm not sure I'm okay with that, but if I say no, well . . . that's not entirely truthful, because I'm supplying the LSD for the evening's misadventures."

"How'd you get in here?" Lucy questioned.

James smiled. He looked around the room for a moment, his eyes settling on me.

"I don't kiss and tell." He winked.

Who does this guy think he is?

"Did you all bring twenty bucks?" he asked, turning his attention back to why we were all gathered here in the first place. We all reached into our pockets and produced the proper funding. "Oh, and . . ." He pulled off his stocking cap, revealing a thick head of disheveled hair, and passed the cap to Shannon, directly to his left. "Put your car keys in here. Nobody leaves until you are no longer inebriated."

The cap made its way around to the six of us, everyone with keys solemnly dropping them into it like an old ritual that had been enacted since the dawn of time. While this was happening, James opened the dental floss, popped the part with the floss out of the canister, and pulled out a tiny ziplock baggie filled with six hits of acid.

"All right, I'm going to hand you one tab each. Put it on your tongue and let it sit there for as long as you can. The longer, the better. I'm not going to partake because someone has to make sure you don't harm yourselves, and in the event you need a redirect, I'll talk you out of the shadows and back to a place of peaceful intoxication."

We all exchanged our money for drugs. Micah and the Dellwood twins took theirs immediately. Shannon was still finishing up her four-course fast-food meal. Lucy sniffed at her tab a couple times, popped it in, and then started moving her mouth side to side, eyes moving around the room the whole time. She looked like a lizard.

I straight-up balked.

I could feel the anxiety building within me.

I wanted to have this experience, but I was also terrified by the unknown. More importantly I found myself intrigued by this James character. He looked like a mad scientist forty years before going mad, yet he spoke so softly and strangely eloquently. *This dude is a dead ringer for Spike Spiegel from Cowboy Bebop.*

"KC!" I heard Shannon shout. "What are you doing?"

Everyone was looking at me. I suddenly felt self-conscious.

"Nothing. I'm tired. It's been a long day." I shot a quick glance at James. He was staring at me, but not in the same way everyone else was. He was smiling. Even his eyes were smiling. His eyes were intoxicating, like two black holes that held secret kinds of sadness and had seen things.

"Why the dental floss?" Micah asked him, causing him to look away from me. I saw a flash of a smile, quickly covered up by a shrug.

"It's practical. I also carry mints, mouthwash, toothpaste, a toothbrush . . . You never know what might happen. I'd rather be mistaken for an eccentric than a drug mule, should the powers that be come sniffing around based on the rapscallion attributes I emanate."

Still chewing, Lucy shot him a thumbs-up. Micah agreed. "I can dig it."

Right then I made an impulsive decision not to trip. I pretended to place the tab on my tongue, but instead I palmed it and stuffed it in the front pocket of my jeans.

"Now what?" Shannon asked, having just placed her hit of acid on her tongue. Everyone looked at James.

"Now," he said, "we wait."

There's a thing that happens when you totally crush out on someone. It's like you can feel your heartbeat in every part of your body. There's a euphoric kind of excitement mixed with sadness and terror. It's hard to explain, but it happens in an instant and then just explodes and grows from there, consuming your every waking thought and sometimes your dreams. You can't escape from it. It takes over and runs the controls that make you . . . you. Suddenly, you aren't exactly the same. You've become a caricature of yourself, like the teenage version of a baby learning to walk and talk. None of your body parts work right, and you say the most ridiculous shit, repeatedly.

With James I felt none of this.

It was different. It was more like somewhere within me, somewhere buried beneath conscious thought, I knew we were meant to know each other. I can't explain how I knew this. I just did. It's like my body was telling me the answer to a question my brain couldn't think up in the first place. Maybe that's why I didn't take the acid. I wanted to see if I was right.

Shit started getting weird a little over an hour after James showed up. Everyone was giggling a whole lot more. The twins were obsessed with the bleachers. They walked up them. They walked down them. Across and back, talking intensely about golf clubs, debating the differences between a Cobra King and a Wilson Staff and other rich sports shit no real human gives an actual fuck about. I think Micah was going over his bass parts because he kept uttering "Shit" and "Fuck" to himself every ten seconds. Dropping acid before a performance sounds like the worst idea of all time, but I didn't know him that well, so maybe this was a regular thing for him. Shannon had somehow gotten down the school's flag and was rubbing it on her face, rolling herself into it and unrolling herself.

"You guys," she proclaimed, "this is the softest thing I have ever touched in my entire life, and I've held the face of a brand-new baby in both hands." Nobody responded. James was sitting dead center on one side of the bleachers, mainly looking at his phone but every once in a while looking up to check out how everyone was doing. I sat directly behind him, but all the way at the top next to Lucy, who appeared to be doing math homework. I could faintly hear music playing through her giant pink headphones.

I walked up to where she was sitting. "What are you doing?" I yelled. No response. I wiggled her headphones, and Lucy jumped out of her seat with both hands instantly balled into fists. She saw it was me and relaxed slightly, removing her headphones. Drum 'n' bass was blaring violently loud through them. I glanced around at everyone. Nobody was fazed except James. He was turned around in his seat and looking up at us.

"What are you doing?" I asked Lucy again.

"Math," she replied. "Wanna get my homework done so I can enjoy the entire weekend."

"Are you sure tonight is the best night to be doing that? I mean, the acid is one thing, the music is another." It was as if she had forgotten it was still on. She quickly turned down the volume on her phone.

"The music helps me concentrate. I can't explain it. It's like it babysits the part of my brain that can't pay attention, allowing the other part of my brain to do what needs to be done."

"Huh" was all I could muster. We stared at each other for what felt like an eternity, both with confused and concerned expressions on our faces. I shot a glance at James; he was still watching.

"All right," she said, sitting back down, "get the fuck away so I can crank Venetian Snares and finish my trig. I'll be down when I'm done." She waited until I started walking away before putting her headphones back on and turning the music up to its original volume.

The twins were dragging these large black square mats into the center of the court and stacking them on top of one another. I made my way toward them, stopping just to the right of where James was sitting.

"Any idea what they're doing?" I asked. He turned toward me, eyes still on them.

"I'd measure to guess they're planning on doing something the opposite of brilliant, involving some kind of unoriginal male energy." He looked at me. Looked all the way down and all the way up. "What's your story?" he asked as the twins blew past us and up the bleachers.

"I don't know how to answer that," I responded, suddenly nervous.

"My apologies," he started. "What I meant was, why aren't you tripping?"

His question caught me off guard. A timid "What?" was all that escaped my lips. He stood up and faced me.

"Everyone else is starting to turn. Just wondering why you aren't a vampire yet." He walked past me and up the bleachers. I just stood there dumbfounded as I watched him dissuade the twins from jumping off the top-row bleachers to almost certain death. I looked around and noticed that Shannon had now gotten Micah to join her in snuggling up all over the flag. I could sense that any minute things were about to get strange.

A few blinks later and everyone was absolutely fucked. I was incredibly grateful for having chickened out on joining them. Don't get me wrong, they all looked like they were having a blast, but something about the whole experience from this side of the sidewalk looked sad. Everyone looked sweaty. They all worked their jaws like they were chewing on something, but nothing was there. They talked incessantly about big plans and ideas. Maybe rooms like this just bring that out in people.

"This is it, man. Like, this show is it, you know? We're gonna blow their goddamn minds. Word is gonna spread like the plague. Someone's gonna tell someone who's gonna tell someone who's gonna tell, like, someone important. We'll get signed. We'll get huge," Micah said. "My way outta this pizza box."

"Oh my God, I know," Shannon said. "I want to get out of here too, away from everything. Goodbye, New Brunswick, I'm too big for you." She waited a beat. "Pizza box?"

I was very glad to be me in that moment, hearing their plans. But what were mine? Why didn't I have lofty visions of an unknown future? Shannon's always had them, since her brother moved away with their dad. She's always wanted to leave this city, this life, and start over somewhere else where no one knew her. She wanted to be an actress or painter or musician; it was honestly hard to keep up as it changed daily, but at least she knew she wanted to do *something*. But me?

As a general antsiness began to befall the group, James rounded them all up in the middle of the court. He then pulled out a large iPad from his messenger bag and placed it in front of them. He put on an animated show about a character named Salad Fingers who liked to caress rusty spoons. Sober, I found it terrifying, but everyone else? They instantly became silent and deeply intrigued. James then pointed at me and motioned toward the back. We made our way up to the top bleacher.

"It is of the greatest importance that we keep them constantly amused. In a moment, anything can happen, and I don't wish for anyone to get hurt."

"Who even talks like that?" I blurted out, instantly embarrassed. But then I doubled down. "I mean, you talk like someone from another era. It's fucking weird."

"I appreciate your forthright nature." He smiled at me. Then he shifted a bit, uncomfortable maybe. "I read a lot. I dig literature from all points in time. Been reading a lot about the gold rush as of late. Maybe that's . . . something."

I stared at him. He stared back, only now he seemed slightly smaller.

So he's human. Just a boy playing dress-up. Putting words in his mouth and a funny hat on his head, trying to figure out who he is, like the rest of us.

The magic suddenly evaporated, and he was reduced to my equal. And he could see that I could see it. I looked away, down at everyone.

I looked back at him. "How do you know I'm not tripping balls?"

"Huh?" he replied, as if the wind had been knocked out of him.

"You asked me why I wasn't tripping. But how do you know I'm not?"

He simply waved his hands toward the five people glued to the bright light on the screen in the middle of the room without taking his eyes off me.

"Fair. Do you do it a lot? Drop acid?"

"Fun fact: I've never actually done drugs myself."

"Same," I admitted, surprised.

"My parents split when I was young. They were addicts. Dad's out of the picture now. I split time between my mom in a shitty apartment complex—where I'd see her get high—and my grandfather, who lives on the golf course where I met Shannon. I don't know, you're around something so much, it becomes you."

I looked at him and admitted, "I'm completely average in every way. My parents are still happily married and siblings well-adjusted. We're not rich, but not poor, either. We just run around on the hamster wheel like everyone else, happy enough, I suppose. And that's cool, and I know I should be grateful, but . . . that's it. I don't have big plans like all of . . . them. I just have this mediocre ability to simply survive."

"I don't think you're mediocre."

We talked for almost an hour straight. I don't know what made me feel so close to him, so trusting of this stranger, but being in this weird situation with a dude actually listening, well, it made me want to open up.

We talked about movies and music and books. We had that in common, a love for the "trifecta," as James called it. Our Venn diagrams did *not* intersect in the slightest, but we were both extremely passionate about the things we were into. He was into '90s alternative music. I was into bands that were still in their twenties and hadn't broken up and gotten back together to tour for the twenty-fifth anniversary of whatever bullshit record came out before I was born. The only movie we agreed was perfect was *Eternal Sunshine of the Spotless Mind*, but we disagreed on the ending. I said it was beautiful and hopeful. He said it was depressing.

It's hard to explain the thrill of communicating with a total stranger about the various likes and dislikes you each have. I imagined an empty vessel, the shape of James in this case, and with each topic of conversation I was able to fill that vessel up with the things that made him him. It was like we were on a talk show, only both of us were the guests, just vomiting out information, not censoring ourselves. It was a rush. I felt high, but in a good way. In an organic way, without having to put poison in me.

"So wait," I said, promptly switching subjects. "What *is* the deal with the dental floss?"

He exhaled. "It's a long story, but it's good."

"I'll be the judge of that."

He blushed a little.

Am I flirting? Is this flirting?

"Well, I have this friend. His family is rich as shit. Every year they go somewhere. This year they went to Acapulco, and each of the kids was able to bring a friend along, which is how I got—"

"How long is this story going to take?" I interrupted. "Because I'm on the verge of unsubscribing." He laughed incredibly hard at that.

"Okay, okay. So this vacation was fucked. The parents spent most of the time drunk and hanging out on the beach or at their pool, while the four of us spent most of our time drinking and trying to score weed and drugs and shit."

"I thought you didn't do drugs."

"I don't. Look, I spent an entire lifetime taking care of my mom, making sure she didn't die and . . . all that. I'm sure it's fucked me up. You know, I just . . . I just want to make sure everyone is okay all the time. You know? So, basically I went along."

I wanted to hug him. I could see that he was good. There was real sadness and worry deep within. I wanted to tell him that it wasn't his job to take care of the world. But I said and did nothing.

I hadn't noticed until now that the way he spoke had changed. He no longer had that formal twang and cockiness hidden under a thin blanket of chivalry. It was almost like he was speaking like me.

Man, this guy.

". . . so my friend was freaking out and had to figure out how to smuggle six tabs of acid back to the US."

"Seriously?" I blurted.

"In retrospect, that wasn't the smartest thing to do. I dunno. I just felt this overwhelming need to get the drugs back to the States so I could prove to myself I could do it. But I didn't stop sweating until I had made it back through customs, picked up my bag, and was safe at home." He looked at his slightly shaking hands. "Just thinking about it makes me all . . . panicky."

I grabbed his hands in mine and said, "If you hadn't done it, we might never have met each other. And I know this probably sounds wild, but I think we were destined to meet."

He really looked at me, and I could see the mixture of sadness and caring in his eyes. I could feel the comfort of this moment, a subtle reprieve from whatever was going on in his life. We were two people floating in space, sharing a moment, trying to figure it all out. It felt like . . . home.

That's when all hell broke loose.

Suddenly, someone was pounding on the main gym doors. Actually, several people were pounding. Panic set in. I looked down, and everyone was cuddled up in one another's arms as if waiting for the bombs to drop. Calm as could be, James said, "Go hide them. I'll deal with this."

I quickly hustled everyone through the back doors to the locker room. I kept the lights off and told everyone to chill. I went back out to the gym and nodded at James. He opened the door and squeezed out.

I returned to the locker room to wait. It felt like an eternity. Micah was crying, and Lucy and Shannon were trying to console him. Waiting for the unknown is the worst type of anxiety. It's like a blank page. It's the sheer variety of possibilities that overwhelms me. I checked my pulse, not that knowing my heart rate would help in any way. It was just something to do.

The door opened and James beckoned for me to come out. "Nobody told me Micah was playing at the thing tonight."

"Yeah, he's in Shifter Focus. They're playing at the thing tonight."

"WHO THE FUCK TAKES ACID BEFORE A SHOW?"

"I DUNNO? MICAH?"

"Jesus Christ! I thought he was just another eccentric." James looked genuinely frazzled. "Micah's band is looking for him. They're on in fifteen minutes." Oh God. Nightmare city.

"He's fucked out of his mind. I mean, they all are. What do we do?"

"Do you have any diazepam?"

I shrugged and started walking around.

James whipped out his phone. "Okay, I'll look up alternatives. Meanwhile, can you calmly tell Micah he needs to start getting ready for his show? I'm gonna try to figure this out."

I walked into the locker room. I turned on the light and acted the shit out of the moment.

"Hey, gang, coast is clear. Just the janitor," I ad-libbed. "James told him there was a crew of us with detention, and our punishment was to miss the Battle of the Bands and clean up the gym. All is good."

Give me my fucking Oscar.

I turned to Micah, who was sobbing uncontrollably in a puddle of his own emotions on the floor. "Speaking of the Battle of the Bands, Micah, I believe your band is playing shortly."

"I KNOW!" was all I could make out between the sobbing. The oblivious twins were feeling each other's muscles. Shannon was staring sadly at Micah, taking in all his sadness. Lucy was staring at him as well, but like Rosanna Arquette in *Pulp Fiction* during the adrenaline-shot-to-the-heart scene. There was a happy hunger in her eyes.

I snapped my fingers at Lucy and Shannon. "Maybe we can get Micah up off the floor already, huh?" The girls whipped into action, as I knew they would, hoisting the limp carcass of Micah into a standing position.

"Let's walk this way," I directed, moving back into the gym. James walked up to us, his hair looking even more disheveled than before.

"Any one of you have any Valium or Xanax? Prozac even?" Everyone shook their head no. "Fuck," he muttered. We walked Micah back to his bass.

"You wanna put this on, honey?" Shannon asked him in her best motherly voice. Micah sniffled and nodded yes. Lucy and Shannon draped the heavy instrument over his body. He came to life a little bit, holding it. So far, so good.

"All right," James continued, making his way toward us. "Where's the nearest Whole Foods or, you know, hippie food joint, or fuckin' pharmacy, even?"

Lucy raised her hand but didn't say anything.

"Yes, Lucy," I permitted. She put her hand down.

"There's a Walgreens like two blocks away from the school. I hang out there on Thursdays."

James looked at me. "Okay, one of us needs to go get some magnesium—apparently it's a natural Valium substitute—and one of us should stay here . . . just in case." The way he said "just in case" shocked me back into reality a bit. Seven of us were illegally squatting on school grounds. Five were tripping on LSD. This was a terrible idea. What the hell were we thinking?

"I'll get the magnesium," I heard myself say. "I know the area. You seem to know what you're doing with this stuff."

James nodded, but I could sense that beneath his seemingly cool exterior he was just as rattled as I was.

"Gimme my keys." I held my hand out. He turned and hustled to where he was sitting earlier in the evening. After a few seconds he said, "Uh, my hat is gone. Everything is gone."

Real panic set in. Adrenal glands doing their thing. Fight or flight.

"I had everything in my bag and there's nothing there." He held up his bag, opening and jostling it for dramatic effect.

"Scavenger hunt," Lucy said, as if remembering something from decades ago. "I think Handsome Eliot and his brother said something about a scavenger hunt."

"Jesus Christ!" I yelled. I stormed into the locker room and grabbed the first twin by the arm. He screamed like a little boy.

"WHERE ARE THE FUCKING KEYS!" I shouted.

"Scary, scary, scary, scary . . ." he began to nervously chant, closing his eyes tightly as if awaiting impact.

The other one tiptoed up to me and said, "It's somewhere in this room, I'm pretty sure, man."

"THAT'S SO HELPFUL." I stared daggers. He inched away like he saw the devil in me. I let the first one go and started opening the lockers. "LITTLE HELP IN HERE!" I shouted. Lucy and James came into the room. Within minutes the locker room was thoroughly trashed. We had found the hat, the iPad, and a few other items that belonged to James, but no keys.

I opened up the freezer to the mini-fridge and *of course*. Stuffed between two plastic ice trays were the keys and key chains. I swiped mine and ran for the back door.

"Stay cool. Be back ASAP."

Everything that came next was like a waking dream. It all happened in record time, yet it felt as if time itself had slowed down, stretched out. When your natural instinct kicks in, you become hyperaware of your surroundings. There are gaps in time. Everything is disconnected and stuttery, yet it all flows tranquil and fluid, like a river in the rain. The colors of the bottles in Walgreens were hyper-vibrant. Magnesium. Bright red bottle like a warning sign. *This is it.* A word shot into my head: *PLACATE.* Keep them calm. Keep them busy. Marshmallows. Pistachios. Water. Remembering slow moments, like snapshots of the truth. It must've happened because I was back at the gym in less than ten minutes with the aforementioned items. We fed Micah the magnesium. Told him it would turn everything right around. Didn't get a chance to witness the effects. We wished him well and sent him out into the school to be devoured by whatever came next. We made the rest of them sit in a circle and fed them marshmallows and pistachios. It seemed to work. They were mesmerized by the marshmallows and seemed to focus extra hard on the shelling of pistachios.

"You're a natural," James said to me, once things quieted down.

"The idea just came to me. There was no thought. I just knew what needed to be done."

"We should get the hell out of here. Micah's probably going to shit the bed, and people will come for us," James said.

"Good thing you were the one who answered the door. What did you even say?"

"That he's ready to go, been practicing all night, super stoked, but should stop at the bathroom first. Like, for real, magnesium can give you diarrhea. Especially at the dosage I gave him."

He smiled as wide as the sun.

"I didn't tell them that part."

I smiled, too.

"Let's get the fuck out of here."

We gathered up the troops and drove off in James's pickup truck, stashing the four of them in the bed while we enjoyed the comforts of cushioned seating and the radio. They howled through the night, believing they'd discovered the hidden secrets of the universe. As for myself, I discovered something infinitely more important. A true connection with another lost soul in desperate need to be seen for who they are.

PEANUT BUTTER SANDWICHES

JASMINE WARGA

Amina was really good at being Gordon's girlfriend. Like really good at it. She always remembered to pack peanut-butter-and-jelly sandwiches with crunchy peanut butter when Gordon wanted to have a picnic in the park (Gordon prided himself on being spontaneous, but he also got super cranky if his blood sugar dropped too much), and she helped him almost daily with his precalc homework. It wasn't like she let him copy her own work—Gordon wasn't like *that*—but Amina did most of the work. All of it, really. But that was okay, right? Gordon was busy worrying about other things. Creative geniuses didn't have time to do their precalc homework.

And Gordon was a creative genius. Amina knew this because he'd told her so. At first, his creative genius had manifested itself in the form of sidewalk graffiti. Gordon said walls were overdone, and so he only tagged sidewalks. He also said there was something *ironic* about people walking on top of his art.

Amina had never quite understood that. She would walk alongside him, feeling slightly uncomfortable that her pink Keds were stepping on his art, but when she looked down at the art, she was always left with a confused feeling in her gut. And it wasn't the surreal, almost sacred type of confusion she'd felt once when she visited the Art Institute and stood in front of a Picasso painting for hours. This was a disappointed kind of confusion.

She briefly wondered why Gordon was wasting all his time on this. By her estimation, all he'd managed to create amounted to nothing more than a scribbled collection of sidewalk chalk ramblings. She'd seen stronger artistic efforts from her little cousins. But then, as soon as that thought entered her mind, she would push it away.

That was mean.

And good girlfriends weren't mean.

And Amina was a really good girlfriend.

She would lean into Gordon on their walk, taking her eyes off his sidewalk chalk, and instead pressing her cheek against his army-green jacket and inhaling his scent. Gordon always smelled like lemons. And Amina loved the smell of lemons.

She'd decided she was done being judgmental of the sidewalk chalk art, but she was still delighted when Gordon announced one day that he was going to stop using his creative energy for sidewalk graffiti and instead start a band.

"What kind of music will you play?" she asked him. They were having one of their spontaneous picnics outside. Amina had packed peanut-butter-and-jelly sandwiches with the crunchy peanut butter.

Gordon's light eyes widened with surprise at the question. "Hmm," he said, "I don't know."

Amina took another bite of her sandwich. "Do you play any instruments?"

Gordon blinked as if Amina's question was preposterous. "No. But I can learn. Everyone has to start somewhere." He rolled over onto his side and propped his weight up with his elbows. Gordon's immense confidence was something else Amina liked about him. She thought that maybe being around it would make some of it rub off on her.

"I play piano," she offered. It seemed like this was something Gordon should know since Amina didn't just play piano. She *really* played piano, taking lessons three times a week and performing in high-profile recitals.

Of course she didn't play "rock and roll" music. That wasn't why Dr. Leyla Aboud and Dr. Mazin Aboud—Amina's parents, or, as she referred to them, "the Docs"—had invested in her piano lessons. But still, she knew a little something about music.

"I know, babe," Gordon said. "But this is different."

Amina stared down at her half-eaten sandwich, ignoring the unpleasant feeling settling in her gut. *Gordon smells like lemons*, she reminded herself. *And he's done with the sidewalk art scribblings.*

After a few weeks, Gordon had assembled his band—his best friend, Tommy, on drums; his friend Marissa on bass; a guy Gordon knew from art class named Pete on keyboard—and Gordon, of course, was slated to be the lead singer.

When Gordon had first told Amina that he'd picked Pete to play keyboard, Amina had felt a little bit sad. Even maybe a little bit mad. But Amina was good at handling feeling a "little bit" like lots of things. A little bit was no big deal. She was able to quickly brush aside those little bits like crumbs, convincing herself that Gordon's choice had been for the best. Besides, how many romantic relationships had been spoiled because of a band? Amina didn't know the exact number, but she was willing to wager that it was a lot more than a little bit.

So the band formed. Without Amina. And the band practiced. Less than Amina thought a new band should probably practice, but they practiced nevertheless. Amina brought peanut-butter-and-jelly sandwiches to their practices. She even brought bottled waters, as the Docs had taught her to be slightly suspicious of public water sources.

Gordon named the band Raging Mice. Amina wasn't sure how she felt about the name. But she pretended to like it for Gordon's sake. And the more she pretended to like it, the more she found herself actually liking it.

The band's first show was held in a local coffee shop, Bean and Ballad. It was less of a show and more of a slot at an open mic night, but everyone was excited. Especially Amina. Even if she was one of three people there. She clapped enthusiastically after each song, even though none of the songs were that good.

But that was okay. Bands took time to get better, didn't they? That's what the practices were for. All those hours logged in Gordon's parents' garage. All those peanut-butter-and-jelly sandwiches that Amina made, bottles of water that Amina purchased, piles of precalc homework that Amina completed for Gordon because he just didn't have the time.

He was busy with the band.

It was at the band's fourth or fifth show—Amina could never quite remember—that she'd heard the first song in her head. A tangle of chords that fit neatly together. Words that felt like a ghost was whispering in her ear. Once when Amina had been in the car with the Docs, she'd heard an interview with a poet on NPR. (The Docs were always listening to NPR.) When asked about writing her most famous poem, the poet had said something along the lines of "I can't remember writing it. It was like it was whispered to me and all that I had to do was write it down."

Amina, at the time, had found that answer to be rubbish. It seemed implausible. But now it was happening to her. She had these words in her head. Words paired with chords. What she was hearing was music.

She didn't say anything to Gordon at first. She wasn't sure how he would feel about it. Plus, she wanted to make sure that she was right—that what was inside her head was actually music.

She plotted out the songs on the piano. Sometimes tweaking them a bit from what she thought they'd sounded like when she had the initial spark in her head. The songs flowed from her fingertips. There was something exhilarating about playing her own music—music she'd come up with!—instead of just following a songbook.

A few weeks later, she wrote out one of her songs and handed it to Gordon.

He looked at the rumpled notebook sheet. "What is this?"

"A song," Amina said.

"You write songs?"

Amina took a deep breath. "I do now."

Gordon couldn't read music, but Pete, the piano player, could, and Amina was thrilled when she heard Pete play one of her songs for the first time. From there, Amina gave suggestions as to what the bass line should sound like, the drum rhythm, and exactly how Gordon should deliver the lyrics she'd written.

Or, rather, the lyrics that had, almost like magic, been whispered to her. But that wasn't something she shared. Not even with Gordon.

Soon enough, the band had a repertoire of four or five really good songs. Like, *really good*. Though Amina of course wondered if she only thought that they were really good because she'd written them.

Amina's stomach was in knots the night of the show where the band was supposed to play their new songs for the first time. They were back at that same coffee shop, signed up for the fourth slot. There were ten people in the shop this time. Apparently one of the people signed up for open mic night was a slam poet with a growing local audience. Amina clutched her soy latte. She was too nervous to drink anything, but she was happy to have something to do with her hands.

The band came on. Everything was how it always was—everyone else in the audience seemed distracted, bending their heads down to look at their cell phones, murmuring to their neighbors, walking up to order another cappuccino.

But then something miraculous happened. People started to look up from their phones. By the third song, someone was even recording the performance. Amina's heart thudded in her chest. She listened as Gordon sang the lyrics—her lyrics, her magical lyrics—as Pete played the piano chords—her chords—as Marissa played the notes on the bass—the notes Amina had suggested. By the time the show was over, Amina was glowing with pride.

After that show, things only got better for the band. They got invited to play at real venues. People started showing up at the shows because they'd heard of Raging Mice and their songs, not just because they wanted a latte.

Gordon wanted to capitalize on this. The band said yes to everything they were invited to. And started to print T-shirts and hats and posters that they sold at their shows. Or, rather, that Amina sold, sitting at a table and hawking the merch.

She didn't mind this, though. It gave her a chance to chat with the fans. She loved hearing what their favorite songs were, the particular lyrics that they couldn't stop humming or scribbling on the outside of their notebooks.

Those are my words, Amina thought. *My whispered words. And people love them.*

Of course Amina worried sometimes that she'd stop hearing the songs. That this gift that had been given to her would suddenly dry up and disappear. Sometimes she'd go two or three days without hearing a single note, and she'd think, *This is it. This is the end.* But it was never the end. The songs always came back.

One day, a particular song popped into Amina's head. It was unlike any song she'd written before. Braver, rawer. It got into her bones. She couldn't wait to share it with Gordon. So when school let out that day, she rushed to Gordon's house. The band always practiced in his garage. She expected to be early but figured she could kill the time by playing around on the keyboard, trying to see if the notes sounded as good aloud as they did in her head.

But when she arrived at the garage, she heard a rustling.

"Hello?" she called out.

There wasn't any answer. Just more rustling.

She pressed the button on the garage door opener she'd been gifted months ago. When Gordon had put it in her hand for the first time, it had felt like an amulet of immense power. A gesture of acceptance. A commitment.

But now, something didn't feel right. The hairs on the back of her neck stood at attention. The garage door opener in her palm was slick with sweat.

Amina had been right to sweat. When the garage door finally

opened, it revealed a very uncomfortable scene: Gordon and Marissa trying to untangle themselves. It was painfully clear that moments ago their faces had been smashed up against each other. Gordon wiped his mouth with the back of his hand.

"Hey! Amina!" he said.

Amina glared at him. She wasn't sure what to say. Her head was blank with white-hot anger. She didn't have a pithy or clever breakup speech. The fury roared in her gut. She squeezed her hands into fists. She wasn't sure what to do with her hands. She wanted to smack Gordon. She wanted to smash everything in the garage.

But she also wanted to play her song. That beautiful song.

And so that's what she did. She walked over to the keyboard and began to play the song she'd heard in her head earlier.

The amazing song. The song that was definitely the best song she'd ever come up with. Her shoulders hunched over the keys, and her body felt like someone else was controlling it almost—like she was simply a puppet. She banged out the song, singing louder and clearer than she ever had. Usually, she was shy when she demoed a song. Careful to remind everyone a hundred times that she was not actually a singer— that was Gordon—and this was just how she imagined it would go.

But this time she sang the song like it belonged to her. Like it was hers.

"Damn!" Gordon said. He'd managed to take several steps away from Marissa, as if by moving he could make her forget his previous indiscretions. "That's an amazing song, Am. I can't wait to play it."

Amina stood up from behind the keyboard. Her movement was careful and precise. "You won't be singing it. This song belongs to me."

"Come on, babe," Gordon said. "That's a perfect song."

"It is," Amina said, looking over her shoulder at him and Marissa. "And it's mine."

"But—but—" Gordon's bottom lip trembled. "How can we win Battle of the Bands without that song?"

A cold indifference rolled down Amina's spine. It was chilling. But it also felt refreshing, like stepping into a cold pool of water. She turned around once more to look at Gordon.

"Please, Amina," Gordon pleaded. "The band isn't any good without you."

"I know," she said sharply.

"Well, what are we supposed to do?"

Amina's eyes flashed. "I don't know. But it isn't my problem anymore."

It felt really good to say that. The words tasted like candy on her lips.

The next day at school, Amina marched up to the booth where they were taking sign-ups for Battle of the Bands.

"Hi, Amina," Lilly said. "You already signed up Gordon a few days ago, remember?"

Amina liked Lilly. They were girls cut from the same type of cloth. Quiet, back of the class, always turned in their homework on time.

"Uh," Amina said, swallowing, "I'm not here to sign up Gordon."

Lilly quirked her head with interest. "You aren't?" Lilly looked down at what appeared to be a complicated spreadsheet. "You also signed the band up for a spot at the merch table. So really, no worries. You're on top of it."

"*I* want to sign up," Amina said, her voice wavering a little. "Myself."

Lilly's eyes filled with surprise, and Amina tried not to be hurt. "You?"

"Yes," Amina said. No quivering in her voice this time.

"Okay," Lilly said cheerfully, pushing the sign-up sheet toward Amina.

Amina didn't have a band name because she didn't have a band. She wasn't even sure how this all worked. But she figured if she'd been more or less managing Gordon's band for the past year, she would be able to get herself up onstage. How hard could it be?

She wrote her name down on the sheet in a clear, neat script.

"See you at the show," Lilly said. "Good luck."

Amina gave her a small smile and walked off.

Now the day was here, and Amina wasn't sure what she'd been thinking. Writing songs was one thing. Singing them in front of tons of other people was another. When she'd first walked into the theater, she'd been greeted by the other kids who were selling merch. They'd assumed she'd be sitting beside them. Amina barely managed to get out that no, she wasn't with Gordon anymore, and actually she was here to perform herself, without stuttering.

And when she saw the rest of the band, she felt completely undone. Marissa was sitting with Pete behind the merch table. The anger roared in Amina's gut, and she looked away.

"Amina!" Pete called out.

She turned back to the table.

"You're competing tonight?" he asked. His gray eyes were soft and kind.

"Ye-yeah," she said, and then shook her head. If she could barely announce that, how was she going to get onstage and sing?

"You're going to do great," Pete said. "You were the best part about our band anyway."

Marissa shifted uncomfortably in her chair. She pretended to be really interested in the large stack of T-shirts in front of her.

"Thanks, Pete."

"Seriously," he said. "I can't wait to hear your new song. Gordon says it's great."

Marissa shifted some more, and Amina smiled. She didn't mean to be mean, but it felt good to for once not be the only one who was deeply uncomfortable.

"We'll see," Amina said. "Good luck to you guys, too."

Pete shrugged. "Thanks. Not sure how it'll go."

"You have all your other songs."

"Yeah. But they're your songs."

"You can keep them," Amina said. "I've moved on to new songs."

Pete gave her a warm smile as she walked away.

Soon enough, it was Amina's turn to wait in the wings. She stood backstage and exchanged smiles with Lilly and with Mina, who'd had her own solo set earlier. But despite Lilly's and Mina's encouraging smiles, Amina's stomach still felt like it was filled with cement.

When she first heard her name announced, she felt like someone had grabbed her by the throat. She wasn't sure she could bring herself to physically move onto the stage, let alone sing anything once she got up there.

But then she felt Lilly's hand on her back, gently nudging her out onto the stage. The lights were brighter than Amina would've expected, the crowd cloaked in darkness. The tech people had set up the keyboard just like she'd asked. She searched around to thank them, but they were nowhere in sight.

It was only her and the big wide stage.

She stepped up to the keyboard. She heard an awkward murmuring from the crowd. They were restless. She was losing their attention.

Amina bent down and grabbed the microphone.

"Hello," she said. "I've never performed this song in public before, but I'd like to play it for you now. I'm Amina, and this song is called 'Peanut Butter Sandwiches.'"

And with that, she started to play. The darkness from the crowd faded away, and all that mattered was her song. She was playing her song. Her own song. And it belonged to her.

Sure, she'd been good at being Gordon's girlfriend. Really good at it, actually.

But the truth was, she was even better at this.

RECKLESS LOVE

JAY COLES

The beat drops. Loud heavy-metal-like music blasts through speakers seen and unseen. Some band called the Grants is running through a song that I'm guessing is called "Heart Shitter," and not gonna lie, it's sounding pretty damn dope.

Some girl in a black shirt stops us and asks if we're here to listen to the bands or if we're playing. And I'm kind of laughing on the inside since Trey and Charity are both carrying instrument cases, and we *just* saw this chick at sound check a little bit ago.

"Ho, what does it look like?" Charity sasses back, snapping her neck to the side.

Trey puts his arms around Charity. "We're playing. Sorry about her. It's her time of the month."

"Excuse me?" Charity whips her head around. "That's rude as hell. Nigga, don't ever say that about a woman."

Now I've got to apologize to this girl for the both of them. She has us sign in and then points us to the backstage area where we can listen to some of the bands until it's our time to shine, bright like the disco ball suspended from the ceiling.

"I'll be right back, bro," Trey says to me. "I'm gonna go get us something to drink. I know a girl here who brought us some tequila in flasks. We gotta get loose."

Charity puts a finger in the air. "Hol' up. I'm comin' with you. Be back, boo." She gives me a quick peck on the lips.

Before I can turn over my shoulder to nod at them, they disappear into the crowd.

The music stops and people are shouting as the band gets escorted offstage for some reason. They don't even get to finish their song.

I'm looking around, trying to see if I can make out anyone I know— either from school or from one of the apps I used that one time when I searched for a gay hookup when Charity and I were taking a break.

Somehow, in a huddle of people grinding, I make out Orlando. Our ex-friend and the ex-drummer of our band, Reckless Love, before he left us for his new band, You Want My Junk or something ridiculous like that. He doesn't see me, but I see him, and I fight for my breath.

Orlando. I can see the diamonds in his ear, the gold pendant around his neck ribbed with various gems. I can see he's growing out his hair. The Orlando I once knew hated having hair longer than a fade.

Orlando and I were childhood friends. We grew up in the same 'hood just a few houses apart. His auntie Ms. Opal raised him, and she'd always smoke with Ma after dinner on our front porch. We celebrated our birthdays together since we're just days apart in January. Orlando and I were so close when we were little that we used to run around naked in each other's houses, and it wasn't weird at all. He was the first boy I ever kissed *and* the first boy I ever hooked up with. Orlando's the first boy I ever came out to. The only one who actually knows anything about me.

It was last year, when we were juniors, and to be fair, it was after Big Blue's party and we were both drunk on some delicious Jell-O shots, but it happened and neither of us complained.

We promised not to tell anyone, though. He was dating Angela Reddington, the head cheerleader, and I was with Charity. Every now and then I feel kind of trash that I've kept this secret from both Charity and Trey, but what I'm nervous about is what their reaction would be if I told them that I'm pretty sure I like guys—that I'm gay, or at least bisexual. *Something.*

But ever since Orlando left our band a few months ago, we don't even talk anymore. He moved away to a nicer neighborhood because Ms. Opal retired, hangs out with a different crowd of people at school. Orlando and I were *something*, but maybe *something* went wrong along the way. He was the closest thing to a diary I've ever had. Apparently, neither the secrets we've kept for and with each other nor the memories we have together are enough to keep our friendship or our *something* alive. He's even unfollowed me, Charity, and Trey on social media and took the link to Reckless Love's Spotify playlist out of his Instagram bio.

Sometimes, it feels easy that we don't talk. I don't have to face the side of me that likes guys because I'm with Charity. Other times, I miss him and what we were and what we had.

A new band called Breakfast of Champions gets up on the stage. It's not Orlando's yet, but his is on next, according to Mr. Bolivar, who's doing the emceeing. The anticipation isn't just annoying me; it's rhythmically shredding me from the inside out. I wanna know what his band sounds like. I've heard them on Insta, TikTok, and Snapchat stories, but you can only get so much from those. I wanna know what he's gonna play.

My heart thuds, no, *pounds* harder than the bass in the song this band is playing. Charity and Trey pop up behind me out of nowhere, each with a flask in their hands. Trey's offering me a sip of his as he sings along to the lead singer.

I shake my head *no, thank you*, but Trey pushes the flask so close to my mouth I can smell the alcohol. "Don't be a little bitch, Q," he shouts at me over the music. "Just drink it."

I roll my eyes and take the flask from him. I don't wanna be a loser, and this isn't even my first time drinking tequila; I just don't particularly like the taste. I take a swig, probably, no, *definitely* making a face like I just downed a bottle of bleach or something.

It causes Charity, my beautiful girlfriend, to laugh her ass off.

"I—I—I just saw Orlando," I tell them, kind of struggling to get the words out because something about seeing him still takes my breath away. Trey spits out a little tequila.

"He's here?" Charity says. "Where his ass at? I wanna fuck him up."

I point out where I saw him, but it's kind of hard for them to see where I'm pointing since it's a little dark and there are a shit ton of people here. "Over there," I murmur. "He didn't see me, though."

"I see his punk ass," Trey mumbles under his breath. "If he come over here, I swear I'mma sucker punch him right in the jaw, bro. That's on my Grandma Gene's grave."

"Nah," I say. "I'm not trying to get kicked out of here before we take home the first place prize."

I take another sip from the flask, almost forgetting what it tasted like. "Honestly, the more I drink this shit, the better it tastes."

"It tastes even better because it's cheap as hell," Charity adds.

"It tastes even better with a hit of some of this," says Trey, revealing a dime bag of weed, pushing it waaaay too close to my face.

Charity slaps his hand down. "Don't be showing that shit in here like that."

Trey smacks his full, bright red lips that look like he's been sucking on cherries since birth. "Fine." He puts the bag away in his pocket.

"Q! Q—it's me! How are you?" I don't see who's calling my name at first, but I feel a tap on my back. I spin around. It's a kid I used to have Mrs. Rasmussen's geography class with. I think his name's Griffin. I don't remember much about him, but what I do remember is that he'd always wear the same dark leather jacket he's in now and how he'd always crack jokes about Mrs. Rasmussen's hair that always looked like she just woke up and showed up to class. And I remember him being out of the closet. Like really, flamboyantly out of the closet.

We didn't talk much when we were in sophomore geography, but by the way he's tapped me and yelled my name, it feels like he thinks we're a lot cooler than we are.

I don't want to be rude, though. "'Sup?" I give him a slight wave, noticing his red curls, which look a lot redder when flashes of light shoot through his hair.

Trey leans in to whisper in my ear, but he doesn't do a good enough job because even Charity hears him. "You know this kid's a homo, right?"

I want to punch him in the damn face. "Shut up!" I shout and push him away from my ear.

"Griffin, right?" I ask the red-haired guy, somewhat unassured because he totally looks more like a Jake.

"Yep. My friends call me Fin. You can call me Fin," he tells me, extending his hand. I meet his hand in the middle, and he shakes mine, and then Trey's and Charity's as well. "You playing tonight?"

"We are," I say. "You?"

"No, I'm just here to watch. My friend Aimee is here somewhere, and she's probably getting drunk and making out with some chick at the moment, but we both love coming to this every year. We look forward to it for months. It's so much fun."

"Nice," I say. I don't know why I'm being so short with him, but even I notice it. So, to compensate, I debate oversharing and telling him about how we want to win tonight because we want to take down our old friend, but I hold my tongue back.

He looks away, then back at me. "So . . . what's your band called?"

"Reckless Love," Charity answers for me. "I came up with the name." *Technically* we all came up with the name, but I'm gonna let her have this one.

"Hmm. Reckless Love," Fin repeats back, like he's pondering our name, getting lost in the mystery of it, like it's some deep, philosophical thing from Socrates. "I think I've listened to one of your EPs or something. You guys ever post on *IndieTrash*?"

"I post on there sometimes," I say. "Like, every now and then. But not too much."

He runs a quick hand through his red curls. Then he points at us kind of aggressively and his eyes get big, wide, and excited. "Oh! Oh! Do you have a song called 'Be with You'?"

The four of us take turns exchanging gazes. "Yeah. We do," I acknowledge. "I wrote it when I asked out Charity." But what no one else knows is that I really wrote it for Orlando. Or for the person I thought Orlando was. Anyway, I'm super damn impressed he knows that song.

"Omigosh! I looooove that song," he says, and starts singing the chorus. I've not heard or even thought about that song in a while, but hearing him sing it—damn, he can really sing it—I feel all the memories rush back at once. "You're so talented, Quinton."

"Thank . . . you?" I say, caught off guard that he called me Q earlier but then used my full name just now. Suddenly, I'm transported back to being a sophomore again, in my studio, which was just my closet, making music with Orlando. Back to a time when we were just chilling in my room. I'm lying across my bed with a notepad, writing lyrics, and Orlando's sitting at my desk with headphones around his neck, producing on some music software. It's been hours and we finally figure out the chorus to our new song. "Quinton," he says to me, looking at me with those light brown eyes that freeze me in place. "What would I do without you?"

It takes a while, but eventually I blink away that memory.

"Well, I can't wait to hear Reckless Love and I'm excited to see what you're all about."

I smile at Fin and tell him thanks. "See you around."

He smiles back. "Of course. I'll be looking forward to it."

He starts walking backward away from us until he turns around and meets up with some bigger girl who's definitely making out with a chick holding a can of Dr Pepper.

"Who would've thunk it?" Trey blurts out. "A homo from Raritan River High School is our biggest fan."

"Stop calling him that," I say to Trey, punching him in the arm kind of hard. The words fall out of my mouth like a forceful glob. I don't know if Fin would even care, but I do know there's something deep within me that hates that word. *Homo.*

Trey winces. "Damn, man, you didn't have to hit me that hard."

"Well, watch your damn mouth," Charity says in my place, craning her neck. Something about her saying this feels like . . . comfort?

"I know *youuuuu* ain't talking, Charity. Bro, remember that joke you said—"

"What? Boy, shut up talking to me." She puts her hand up in his face. "That was a joke I was reading from Twitter. And I told you that it was problematic. Remember when YOU said—"

Trey and Charity start going back and forth between the two of them about who's more problematic, like that even matters right now. But all I can think about, all that's popcorning around in my head, banging up against every inch of my brain, are the memories of when Orlando and I would be in my mini-studio, making beats and writing lyrics and creating these beautiful things that would come alive through Reckless Love. Beautiful things we'd post on places like SoundCloud and Tumblr and share with the world. Beautiful things we brought into the world together. And now they're out there somewhere, abandoned. And now I'm thinking about just how messed up that is.

The audience erupts in applause for the band onstage who just finished their performance. I've tuned out a lot of it, but I'm sure it's worthy of applause, so I join in on the clapping. The band takes a bow and waves at the crowd before getting their guitars and basses and drumsticks and going backstage through a thick black curtain. Mr. Bolivar, who's been announcing all the bands, comes out again.

"Let's give it up again for Breakfast of Champions." People start clapping and cheering again. "Weren't they just . . . amazing? I'm sweating from how much I was dancing to that last tune. I'm so excited that tonight is just beginning. Without further ado, please welcome our next band of the night, I Want Your P.S.!"

Fuck, fuck, fuck. "This is it. This is Orlando's new band. *Shit*," I say.

"Are you nervous or some shit?" Trey asks me, again getting waaaay too close.

"No, why?" I shake my head at him before returning my gaze right as Orlando comes out and takes his place at the drum set.

"For one, you're balling up your fists, and you haven't stopped jiggling your leg since they said the name I Want Your P.S."

He's right. I take a deep breath and undo my fists. I try to tell myself to be calm about this, but it just feels kind of nerve-racking—the uncertainty of it all.

The crowd goes completely nuts for them, chanting their name as each band member takes their place. "P.S.! P.S.! P.S.! P.S.! P.S.!" People scream in unison, especially the group of white girls huddled up next to us who keep shrieking, not even screaming, *shrieking* in a cacophony. I know what P.S. means when you're writing a letter, but I wonder what it means for them.

"Doesn't it sound like people are shouting, 'Penis! Penis! Penis!'?" Trey asks me, kind of chuckling.

I shush him, even though I kind of want to laugh with him.

Their lead singer is some really muscular Asian guy with spiky hair and a sleeve of tattoos. He clears his throat into the mic, and I can tell that he's chewing gum, like he's the textbook definition of a punk kid. "All right, all right, friends," he hums into the mic, an acoustic guitar strapped across his chest. "My name's Goga Zheng, that's Catherine James on bass, Hector Perez on electric guitar, and my boyfriend, Orlando Alexander, on drums. And we are—"

"I Want Your P.S.!" every member of the band recites in unison.

My jaw nearly breaks as it falls open. One glance at Charity and Trey and I can see that they feel exactly as I do right now.

"Boyfriend? Orlando's gay?" Trey goes. "Yooooo!"

Apparently he's out now. I don't know how I should feel about that. I just swallow down hot spit.

Orlando clicks his sticks to count down and then they start to play. From the first notes, something feels familiar about this song. It's smooth and mellow, like the sound of rustling leaves in the fall, but I can't quite point out what exactly is familiar about it.

Then the lead singer starts singing the lyrics in a low voice that's slow and sweet, like molasses.

"Baby, open your arms and fall into me. Baby, receive me and let me in. You are the one. You are the way. You are the keeper of my heart."

What. The. Fuck. These lyrics—they're mine. I mean . . . ours. I wrote this song with Orlando just moments before we shared our first, secret kiss. And now someone else is singing them. I feel like I'm being split at the seams and all of my insides are spilling out for people to see. My fists ball up at my sides all over again, and there's something building, building, and building deep within me, and something really wants me to act on it.

"Those are my lyrics!" I shout to Charity and Trey.

Charity's eyebrows rise and Trey's eyes widen. "What the fuck?" he says.

"I know. We wrote this song together," I tell them. Orlando owns the rights to sing this song as much as I do, but something feels wrong about hearing this random person sing lyrics that are 50 percent mine.

I run outside to catch my breath. I sit out on the curb in front of the building. It's dark out and the stars shine bright in the sky like the disco ball inside. The wind blows and I hold my elbows. Cars zoom past on the road across the way, and I can hear crickets chirping in the patches of grass nearby.

"Hey, you okay?" a voice says from behind me. I glance over my shoulder, expecting it to be either Charity or Trey, but it's not. It's Fin.

"Yeah," I lie. The truth is, I'm not okay and I don't know why I'm not.

"I know a lie when I hear one," Fin says, sitting down next to me. "Were you not feeling I Want Your P.S.?"

I stay quiet.

"They just announced that they're uploading a new album to Spotify and are about to sign with a record label."

"Cool," I say, sighing.

A silent beat that feels like forever.

"But I'll take Reckless Love over them any day of the week."

I kind of laugh, but don't say anything else.

I don't know how Orlando did this, how he allowed someone else to sing our song. Suddenly every single one of my limbs feels super heavy and I'm numb. "They stole my song," I admit to him, this kind-of-stranger, unsure of the reaction he'll have.

"What?" Fin raises an eyebrow.

"The song they sang. It's mine. I wrote those words."

"Oh my God." Fin puts a hand to his mouth. "How'd they—"

"It's a long story."

"Good thing I have time."

I look at Fin, and he's smiling at me in this weird way. I look away kind of quickly, hesitating on opening my mouth. I have a tendency to overshare. "An old friend is in I Want Your P.S. We used to write songs together. We were the best of friends, did everything together, like two peas in a pod, but somewhere along the way, our pod split, and we started growing in different directions. And then one day, I got a text that he was leaving Reckless Love to start his own band. We haven't talked in months. Ain't that some shit?"

"That feels tough, Q. I don't exactly know what you're feeling, but I definitely understand what it's like to lose a childhood friend. I had this friend, Ray, that stopped talking to me once I went public about being gay."

"That's messed up, man."

"After a while, you get used to the ways the world shits on you. But it did sting to lose Ray. I didn't think there was anything in the world that would make us stop talking."

"Yeah," I say, staring up at the night sky, admiring the constellations.

He puts a hand on my shoulder. "What would make you feel better?" he asks me. "I admit that I feel kind of powerless right now, but maybe there's something I can help you do." He whips out a shiny object, and it takes me a while to realize that it's a pocket knife.

"What—what are you doing with that?"

"What do you *want* me to do with it?"

"Orlando's singing my song. I'm not gonna kill him for it, though," I say. "Prison doesn't exactly sound like a place I'd like to be. I've heard stories from my pops about the one time he got locked up for dealing when he was my age."

"I don't mean kill him, O.J.," Fin says. "But we can fuck some shit up if you want. Sometimes that's exactly what you need."

I think for a moment. "Nah. I'm okay," I mutter, feeling like I'm sinking within myself. I just want to stay here, staring up at the sky, wondering about all the things we can't see up there, forgetting about what Orlando's doing inside.

"Loser." It feels funny that he's calling me that word, like I'm boring him. It's a word some people call him, but sitting here with him, while my girlfriend and best friend are both enjoying this night in there, he's not boring me at all, and it's easy to talk to him. Even easier to talk to him than to Trey or Charity at times.

"Who you calling a loser?" I play-punch him in the arm.

He just laughs, showing teeth and all, and our eyes lock for a moment; then I look away again.

"Fin?" I ask, picking at a hole in my dark jeans. "H-how did you know about you? How did you accept it?" It's a question I've always wanted to ask someone.

"What do you mean? About me being gay?"

"Yeah," I say. "You don't have to answer if that's too weird of a question to answer. I don't want you to feel—"

"Not weird at all," he interrupts. "It's who I am. But I do answer that probably every day. The thing is, you never really stop coming out to people. You just keep doing it over and over and over again forever and ever until you die."

I swallow whatever lump is lodged in the back of my throat. "That feels sad, bro," I say.

"It can be. But good thing I like talking about myself." He laughs. Our eyes lock again, and I finally notice how deep and electric blue his are.

"Yeah, good thing." I feel like there's more he wants to say, so I wait. I want to listen, to really hear him.

"But I started thinking about it in the fifth grade when I got my first boner after a kid that I was friends with got changed in front of me. Then, when I eventually read the Harry Potter books, I kept imagining Harry and Draco making out every time they interacted. But what confirmed it all was when I had my first kiss with a boy, and even after already having kissed girls, my first boy kiss felt like the truest, realest kiss in the whole world to me."

Damn. I feel that. That's how I felt when Orlando and I kissed. But I can't be gay. I don't know another gay person besides Fin, who I barely know. Besides, I'm dating Charity, and I really, really, really like Charity. No, I love her, and I love when we kiss and do other things that you do before sex, too, ya know? I love imagining the two of us doing it some-day. But I also loved doing all of those things with Orlando, even if it was in secret. Part of me really liked that we were secret. We were *each other's* secret, even if it was really, really wrong. Now it's like we're each other's memory we want to forget.

An owl hoots somewhere that sounds nearby. Fin studies me.

"Why do you ask?"

I have to come up with some sort of answer. I don't wanna be a dick. "Umm. I just feel . . ." I struggle to legit find the words to say. They're there somewhere in the abyss of my thoughts but won't come out. *Come out, come out,* I want to shout at the words in my head. Still nothing. It's like there's something, like a beautiful butterfly, trying so desperately to reveal itself, but its wings are caught in my throat. "I love my girlfriend very much, but I've been keeping a huge-ass secret."

"Can I guess?"

"Sure?" My voice fills with curiosity.

"You're in love with me," he says seriously, but then laughs like he's joking.

I shake my head at him, at him joking when I'm being vulnerable. "Orlando and I had sex, and I never told Charity."

"Ugh. Straight people," he says, smacking his forehead. "For some reason, I'm always finding myself in conversations like this. That's how Aimee and I became friends."

"But I liked it, though. He was the first and only boy I've ever done anything with that I actually had feelings for. The idea of being with a guy in that way excites me the same way being with a girl does."

"You're probably, I don't know, bisexual," he says. "But you're defi-nitely not an alien. And that's really okay."

I swallow my spit. "Bisexual?" I say, as though I've never really thought about it before. But that's not true. The thought has crossed my mind before, but for some reason, with Fin saying it to me, it feels like a totally new thought. Like I'm thinking about it in this brand-new way, seeing myself with brand-new eyes.

"Yeah. 'Bisexual' means you like—"

"I know what it means . . ." I interrupt him. "But thanks. I just feel some type of way that you're now the only other person that knows about Orlando and me, and I feel some type of way about he and I not being friends anymore."

"Look." He settles closer to me. "Sometimes, people stick around. Other times, people don't. It's up to you to let the people go that don't want to stick around. No matter how much you might think they're great, some people just aren't meant to stick around."

This Fin kid is actually really wise, and I don't entirely know why I'm so surprised. It's not like I've tried having a real conversation with him this deep and intentional at school before. But what he's saying makes a lot of sense, even if it does feel really hard to hear.

"You're right," I admit, kind of huffing out the syllables.

"And you're the one who chooses who knows about you being bi, or whatever you end up labeling yourself," he murmurs, lighting a cigarette and taking a huge puff. "When we're born, we're so obsessed with putting ourselves in something. We're so obsessed with putting ourselves in boxes. When we're young, we put ourselves in cardboard boxes and imagine that we're on spaceships or in whatever dreamland that makes us happy. When we're adults, we put ourselves in these metaphorical boxes to hide from who we really are. Let yourself out of the box, Q. You can't keep yourself in there forever."

Damn. He's right about that, too. Fuck . . .

A beat of silence—so quiet I can hear applause coming from

inside—so quiet I can hear my stomach rumbling a little bit, reminding me that I need to eat something. I watch the smoke from his cigarette funnel around us, and suddenly our gazes lock again.

"I . . . I like your eyes," I blurt out awkwardly. There's no taking this back, even when I instantly regret saying it.

He looks puzzled at first and smiles. "Thank you. Red hair and blue eyes, the rarest combination a person can have. We make up, I think, less than one percent of the world's population. Pretty cool knowing there's less than one percent of people like me out there. Scary, too. Now imagine what percentage of the less than one percent is also gay, like me."

Things go quiet for a long minute.

"It is pretty messed up that he's doing your song like that." He finishes up his cigarette and flicks the butt onto a patch of grass.

"Thanks . . . Charity and Trey probably think I'm overreacting." But they don't even know why I'm out here. Neither of them has even come to check on me. "Fin. You're actually pretty dope, bro," I tell him.

And he grins nearly from ear to ear.

"You still have that pocket knife?" I ask. "I feel like fucking some shit up."

He grabs my elbow and helps me up off the curb. Though my ass has fallen asleep, I grab the pocket knife and lead him to the parking lot, strolling through to find Orlando's Honda Civic. When we do, I stab at one of his tires. At first, I feel really bad, like I just committed a crime that I didn't even want to commit. But then—maybe it's something about hearing all the air whistle out—it starts to feel really good.

I poke out his back tires, then slash away at them like I'm an angry explorer fighting my way through the jungle. "AGGGHHHH!" I scream at the top of my lungs—surely things are so loud inside no one can hear me—and for the first time in a long time, I feel good. I feel infinite. I start kicking away at the doors of the car, the side mirrors, the trunk, the front license plate that says SWINGER that he didn't have the last time I saw his car. The I Want Your P.S. bumper sticker that he *also* didn't have before. Kicking the car barely does anything, but it feels good.

"We should piss on the driver-side door," I joke. That would be another total dickhead thing to do.

"Me first," Fin says, whipping out his dick through his pants zipper to start streaming all over the front of Orlando's car before I can even say that I'm kidding. "This is for always asking to see my math home-work freshman year." I'm kind of surprised he remembered that. And I'm dying laughing standing here, taking in the fact that he actually is peeing on Orlando's car.

"You're so fucking wild, Fin," I say through a small chuckle.

"Your turn. *Finish him,*" he says in a voice similar to the one on *Mortal Kombat* when you get to use a final combo to do something super sick and gory to your opponent.

I take a deep breath. I don't know if I can actually do it. I was mainly joking, but I'm impressed that he really did it. I glance around to con-firm that we're alone; then I whip out my dick and start peeing. When I'm done, I zip back up and give the car the finger.

Fin wraps me up in kind of a hug.

"I'm so proud!" He's acting like I'm some little kid and he just taught me how to ride a bike. In a way, he did teach me something, and for that—I'm grateful.

His arms feel warm around me, and I really want to tell him that I'm scared of what comes next, but before I can say anything, someone's shouting at us.

"There you are! There you are! We've been lookin' for you, bro," Trey says, running toward me with Charity. "We're on next."

Shit.

"You've been with Griffin this whole time?" Charity's nose kind of turns up and flares. I can tell she's pissed. My smile fades. I don't even wanna really play anymore.

"No—I mean, yeah," I say. "I came out here to get some air, but then Fin came to join."

"Why are you holding a pocket knife and why does it smell like pee over here?" Trey asks.

"Mind your business," I tell them. "We've got a show to do." I return Fin's knife and push past them, heading for the entrance of the building.

"Wait. Wait. Wait!" Charity screams at me. "Before we go in there, we've gotta do our thing."

I almost forgot. Before every show, the three of us do, like, a team handshake that's waaaaaay too complicated, but we've never not done it before a show or performance, and despite me being in a weird place right now, I can't let that stop us from doing it right now.

"Good luck," Fin tells us.

"Are you not coming in?" I ask, concern probably obvious in my voice.

"Oh, I am. Just after I finish this cigarette," he says. I look down at his right hand, holding a new cigarette.

"Well, see you inside," I say to him before turning away and walking toward the building, emotionally preparing myself for this performance. I'm sure Orlando's somewhere around, and while neither of the songs we've prepared to do are ones that I wrote with him, one of our secret songs, one is a song I wrote about love and how love has this way of lying right to our faces—a song that I listen to when his face inevitably pops up in my head at night, when I'm winding down and trying to shut off my brain to sleep.

As we get closer, I can still hear people cheering. There's a girl with a clipboard and a headset who's all like, "Umm, are you a part of Reckless Love?"

"Uh, yeah. Why?"

"Well, we needed you and the rest of your band backstage like five minutes ago. Follow me."

I wait a little bit for Trey and Charity to catch up before I follow this girl through some hidden, really bright hallway, up a small set of stairs, and around to where the stage entrance is.

"Take your places, everyone," someone shouts around us, but I'm too focused on my thoughts.

Trey yanks at my shoulder. "What's goin' on, bro? You seem . . . not like you right now."

Charity gets close to my face. "Is this another one of those anxiety-attack moments?"

I've not had an anxiety attack since last summer when we went to see that one horror movie about the killer clown. Yet she keeps bringing it up.

We listen to Mr. Bolivar's muffled voice introduce us, reading the blurb about us on our website word for word. The blurb we wrote back when Orlando was still a part of us. I make a mental note to change that at some point also. I hear people stomping their feet and cheering our name. It's so loud it feels like the floor is rumbling, and I can feel it in my legs and stomach.

"Ready?" the annoyed girl with the headset says, lines forming on her forehead.

"As ready as I'll ever be," I mumble under my breath so quietly no one hears.

Thankfully Trey answers for the three of us by saying, simply, "Yep."

I listen to her countdown before the curtain opens and we're exposed, before we have to resume our places and perform.

Five.

Four.

Three.

Two.

One.

"Showtime," she says, and the thick black curtain pulls back slowly and then all at once.

"Welcome to the stage, Reckless Love," Mr. Bolivar announces. Everyone's screaming their excitement at us. People even have signs with our faces on them.

I approach the mic at the center. Trey gets on the drums, and Charity sets up her bass.

I clear my throat into the mic a little. "Hey. My name's Quinton Kerr, that's my bro Trey Watson, and my beautiful girlfriend, Charity Carson, and the three of us are Reckless Love. Our first song is one we wrote just for tonight called 'How Could You.'" It's not a rager, like all the other songs have been. It's more of a relaxed, slightly medium-tempo ballad.

"One, two, three, four." Trey clicks away with his sticks. And then I begin strumming my guitar between a C and F chord. Most of the song uses those two chords.

"There are days that I pretend that I'm okay, but I'm not, and that's okay. You've seen me bare and you've seen me there. You are the one that hurt the most. How could you? Oh, baby, how could you?"

A brief and slow instrumental break.

"I loved in the shadows of the night, waited in the dying light. Running in between our history and a future mystery. I'm not losing sleep. Even though you cut me deep. How could you? Oh, baby, how could you?"

My eyes scan the crowd. I see Fin there with his friend Aimee, and they're swaying with each other from side to side like they're at prom. It seems like people are actually enjoying this song that we came up with in Charity's parents' garage a few weeks ago when we first found out about this event.

I make out Orlando in the crowd, and he's holding hands with that Goga guy from his new band. I close my eyes as I sing, transporting myself into the music, away from here, so I can focus.

When the last C chord rings out, the whole crowd's cheering with applause and loud screams. I even catch a few people in the front row wiping away tears from their eyes. And shoot, before I know it, I'm doing the same.

There's something about the lyrics that just hit me all over again hard in the gut.

I loved in the shadows of the night, waited in the dying light. Running in between our history and a future mystery. I'm not losing sleep. Even though you cut me deep. How could you? Oh, baby, how could you?

We're backstage with all the other bands, huddled up waiting to hear the results on who's winning the first, second, and third place prizes. I summon the courage and confidence from somewhere, maybe deep within the core of the earth. "Guys, I have something to tell you both."

"Shhhhh! They're about to announce the winners. What if it's us?"

"No, listen to me, Trey," I say. "This is important, too."

"What's wrong?" Charity asks. She grips my hand, her fingers interlocking with mine. I don't know why something always has to be *wrong*. But her words trigger something inside me, and instantly, there are tears streaming down my checks, dripping off my chin. This feels so fucking hard. I play back some of Fin's words: *You can't keep yourself in a box forever.*

I swallow hot boiling spit before opening up my mouth.

"I—I—I'm . . . I think that I'm bisexual," I say, stumbling over the words like rocks on a sidewalk. "And I don't want anything to change between us, but I just thought that I had to be honest with myself."

"Holy shit!" Trey says. "You're serious."

"I am," I say, unsure of why I'd say that as a joke. "I've known for years that I at least liked . . . guys." I get that feeling like my entire body wants me to throw up, but I don't and can't.

"Whoa" is all Trey says next, but Charity seems absolutely stunned.

I take a deep breath. "And there's something else," I add. "I hooked up with Orlando when you and I first started dating, Charity," I admit.

She lets go of my hand, which is sweating bullets now. "What? What do you mean?" She wrinkles her forehead and takes a step back.

"Like, you know—" Suddenly, my words leave me for a moment. I don't want to talk about everything I did with Orlando right now.

"Butt stuff!?" Trey blurts out loud—so loud other people who are waiting to hear the Battle of the Bands results crane their necks around to listen. "What's everyone looking at? Mind your business," Trey shouts. Everyone turns back, returning to their own conversations again.

I nod at Charity like we've got this telepathic way of communicating the truth.

"You did it with Orlando? But *we* haven't even done it. You said you wanted to wait to do it with me."

"Ohhh. Shit." Trey puts a fist up to his mouth like he's watching someone get sucker punched. In a way, my news is sucker punching.

"I know I said that. And I feel like a dickhead for doing stuff with Orlando."

She looks puzzled, and I can see the tears pooling in her eyes. She's hurt, pissed, sad, all of these at full capacity. "I don't . . . I don't even know what to say right now, Q."

"So, you're telling us that you're bisexual? That's actually kind of dope. Give me a hug. Thanks for telling me." Trey opens his arms, and I meet him there for a hug, feeling a mixture of happiness, relief, and curiosity.

"But are you breaking up with me?" Charity asks once Trey and I break away.

"No," I say. "I mean—I don't know—I mean, maybe, but I don't want to. I don't think I want to. All I know is that I had to come clean, come out, I had to tell you the truth."

Charity pulls me to the side, and she lifts up my chin. God, I love her dimpled smile, her freckles around her nose, her medium-brown skin like caramel, and the way her hair curls into coils. "I know I'm supposed to say something supportive. I don't know. But right now I don't think I can. This is a lot. I know it's a lot for you, but it's also a lot for me."

I look down at my shoes. I feel so damn bad. "I know it's a lot. I'm sorry."

"I just think . . . it would've been nice to know all of this sooner. My cousin just came out a few months ago and she's eleven. But everyone's different. Maybe you weren't ready. I get it. Sorry, I'm externally processing all of this. Can we—can we just talk about this later?" She wipes away more tears, and I want to wipe them away for her, but I don't want to attempt to do it and have her reject my help by swatting away my hand.

"Sure. Yeah . . . we can talk about it later. Are we . . . good for now, though?" That feels shitty to say, or at least the way it comes out does. "I don't want to go out there and accept first place if you're mad at me. You matter more than any Battle of the Bands prize."

She smiles, and usually I'd see the gap in between her teeth, but this one is tight-lipped and bittersweet, so I can't. "Yeah. Yeah, we're cool."

Trey signals us to come back over toward him and wait in anxious expectation for our band name to be called. He's nearly biting his nails, and it's kind of funny, watching him, but the whole time I can only think about one thing, thanks to Fin, and that's that maybe the liar this whole time wasn't love and wasn't my sexuality and wasn't the world and wasn't Orlando. Maybe this whole time it was me? Maybe I was so content with this secret box I put Orlando and me in that I lost myself along the way—or pieces of myself. I've been keeping the real me hidden all this time, and I'm finally ready to break free.

That's what this is.

My breaking-free moment. I'm peeling back the tape of the box I've put myself in.

I'm ready to break free, and opening up to Trey and telling Charity the truth feels like a big first step for me. I know I've got a lot to work through with Charity and there'll be a series of bumps to ride in the days to come, but I'm ready for them. Until then, I'm content with being here with my best friend and my mega-awesome, fantastic, beautiful girlfriend who didn't completely explode on me when I told her that I'm bisexual and that I did things with Orlando behind her back. I don't

171

expect things to be easy, and I'm silently praying that Charity won't break up with me after tonight. I don't know what the future holds for us and our relationship, but I'm okay with not knowing right now. I'm just so fucking pumped that I have them—OGs who don't take the easy way out, like Orlando, who love me enough to stay here even when things are messy.

THE RIDE

JENN MARIE THORNE

Have you ever felt that moment
The beat where your heart stops thrumming
Your thoughts start coming
And your world won't ever go back, go back?

Have you ever lived that feeling?
It's almost too raw and reeling
In a blink you're smart
It's the start the start of the end of what's gone and
Have you ever felt that moment that moment that moment
*   that moment that—*

My boyfriend of two years is talking to me.

Talking? Ranting. In my direction. I cannot hear a word coming out of his mouth, but I can sense that he is not going to let up anytime soon.

I'm watching his lips. I had them memorized long before I even kissed him, that perfect valley in his perfect upper lip, and now all I can see is a bubble of spittle that forms and pops in the corner of his mouth over and over and over again as the rant continues apace.

The wind blows past the front stoop and his blond hair hardly moves. He's wearing gel. I am dating a guy who wears hair gel, not just for shows but for school, for trips out to the store to get a soda. And he wears it specifically to look dirty. To look like a *real* person who's, like, *lived.*

He stops talking, and the sudden silence startles a blink out of me. He stares at my hand.

I'm holding my keys.

"You gonna lock the door or what?" he asks.

I turn away, fitting the key into my front-door lock with completely numb fingers, and he starts up again.

"They're such complete posers, you know? Like they seriously think you can make music that matters from, like, the carpeted basement of their subdivision Tract House Number Two."

Okay, so, I've caught up now. He's talking about Safe & Sound, which I should have immediately guessed, because he's always and for-ever talking about them. You would think he wrote fan fiction about them, they take up so much space in his brain. He wants me to nod and agree and cheer him up—*Yeah, Aaron, they're a high school band, they're all gonna work for like an ad agency one day, you and Big Talk are the real deal*—but instead I hear my own voice, a flat drone, saying, "*I* live in a subdivision."

"Yeah." He rolls his eyes slowly, languorously. "But. You know what I'm saying."

He lives in a McMansion on a wooded eight-acre property five miles outside of town, but because he dislikes his parents, he thinks that lends him an air of authenticity as a musician, and holy, holy, holy . . . I cannot breathe. How am I dating this person? How has it lasted two years? What is happening?

My heart is beating so fast that stars are gathering, but my boyfriend doesn't notice. He's ambling toward the car, speculating about what songs Safe & Sound will play, snickering to himself. He can only amble, can only snicker, not belly-laugh, because his pants are so tight that I had to zip them for him.

I zipped. His pants. For him. No less than ten minutes ago. Oh my *God*.

He's stopped talking again. "What's the matter? Are we going, or . . . ?"

I just blink.

He blinks back. "Were you . . . ? Did you want to change clothes? We don't have that long, Jess, but I mean . . . I guess I can wait."

He leans against the hood of my car, checking his phone.

I inhale fire and exhale: *"Why would you think I wanted to change clothes?"*

He doesn't look up from his texting. "I was just surprised that's what you chose to wear."

I'm wearing jeans and a black tank top and black boots, and there is nothing wrong with what I'm wearing, and I finally, *finally* know that.

He must sense the gamma waves of rage radiating from my every pore because he looks up slowly and pockets his phone. "No, you're right, you . . . I mean, it's not like you're going to be onstage, so who cares, right? It's cool that you're willing to, like, fade in when you need to. Ahhhh, you're perfect."

He steps forward, half smiling, head cocked, beckoning. I vaguely remember this expression working in the past, the gravitational pull of it, the way I would step forward and melt against him.

I walk briskly toward my beige Buick, an ancient hand-me-down from my grandfather that Aaron mocks at least every third day, begging me to upgrade to something cooler, even though he hasn't so much as attempted to learn to drive, let alone get his own damn car, and therefore has no grounds for complaining.

He's still squinting at me. He throws his hands in the air. "What, are you pissed about the subdivision thing? You know you're better than this."

He gestures to my house, and I open my driver-side car door, and before he can languidly reach for the passenger-side handle, I throw myself across the seat and slam the palm of my hand down hard on the ancient uncool manual lock. *Shump.*

He gapes at me through the closed window. "Oh . . . kay?"

I turn the ignition.

"Haha!" He raps on the glass. "Real funny, okay, enough, let's get there. I want to beat Safe & Sound to sound check."

I don't look at him. I check my mirrors and hit the gas. Behind me, I'm not sure if I'm imagining it or if I can really hear Aaron Crenshaw scream, *"What the fuck, Jess?! You're my ride!"*

I begin to laugh. And laugh. Only vaguely hearing it. I drive and I turn on the radio, a sharp chop to the on button, just like the one I gave to the lock to keep him out. It's the crackling college station, the only one Aaron ever lets us listen to, but I breathe in an electric breath and switch it to his worst nightmare, to Hot 98, and crank the Top 40 up to eleven.

They're playing a terrible song. Truly awful. I laugh and listen and try to sing along, but I can't even find a tune.

Where in the hell am I even driving besides *away*?

I blink and see a strip mall, a line of trees dressing up the parking lot, the place with the crafts store and the Starbucks where my friends and I used to hang out and feel grown up before I leveled up to a boyfriend and weekend plans. I wonder if Lydia's there right now, drinking a chai latte and playing snap with some new friend.

Jesus, Jess, probably not, it's, what? Five? And I'm pretty sure I just ran that red light.

I blink hard. This is bad driving. At least now I know where I was heading in my fugue state. The school. "The venue," Aaron called it this morning, like he was on a world tour and this was the next stop. I haven't delivered him to *the venue*, but I did drive there anyway, like I'm on autopilot, like I've been programmed to arrive at this destination at this exact time, and good Lord, it would explain so many questionable decisions from the past two years if it turned out that I was, in fact, a robot.

There's a fair number of cars in the parking lot already. About half have parents sitting in the driver's seats, scrolling on their phones or, in a few particularly sad cases, napping. I don't pull in. I speed up, drive past. I make a right. When I get to the corner, by the old playground, I make another right. And then another, and then, hey now, I'm back where I started. And then I do it again.

On the third circle of the block, I panic. I don't know what to do. I pull in. I park. I get out of the car and follow a couple of freshmen carrying ukulele cases into the auditorium entrance. The bustle of a whole lot of musicians getting ready buffets me as soon as we enter the dank, dark, velvet-draped space, the site of so many stultifying assemblies and earnest attempts at musical theater glory, and Jesus—these aren't my thoughts. They're Aaron's! He's infected my brain. *The Addams Family* was really good last year! *He* was the one who was too cool to come see it, not me.

177

I'm at the stage. I'm climbing up and walking into the wings, only because the people I was walking behind were heading in that direction. They stop and talk to a girl with a clipboard, and only then do I realize that I am not in a band and have no reason to be here and turn to leave.

"Jess!"

I turn back, my neck tingling. Aaron's bandmate April sits perched on a tall crate, her shiny blue bass guitar propped jauntily behind her. She's wearing jean shorts over bright green fishnets and her usual dirty white Converse sneakers. Her blond bob forms two sharp V's pointing straight at her bright pink lips. It looks freshly cut. She might have done it herself.

Her shirt is super slouchy. At this angle, I can see her fuchsia bra strap, her shadowed collarbone, her—

"Jess?" She smiles. I'm staring. "You okay?"

"I'm here!" That is not an answer.

"Yeah. I'm glad." Her eyebrows are sky-high.

This is awkward but, to be honest, less awkward than usual. The new usual. This might be the first time we've had a one-on-one conversation, just the two of us, since the night things got weird. Pleasantly, unexpectedly, completely weird. Jay's party.

Speaking of whom . . .

"Yo yo yo, where's A-Man?" Jay appears, hand raised for me to high-five.

I do it. I high-five. My hands are regaining a little bit of feeling, so that's something. Then I realize what he's asked me and say, "Um."

"So we missed sound check. I know, I know, I swear they told us the wrong time, it was *not* my bad. He's gonna be pissed. Is he in a good mood?" Jay leans in, hands clasped. "Please tell me he's in a good mood."

"I'm going to guess that he is not in a good mood." I close my eyes.

Why did I come here? There is no point in me being here without Aaron. I should have just driven him here and *then* driven away, never to return.

Wallace lopes slowly over, twirling one of his lucky drumsticks, nearly ramming into three passing musicians, and yay—the band's all here! Except it isn't! I've just completely screwed them all over and then *turned up* to . . . what? To stare at them?

Even Wallace is staring back, his drumstick steady in his hand. "Damn, Jess. You look how I feel."

I have turned into Wallace.

A voice booms over the speakers, drowned instantly by a loud screech of feedback. Mr. Bolivar steps back, muttering to himself, then tries again more cautiously.

"All right, all right! Are we all ready to rock out?"

The audience sounds like they're not sure whether to snicker, groan, or cheer, and I use the momentary distraction to do what I apparently do best: *flee the scene.*

The backstage bustle forms a tight tunnel around me as I make my escape, hardly feeling my feet, like I'm standing still on a moving walkway at an airport, heading to my gate, everyone else heading in the other direction. The auditorium is filling up. The lights are dropping in the mezzanine. I go the other way, out the stage door.

Outside it smells fresher, the world is wider, it has just started raining, fat plops landing right on the crown of my head and dripping down my nose, and a girl is running past me, clutching a camera. I know her—we have physics together. I could say, *Hi, Raven,* and follow her in pursuit of normalcy, but she's already sprinted inside and I think I'd better stay out. I can breathe for a few minutes until I'm cool to drive . . . home, I guess? I'll go sit on that bench over there that nobody ever sits on except kids whose parents are late picking them up.

Stranded people. People who have lost their ride.

I start to laugh. I lean my head into my hands and keep sinking until my hair is dangling between my legs, and I'm laughing and laughing but no sound is coming out.

"So I'm guessing you broke up."

I jolt upright. It's April. Her voice sounded smug, but her face is sympathetic. I don't know why, but I'm disappointed. In that split second before seeing her, I'd hoped for more. A happier reaction. Which is asinine—she just wants to know where her band's front man is. They were fourth in the lineup. The clock, it is a-ticking.

"Um. No?" It has occurred to me that she's waiting for an answer. "I don't think so. I mean, I think that will . . . result from this. But the words were not spoken, so—not officially broken up. Yet."

I am babbling.

"So what is the 'this'?" April steps closer, thumbs stuck in the waistband of her shorts.

"I don't know," I admit. "We were talking—he was talking—and then something kind of—"

"Snapped?" She nods, unsurprised. "Was he talking about Safe & Sound?"

My mouth falls open. "How did you—"

"He's always talking about Safe & Sound. They are his unwitting archnemeses. Once I thought about telling them, but . . ." She shrugs, smiling. "So that's what did it after all this time."

I blush sunburn hot, feeling nuclear-radiation levels of embarrassment. All this time. Two freaking years. Longer than that, really. I fell in love with Aaron on the sixth grade sleepaway weekend, when he brought his guitar and performed "Wish You Were Here" on the steps of his cabin. All the girls, including Lydia, were sighing over him, and a couple of the boys, too. Nobody but me seemed to notice that he mixed up a couple of the lyrics, but it endeared him to me even more, that lapse in perfection. I was the one who got him.

It took me a few years of languishing in obscurity to *really* get him. Snag him, snare him, catch his attention and keep it. In the end, all it took was wearing a T-shirt my aunt gave me for Christmas, a picture of somebody named Edie Sedgwick—one of Andy Warhol's muses, apparently—against a stripy background. My aunt worked in fashion and her gifts were usually completely OTT, but I liked this one and Aaron liked it, too.

He got up from the seat behind me when French class ended and leaned in to murmur, "Ton chemise est chouette."

Ta chemise, my mind corrected, while my body disintegrated into dandelion fluff.

That's when the flirting started. And then the invitation to their first show. And then hanging out afterward until everybody else had left, and *finally* kissing Aaron Crenshaw, which was not exactly like I'd expected it to be, but that was fine, we'd figure out our way around each other, I thought. And then I was the envy of the school, the perpetual plus-one, the support, the weekend muse during fevered writing sessions. The unpaid therapist, the lunch and dinner buyer—he was the brokest rich person anybody knew. It was a funny little quirk; all of his personality traits were charming until, abruptly, they weren't.

Had I been drifting away sooner than this morning, though? Were there moments in the past few months when I tuned out while he talked? I would go through my homework for the next day, write mental haikus, daydream about sitting on a long pier, far away, completely alone, and he wouldn't even notice that I wasn't listening. I was a warm body, a human sounding board.

Was that what made me linger at Jay's party that night last month? Aaron wanted to leave early—somebody had pissed him off—but when we got to his house, he realized he'd left his acoustic Fender back at Jay's, so I had to go back and get it. The party was still going. I asked the linebacker playing "Brown Eyed Girl" on the guitar to hand it over, slunk back past the kitchen, and saw April sitting on the counter.

She wasn't drinking but still seemed like the most relaxed person at this party, as if I were finally spotting her in her natural habitat. Her lips were parted in concentration as she scrolled through her phone, editing the party's playlist.

She glanced up and saw me and brightened, sun sparkling on a river. "You're not leaving. Stay!"

I stayed. And she stayed. Oh man, did we both stay.

Now, here, she squats down in front of me, her hands pressed to the bench on either side of my legs, her mouth inches from mine. I could just lean over like she did that night and . . .

She glances back at the school with a grimace. We both flinch, hearing the dum-dum-dum of a bass line kicking into gear. "That'll be Shifter Focus."

My heart starts popping like corn.

"Listen, April," I say quickly, to make up for the fact that I should have said it a good half an hour ago. "I'm really sorry, but I left him. At my house. I have no idea how he's going to get here, *if* he's going to get here, and I know you're fourth on the roster—"

"Twelfth."

"Twelfth?" I blink. "Jesus, how many acts are there? Anyway, maybe that's good, you've got time to go find him, or . . . ?"

"You know the stage manager, right?"

"Lilly? I know *of* her."

April scratches her cheek. "Yeah, well, she runs a tight ship. I'd guess act ten is already up."

How is that possible? Time has lost all meaning. "I've screwed this up for you guys. I am so, so sorry—"

April presses her index finger to my lips, once, way too briefly, extends her hand again, and hoists me to my feet. I'm so caught up in the feeling of her arm sliding around me, her wrist bangles tickling my waist, that I don't immediately process the fact that she's herding me back toward the school.

"What are we . . . ?"

"I have an idea. Just . . . trust me."

Wallace and Jay are waiting just inside, leaning on the walls to either side of the stage door.

"Aaron?" Jay asks.

April shakes her head.

"Sorry!" I blurt. "I'm so—"

"Don't be sorry." Jay snorts. "Just . . . we get it."

I stare at him, his over-it slump, then take in Wallace's dazed smirk, April staring at her feet like she's trying not to laugh.

The entire school rotates around me. "Does *no one* like Aaron?"

The remaining members of Big Talk let out a noncommittal whining noise. Out past them, I hear cheering from the audience, stagehands ushering one band offstage and the next band on.

"Big Talk?" someone calls from deeper backstage. "Anybody see Big Talk?"

None of us answer. We all stand in place, locked in indecision.

Then, of all people, it's Wallace who straightens up and claps his hands like he's taking charge. "Okay. Time's up. You'll have to sing it."

I glance at April, hoping she'll be up for stepping up, only to find her eyes locked on mine with the exact same expression. Wallace is pointing at . . . me?

"What? Why? No!" I laugh. "Are you . . . what? I am not in the band."

"You're not *not* in the band," Wallace says sagely.

"Why don't you do it?" I nod at Jay.

April snorts. "Have you heard him sing?"

"If you like the sound of cats in heat having a fight, I'm your guy!" Jay beams. "I can riff and fill in Aaron's guitar part, so don't worry about that . . . Oh, *snaaaaaap.* I can finally do Aaron's guitar solo. He never lets me play his guitar solo!"

I reach quickly for April. "You sing it, then."

She glides out of range. "I *can* sing backup, just . . . not lead vocals. Not while I play bass. Two different rhythms and my brain is all: *Malfunction.*"

"Wallace?" I plead.

He scratches his chin. "I don't know the words."

"To which song?"

"Any of them."

"What songs are you even playing?"

"We had two ready, but now I'm thinking . . . one will be fine. 'That Moment.'" April stares at me, unblinking. Accusatory. "Our only good song. *Your* song."

My cheeks flush. "What?"

"Big Talk," the stage manager calls, then mutters behind her, "Um, can you not touch the curtains, please and thank you?"

April scratches her hair. "Okay, we don't have time for this. Jess? Please come sing the song you wrote."

"*I* wrote?" I let out a weak laugh. "Aaron writes—"

"Aaron writes all our songs, yes, except for that song, which we know *you* wrote because it's actually good." April blinks. "And because the style is an awful lot like the poem you wrote for the lit mag last spring."

She read my poem.

"Plus the chord progressions. Some of them were Aaron chords, but some of them were . . ." Jay waggles his hand, thinking.

"Better," April fills in.

I sputter in lieu of reply.

Did I write "That Moment"? I honestly don't know. I'd started sitting with Aaron while he composed on the weekends, and I guess I got a little frustrated when he was pacing and stuck and being a Struggling Artiste—in fact I could not take it for one second longer—so yeah, maybe I suggested a line or two and some chords to go with them, but . . .

"Big Talk?! *Last* chance!"

"Yes," I say.

"Yes?" Jay jumps twice. Wallace straightens, drumsticks ready. April bites her lip.

"Fuck it. Yes!" Oh God, what have I just done?

April springs to action, leading us all to the thick velvet curtains, behind which the band before us is clearing out.

"I'm not the world's best singer," I mutter to her, heart thudding. "I'm not even my family's best singer, and I am an only child."

"You're fine!"

"I've watched Aaron perform enough, though. I can copy him."

"Or just . . . not?" She links arms with me and pulls us both past the curtains, onto the stage, Wallace and Jay trailing behind. "Be *you*. I like you! I . . . *really* like you."

The lights are blinding, but I manage to find the mic stand. There are people out there, a great murmuring sea of them. There is a judges' table. We are very much in this for the participation prize.

I glance back at April. She swings her bass over her shoulder and shoots me a wink. That's probably as close to a cue as I'm going to get.

I lean into the mic. "We're Big Talk, I guess?"

And Wallace immediately jumps into the *beat beat beat* lead-in, and that's all I've got, no time left to panic—I sing!

Not well, but I did warn her. My pitch is more approximate than precise, and I can't figure out how close to get to the mic, but you know what? This *is* a good song! My voice is carrying, and I'm straight-up bouncing on this rhythm or whatever the cool kids say, and I know it by heart because I'm pretty sure April's right. Which of these lines did Aaron write? Did he come up with a single bar of this?

This *is* my song and I'm owning it, and I have to assume the crowd is into it, and April's on fire, and Wallace is solid, and I drop out now while Jay does his guitar solo, and off in the wings . . . holy shit.

Off in the wings and then out of the wings and onto the stage bursts Aaron. No guitar. His hair is sticking up, his tight pants are ripped at one seam, and there are sweat circles ringing his armpits. Did he run here? He's running toward me now, his face white and gaunt and dripping with fury, some avenging spirit, and I think for a second he's going have a lovers'—ex-lovers'?—spat with me right here, live onstage, but he's looking straight past me at the microphone stand. And *now* he's charging.

Oh hell no. Two more bars and my vocals come back in. *My* vocals.

I grab the mic with both hands and plant my feet for impact.

"Do you know that day and that way that you pay for the crimes in the times when you waited, you waited for more than you had—and now it's all here . . ."

April's come in on her backup harmony, but Aaron's joined in now, too, his sweaty hands trying to pry each of my fingers off the mic, his mouth so close and so humid my hand is starting to slip. He bumps me with his hip like he can pinball me offstage.

"It's all here . . ."

He's staring right into my eyes as he tries to outsing me, his pupils tiny little furious specks. But I know the truth. He can't see anything beyond this performance and himself—not right now, not ever. The world doesn't exist outside the circle of Aaron.

He can't even see that he's standing inches away from the edge of the stage.

"And it's clear," we sing together.

I step forward, tipping the mic stand. He steps with me, chasing it, one inch, two—and *shump*.

He falls off the stage.

"Have you ever felt that moment, that moment . . . !"

I spin to face the band. Wallace, Jay, April, all concentrating, grinning, elated, living this moment, this moment, this moment, the four of us totally in sync.

I can't see past the lights, can't hear past our music, but I imagine that Aaron has managed not to smash into the remaining judges, that he's being helped up and fighting off assistance, that his attitude has rankled the wrong people, that he's being hurriedly escorted off the premises as we hit the last few bars of this kick-ass song.

"Well, I know that you've felt it now."

The audience whoops and stands to cheer, probably more for the spectacle than for our actual performance, but I don't care. I turn, exultant. We did this!

April shoves her bass away and runs to me. I throw my arms around her, lift her half an inch off the ground and spin, and before we make it full circle, my mouth finds hers.

It's just like it was at Jay's party.

This kiss isn't a letdown with room for us to get to know each other; it's electric and ripe and Technicolor perfect. It is fully formed.

She holds my hand as we wave to the audience and walk offstage, which is helpful because it keeps me from floating away.

Have you ever felt that moment that moment that moment that moment—

Well, I know that I've felt it now.

THREE CHORDS

ERIC SMITH

Three chords.

That's all it takes for my heart to practically seize up in my chest. There are certain songs that, almost immediately, you can recognize from the opening few notes. Like some of those classic jams by Bruce Springsteen, John Mellencamp, or Arthur Crow that my dad rocks out to in the living room, the saxophone lick in "Born to Run" and the opening chords of "Jack & Diane" sending him into a disaster of a dance party. Something pure and joyful and embarrassing. Or the classic pop-punk my older sister loves, the Ataris or New Found Glory or the Starting Line whisper-singing the beginning of "Best of Me."

I catch my breath as the audience notices what she's playing. As *I* notice what she's playing. Well over a hundred students from my new high school go from a bunch of quiet, softly muttering classmates to an excited, surprised mob as this girl starts to play "Written in the Stars" by the Field Notes.

It's normally a fairly slow-paced pop-punk song, with sharp chords and epic choruses, the sound of three singers bursting into harmonies, but this . . . this is something different altogether. It's just her and an acoustic guitar, the song stripped down, totally raw and reinvented, and when she sings, the audience gasps. The recognizable notes in the strumming of her guitar, in her unique transformation of the song . . . I thought that was enough. But it's in her voice. My God. It's a gentle, soft thing, and the lyrics flutter from her lips, sounding delicate and otherworldly, the words rustling through the school theater like butterflies.

It's an indie-folk-rock cover of one of the most popular singles on the radio right now, instantly familiar to everyone who hears it, from the first three iconic chords to the way she's twisting the song with her voice, making it sound like something brand-new yet totally recognizable.

And I should know better than everyone.

'Cause I wrote it.

I grab hold of a thick black curtain, hoping that the velvet fabric might wipe away some of the sweat from my palms, steadying myself with that hand and gripping the neck of my guitar with the other. From here, on the side of the stage, I watch her. I've seen her before, in the hallways, looking cool and hip in this effortless way, but I don't think we've ever spoken a single word to each other. The school's stage is dark, and she sits on a stool in the middle of it, a single spotlight shining down on her, and even the cheap school-theater lighting can't wash out her olive skin and her bright green eyes. When she has them open, that is. When she doesn't have them shut as she sings high notes in a raspy gasp that makes my heart flutter even as my stomach is sinking.

Does . . . does she know?

She can't.

I've kept a low profile all year. I couldn't keep going to my old school, the private school where everyone knew me, knew what happened. The only real friends I've made here are Lilly, who is off running this whole event behind the scenes; Hailey, who is up running the lights with her pals; and Ken, the one person who has been desperately trying to get me back into music. Ever since I was booted out of the Field Notes after we got signed, not fitting the "image" the label wanted, he's seemingly made it his mission. The old crew, they're all wildly handsome and spend more time in the gym than they do working on the music, while I couldn't care less about how I look. And there's the fact that I didn't want to change any of my songs. The studio that recorded our first EP was overproducing them, making them into something they weren't.

And to think it's the same studio offering up recording time for whoever wins. I do not want to be in there with whoever is behind the board. They might recognize me. And when me and the guys were there, we didn't sound like people anymore.

But this. This girl here. She sounds so real.

Funny, my desire to sound real has left me living this fake life. I'm perfectly aware of the irony in all of that. Not telling anyone too much about myself. Steering clear of social media. Dyeing my hair, growing out the weak amount of scruff on my face, like some kind of badly drawn villain in a comic book or Law & Order episode. My hair is light brown these days instead of black, and that, combined with the scruff and the nonprescription glasses, make for a solid Clark-Kent-only-brown-and-slightly-more-emo disguise, I guess. Trying so very hard not to be seen for who I am. Everything about me washed away after my face became way too recognizable at my old school, where all my friends—

No.

Where all my *bandmates* went. They're not friends anymore. Friends call. They return texts. They don't unfollow you across all of social media and stop responding to your emails, when it's *you* who *made* them.

I hear some harried footsteps behind me and turn to see Ken, the shock of pink in his thick black hair bobbing as he runs, a look of concern on his face. We've been friends since before the Field Notes took off, connecting at local shows, back when the band played in small cafés and little venues. And now he's my partner in whatever this band is that we're trying to start. Acoustic duo?

He's the only one here who knows who I am.

Well, at least I thought so.

He bends over, his hands on his knees, and raises a single finger in the air as he tries to catch his breath. His eyebrow piercing catches a glint in the dim backstage lights.

He clears his throat and looks up at me, worry all over his face.

"Steve—" he sputters out.

"I can't do this." I shake my head, the words just tumbling out as that girl keeps singing my song in the background, the strumming of her guitar gorgeous and familiar. I'm not sure what's worse—that she's playing the hit song I wrote that's gone on to make my former best friends famous without me, my name just a dead link on the group's Wikipedia page, or that she's playing and singing it better than I ever could. Every breathy note, every strum . . . it feels like a punch in the stomach. But a punch that I miss, for some reason.

A nostalgia punch? I don't know.

Ken's never made a big deal out of it, out of me. He's joked that once we record some of our songs, people will notice me, that music blogs like *IndieTrash* and message boards will run with the whole "ex-songwriter of the Field Notes" thing, but I don't know. I really don't think anyone will care. I hope they won't, anyway.

Under the radar is safe. It's cozy.

"I just . . . I don't think I can do it." I swallow.

"Dude, no one here even knows who you are."

He says this with such brutal finality that I feel like I might collapse in on myself like the star that I'm not. Anymore, that is. I turn back to the girl, the song nearly over, and I catch a sob in the back of my throat that surprises me. I put a hand up to my chest, worried that the strangled sound could be heard across the stage. Ken grabs my shoulder and I shrug him off.

"Hey, sorry," he says. "That came off a little—"

"Yeah, it did," I snap. The song is winding down, and the girl strums a final chord, singing the last lines of the song, my song, in the utter silence of the theater. I can hear my own heartbeat, hear the sound of Ken breathing gently next to me. I watch as she closes her eyes, holding that final note, her voice a hum that vibrates across the walls and over my skin. There's a beat of quiet in the theater as she looks up and opens her eyes, looking toward the audience, that flash of green illuminated by the pale fading stage lights.

And the applause is fierce and loud and rolls like thunder.

I see several students jump to their feet, screaming and cheering. Someone shouts, "Yeah, Megan!" and I'm pretty sure I hear several others yelling something similar. Megan. A teacher brushes by me a little too roughly, thunking against my guitar case, the guitar inside making a loud musical thud as his leg knocks into it. It takes me a second to realize it's one of the music teachers, one who is consistently correcting and prodding at me in his class, and it has taken everything within the fiber of my being to not do the whole *Don't you know who I am?* thing to him.

I mean, I know I'm no one right now. But I was.

He doesn't even turn around to apologize, just pushes ahead. He says something inaudible to Megan before taking the microphone, and her face lights up under whatever compliment he hands out.

"Let's give it up for Megan Talley, everyone!" Mr. Bolivar says, gesturing toward her proudly. He's beaming, and the house lights go up with an audible snap. Both he and Megan wince for a second and continue waving to everyone as the applause starts to quiet down. I can make out the judges now, sitting in the front. There's that guy who goes here and works at Atomic Records, who I swear seems to actually hate music. The vice principal, some social media influencer I've never heard of, and . . .

My heart hammers in my chest.

Melissa Nuvel. From the band You Try Smiling. She has her feet kicked up on the table and is just beaming at the stage, her smile like a second spotlight.

She glances toward the curtains, and for a minute, I think she sees me as a bit of light reflects off her thick, chunky black plastic glasses. I don't think any of the other judges know who I am, but she sure as hell will.

She helped produce the Field Notes' first EP, the one that got us signed. She worked with our songs when we were bickering over them in the studio. Smoothing out the choruses, the verses . . . I know I've seen her on countless "one-hit wonder" lists and articles, but behind the scenes, she works with a lot of musicians. Like how the dude who wrote that "Closing Time" song writes for Adele, Phantogram, and the Chicks.

"Tough act to follow," Mr. Bolivar says to scattered laughter.

"Oh, to hell with this," I mutter, turning to walk away.

Ken presses a hand to my chest. "Come on, man. Don't bail."

I sigh and glance at my guitar case. It's peppered with logos of bands we played with during our rise up, first playing in small venues that made us buy our own tickets, then headlining at medium-size clubs, with groups I loved opening for us. There they were, on the case. All Time Low. State Champs. Sleepaway. The Wonder Years. Boys Behaving Badly. Yours Truly. The Echo Screen reunion. That acoustic show with the Rocket Summer that felt like a dream. Why did I bring this case? All these memories now like battle scars.

"Next up we have . . . the musical stylings of . . ." Mr. Bolivar squints at the postcard in his hand and looks over at me and Ken.

"Once Br—" Ken starts.

"Once Bitten!" Mr. Bolivar exclaims, and motions for us to join him, smiling as though he didn't just rename our duo after that awful old vampire movie.

Ken groans, and then looks over at me, his gaze expectant.

Anxiety fills me. It would be so easy just to walk in the other direction, walk away from the music. The Field Notes guys did it to me, just turned, leaving me to my own devices. Toiling alone.

"Hey," he says. "You coming?"

I look down at my guitar case again and exhale through my teeth. I pluck out my guitar, gripping it around the neck, the metal strings digging into my fingers. It's the same guitar I recorded that EP with, the same guitar that came with me on that first little tour, played all those shows, that ended up getting us signed . . . It's nothing special. A hundred-dollar Yamaha electric guitar with a rosewood edge, and a white plastic fretboard that's scuffed to all hell. Older than me by a decade, bought at a pawnshop in Newark with some birthday money when I was twelve.

Nothing special, but special to me.

I could have let it go when everything happened. Thrown it away. Tossed it in the basement of my dad's house, brought it back to that pawnshop. Lord knows I have plenty of other guitars around the house, for when the mood strikes. But it's like an old friend that I lost touch with, and there's something strangely comforting in just knowing it's around. Maybe that's why I brought it instead of any others.

Part of me still wants to be here.

I walk with Ken onto the stage, a smattering of applause following. I see the judges, and I can't help but zero in on Melissa. My mind flits back and forth to the last time I was on a stage, with the roar of an audience in front of me, to those moments in the studio with her, fussing over the songs that would make them famous. My feet squeak a little against the dark amber wood on the stage, bits of white tape stuck here and there. The last stage with the boys, it was dark gray and scratched to the point you could see the layers of past paint jobs beneath it, from the hundreds, if not thousands of people who had graced it. This stage . . . it's too clean. It hasn't seen things.

I've seen things.

An audience of a thousand. Camera flashes like lightning. Stadium amps the size of people and people with personalities the size of stadiums.

I grab the stool Megan had been sitting on and move it away from the microphone, and Ken takes the mic, standing in front of it. The stage darkens, and a spotlight shines down on Ken. I think about Hailey and her friends up there in the loft, fussing over lighting and soundboards, working their magic. I try to scoot away a little from the beam.

A few people in the audience notice and chuckle, and Ken reaches out and drags the stool with me on it closer to him. The audience laughs, and I glare at him.

He smiles down at me and then looks out to the audience, holding the microphone.

"Hi, we're Once Bright." He glances off to the side of the stage, and I look over to see Mr. Bolivar shrug. Ken turns back to the crowd. "And we hope—"

But I can't hear anything else he's saying.

Because there she is.

Standing right up front, looking right at me, and I swear, even in the dimly lit theater, I can see those emerald eyes looking up at me. How did she get here so fast? Did she just stash her guitar on the wings of the stage and run into the audience? Now that she's no longer in profile, I can see that her hair is buzzed along one side, the rest cut short. She's wearing a dark jean jacket littered with enamel pins that I can't make out. But she looks up at the stage at me in a way that would be impossible at a show with the old band, the house lights blinding us from the people right in front of us.

I give her a quick nod, and her eyes flit away from mine before looking back up at me. She's smiling, and then I watch as the expressions on her face shift and change, from what felt like a flirty glance to a dawning realization and confusion.

She's seeing me for the first time. Really seeing me.

And she knows.

Someone here at this school sees me—someone other than Ken knows the truth about me—and it sends a shock through my system. I don't think I'm ready for this. I'm not sure I can live up to whatever expectations she might have, if she even has any.

I still have the music in me someplace. I know I do. But I don't think it's here, on this stage right now. And it's in that moment, being seen for who I really am—someone forgotten, someone cast aside, someone who was so damn close—that I'm just frozen.

"Hey. Steve." Ken motions.

"I . . . I can't . . ." I manage.

I look down at the strings. New. Not snapped like they were just a few months ago. Before Ken brought up this duo idea. He had the voice, but he couldn't play. He knew I could play. He saw us open for the Spark & the Fire two years ago, owned our EP. The one Melissa Nuvel helped us with, the self-released recording we'd tossed up on Bandcamp and Spotify, before the labels came knocking. The one I recorded on. Not the new EP without me, not the album that's absolutely everywhere.

The practices and songwriting sessions were long and fun. I grew calluses on my fingers again. I felt happy.

"Steve?" Ken tries again. The silence that looms ahead of us, in the audience of my classmates, feels heavy and thick. I hear some soft muttering and the shuffling of feet. I catch the judges looking at one another.

And then I hear a boo.

Then another.

They sound like a thunderstorm in my head. There's this part of me that knows it's just a few jerks, people who are inconsequential to me, to Ken, to anyone here. Probably just came to the Battle of the Bands for a laugh. But this other piece of me knows that deep down, maybe I deserve this. Maybe I don't belong here, maybe I already had my shot, and this is a space someone else should have been in. And maybe I should put this guitar away and find the music somewhere else, some-day down the line when—

"Shut up!"

I look back into the audience, and my eyes flit down to the green-eyed folk singer with a half-shaved head and an unearthly voice.

The girl.

Megan.

"All of you, shut up!" As she shouts, a hush falls over the theater. She holds a power over them, the same power she had when she was singing. And I wonder, who is this girl? I mean, I've seen her before in the halls, but I never saw anything that would explain this hold she has over the crowd. Then again, I'm not exactly someone in touch with school gossip.

She looks back up at me.

"Play," she says, loudly and forcefully.

"Play!" she shouts when I continue to sit frozen, and she looks around to the people sitting near her.

"Play, play, play . . ." It starts with Megan and her friends and quickly takes over, flowing over the theater, until it becomes a roar echoing from the back near the doors. I feel a hand on my shoulder, and I look up at Ken, who is a blur, my eyes full of tears now.

"Hey," he says. "You okay?"

Play.

"I just . . ."

Play.

"I forgot. I forgot how much I love this. I miss it."

Play.

He squeezes my shoulder and gives me a shake.

Play.

"Then show them," he says.

Play.

And so I do.

I hit a power chord on the electric guitar, the crunch loud and glorious, and launch into one of the songs we've been working on since winter break. Megan cheers, and everyone else joins in, the sound swelling up around me as though it could lift me up from this stage.

I turn to Ken, who is beaming at me. He nods and grabs the mic, the song starting with him singing a low hum that builds into him bursting into the opening verse. He stomps his foot and pulls a little tambourine out from behind his back, keeping an impossible drumlike rhythm while he sings, and the cheers grow louder. It's a remarkable talent, and he handles it like Aaron Gillespie of Underoath or, if my dad were drawing comparisons, Karen Carpenter.

The song, and our little duo really, is a bit like Dashboard Confessional mashed together with Shawn Mendes, some emo and pop blended in one. We'd talked about adding an actual drummer, but Ken's brilliant way of keeping rhythm with his stomps and tambourine . . . it's just unlike anything I've ever seen. He sings, his honeyed voice full of melancholy and joy and things you can't describe, and I watch as the eyes in the audience shift to him, gripped by the magic he's conducting up here. Melissa looks right up at him, her eyes wide. I don't know if we'll win, but I'm not sure I really want us to. Maybe something will happen for him after all of this.

Maybe he'll leave.

Maybe . . . I've found the music only to lose it again, to be left behind again.

He hits the tambourine hard and smiles at me, lost in this moment, and I shake my head as I keep playing. He won't. He wouldn't. It's in the way he loves the music, in the way he loves his friends. How he showed up for me when things went south, expecting nothing. How he's been there since the start. How he's never pushed me to tell people who I am, who I was, even though that might mean a bump of fame for him.

However small all that might be.

It shows how big a person he is.

I keep playing along, the power chords crunching during the verses, full chords thrumming over the chorus. I even have a little solo, but as Ken dances onstage to it, keeping rhythm, the eyes are still on him, and I love it. He shines.

My eyes flit to Megan, and in a sea of people watching Ken, she's still looking up at me.

She sees me.

Really sees me.

And I'm glad.

MERCH TO DO ABOUT NOTHING

PREETI CHHIBBER

ROCK YOUR MOUTH

Wah-wah-wah-WAH-WAH-WAH—

Karan looked up from his phone, waiting for his eyes to adjust after staring at the blue light of his screen. A tall, grungy dude stood in front of his table, muffled sounds pouring out of his mouth like molasses and dying halfway across the loads of homemade band merchandise sitting between them. Karan pulled rolled-up bits of napkin out of his ears.

"What?"

"Bro, I asked how much the buttons were."

Karan glanced at the spread and sighed.

"Do you mean the big I'M A CHUMP ones or the small ones that just say FARTS 'N' MUSIC?"

"FARTS 'N' MUSIC, obviously."

"A dollar."

The kid pulled a dirty wad of bills out of his hoodie pocket and shoved a particularly greasy one toward Karan, waiting for him to take the dollar before grabbing a pin and fading off back into the seats.

So, this was working a merch table. Granted, the back of a high school theater probably wasn't the *exact* same experience as a real venue, but he figured a merch table was a merch table. Karan put the dollar into his very light envelope of cash and grabbed a few napkins out of the stack he'd brought with him from home. He methodically wiped his hands, and then tore two strips off a clean napkin to roll into new balls to stick right back into his ears and dampen some of the screeching currently coming off the stage. And he did mean *screeching*.

"*YOU! YOU! YOU ARE HELL! I CAN'T STAND YOU. OUR TONGUES DANCE BUT OUR HATRED IS ETERNAL —!*"

How was this only the first band? When his friend Jonah had asked—okay, had sort of blackmailed—Karan into selling merch for his band Chump 2.0 at the Battle of the Bands, he'd known it'd be a slog, but *man*. They were only one band in and he could feel his blood starting to enter a constant state of vibration.

It was also possible that he was just stationed too close to a speaker, but whatever. It was definitely the bad music.

Was it really only this afternoon that he'd had the prospect of a full, glorious, plan-free weekend ahead of him? He looked down at the text Jonah had sent him again: *U SELL MERCH OR UR MOM FINDS OUT WE WENT 2 THE BCH INSTEAD OF FRENCH CLASS LAST WK*

Jonah was the worst. Last time he'd trust the argument that skipping school was "the only way to stick it to the man." More like "the only way to make my friends do shit they don't want to do."

WAH WAH WAH WAH WAH WAH —

Karan jolted out of his musings, expecting to see another random flannel-wearing pest in front of his table, but was surprised to realize the movement and vocals were coming from someone at the table next to him. He pulled out one of the bargain earplugs.

"*HELLO!*" The person standing in front of the neighboring table was frantically waving a hand, trying to get the attention of an Indian girl who seemed to be there to, well, sell merch. Or he'd have assumed as much if she wasn't sitting behind the table, head down, curved over what seemed to be a book with approximately two thousand pages. "*Hey!!*"

"Huh? What? Oh, hi. Do you wanna buy something?" The girl folded over the corner of the page and shut the absolute unit of a tome sitting on her lap. Then she turned toward her customer, and Karan saw her face. And while his brain didn't register it, his heart did, and he fell in love a little bit.

ROCK YOUR MOUTH, CONTINUED

Saru bit back the sigh that was trying to make its way through her lips. She'd just gotten to her favorite part of *The Secret of the Undercurrent*, book two of the best series in the world: Space Crowns.

Prince Deverindara of Mahabali was *about* to give up his throne for the sea sprite Sonal! But *no*, Saru was here to do a job, so she paused in her reading, folded down the top corner of the page, closed the book, and turned to face the woman leaning over the table.

"Do you wanna buy something?"

"*Yes.*" If words and emotions could be physically manifested, that one would have been dripping with actual disdain.

Saru took a deep breath in through her nose, held it for three seconds, and then exhaled.

"Okay, which one of these do you want?"

"I need a medium in that shirt." The woman pointed at Saru's personal favorite piece of merch, a shirt with a unicorn and the name of her sister's band, Breakfast of Champions. Saru gestured for her to take it.

"It's twenty bucks."

The woman held out a credit card in response.

"Uh, sorry, no cards."

"Why?!"

"Well, this is a pretty homegrown, grassroots-type situation. We don't have card readers."

"Guh, *fine.*" She reached into her pocket, presumably to pull out some cash, but before she could, a concertgoer shoved by her and she fell forward, bumping hard into the table, which then bumped into Saru, and her book fell to the disgusting, sticky floor with an unnerving *splat.*

Books should not go *splat.* Saru reached out and peeled the book back off the linoleum, and it sounded like someone sucking their teeth, which made the whole thing worse. The floor was so gross, it was like the high school auditorium was trying to bring the atmosphere of an actual club or something. Maybe the scene kids had spilled soda and snacks on the ground in the name of authenticity?

Saru let out the hefty sigh she'd held back earlier. She was *supposed* to be on her way to her local bookstore, picking up the new book in the Space Crowns series, which was dropping at midnight. There was no way she'd make it at this point; people had started lining up *this morning.* Plus, her sister's band hadn't even gotten close to going on yet. She was going to have to wait a full extra *twelve hours* to find out what happened between Sonal and Deverindara and it was *infuriating.* Gita owed her so hard. But her sister knew that.

"Saru, I will do your chores for the next three months. *Please*, you're our only hope. Tejas got food poisoning and can't sell our merch, can you *please please please please.*"

"Gita, but the book—"

"Will wait! The Battle of the Bands waits for *none of us.*"

Saru had rolled her eyes at that one. Didn't Gita know about *spoilers*?! But Saru had acquiesced as she usually did. She could play the Good Sister.

So now, instead of screaming in frustration, she turned back to help her customer, only to find a crisp twenty-dollar bill in place of one of the unicorn tees. Great, that worked perfectly for both of them. She did another quick breathing exercise, tuned out the crowing onstage, and reopened her book.

. . . Only to feel an itching at the back of her neck, like someone was staring. She looked to the kid at the table to the right of hers. He was on his feet, pumping his fist to the music, and paying her not the least bit of attention. She panned back to glance to the left, and *oh.* The scruffy-looking Indian kid at Chump 2.0's table had clearly been staring at her. No *way* was picking at a tabletop that interesting.

"Can I help you with something?"

"Hmm?"

THE GREATEST PLACE

Crap.

The girl definitely knew Karan had been staring like a complete weirdo. But in his defense, everything about that interaction was distracting. He didn't want to be here, either, but at least he could interact with a customer without coming off as a complete misanthrope. Just, like, 60 percent of a misanthrope, he thought.

"Hmm?" he'd responded to her, like *hmm* was a word that meant anything.

"I asked if you needed something!" she yelled back at him over the music.

"Nothing. No, why would I—I mean, no. I don't need anything. Just, uh, selling merch. Same as you." The band chose that moment to end their set, but his unprepared butt kept yelling. "Sort of." And that was painfully loud.

If he thought she'd looked irritated before, the "sort of" qualifier at the end of that sentence seemed to really piss her off.

"Well, apologies if my customer-service skills aren't up to your standards, person I've never seen before in my entire life. But if that's all you had to say, I think I'll get back to *sort of* selling merchandise for my sister's band." And with that, she opened that massive book again and started reading. She was punctuated by the sound test of a *very* aggressive guitar twang. The next band on the roster must be setting up onstage, and the crowd was swapping one set of fans for another, though Karan couldn't really distinguish a difference.

He mentally groaned. Just his luck to end up next to a stuck-up, sensitive brown girl. They were going to be there all night; maybe he should try to apologize.

"That's not—sorry, that is not what I meant. I just—this sucks, right? You don't want to be here, I don't want to be here. Same. Same." Why was he talking so much? He tried to send a smile in her direction. Nothing, no recognition that he'd spoken whatsoever. He swore he could feel an actual ice wall between the two of them. He drummed his fingers on the table. *Ugh*, this was *so boring*. His eyes flickered back to the girl next to him. She was leaning her head in her hand, and her hair had fallen around the slope of her shoulder and pooled onto the table. The lights of the stage reflected against her glasses, barring him from seeing if she was actually reading or just daydreaming. Then she turned a page. Actually reading.

What could be that big and that interesting to be able to block out all of the hectic sounds and sights of the Battle of the (Too Many) Bands?

Karan narrowed his eyes. At least it had to be more interesting than what he was doing . . . which was a whole lot of nothing because, really, how many people were going to spend money on a band they hadn't even seen yet? He took a deep breath to fortify himself. Why did talking to another human being always feel so awkward? He pulled the napkins out of his ears.

"Look, really, I'm sorry! I didn't mean anything by the 'sort of,' I swear."

Karan saw her shoulders shift slightly. She'd definitely heard him.

"You've got to tell me the secret of being able to ignore all this crap. What are you reading?"

THE GREATEST PLACE, CONTINUED

Well, those were the magic words, weren't they? Saru tried to keep the corners of her mouth from going up. She just really loved talking about this series. It was her happy place! Even if it meant talking to a guy she'd already written off as a jerk. She dog-eared her place again and closed the book, wincing as her finger grazed a spot of unidentified stickiness on the cover. She needed to get some Wet-Naps. She wiped her hands on her jeans and turned to face whatever-this-guy's-name-was.

"It's the Space Crowns series. I'm Saru." She gave him a mini-wave in lieu of a handshake.

"Hey, Saru. Karan. What's Space Crowns?" He nodded in the direction of her book. She, honestly, was taken aback. How did anyone not know Space Crowns? Oh no, maybe he *didn't read.*

"I'm sorry, did you just ask me what one of the best fantasy series *ever* was? One that's been turned into four movies already, and inspired Shane Crawford's last album? And the new book comes out tonight and I'm missing it to be *here.*" She tried not to sound *too* angry. Her mom was always telling her she was too "spirited" for her own good.

Karan looked semi-abashed, but also annoyed.

"Well, maybe I just live under a rock." As if it knew, an intense guitar riff punctuated his frustration.

"*Please* tell me you've heard of *Mars Man*? It's the first book and what they called the first movie, or—"

"Yes! Oh man, I liked that movie, I think? I think I saw it." Karan had scrunched up his face, and Saru couldn't help but notice that he was kind of cute. He had that flop of Punjabi curls on his head, and the stubble of a few-days-old beard on his face that told of a kid too lazy to shave on the daily. But she could see the high cheekbones and full lips. Honestly, he wasn't so off from the description of Prince Deverindara.

Deverindara's jet-black hair curled and gleamed in the sunlight. His beard shone, and his eyes were dark and cunning. His mouth held a smile so sharp it could cut the world itself in half.

So, his face was good. The jury was out on the smarts part. She bit back a grin. Then her brain caught up with what he'd just said.

"You *think* you saw it?"

* * *

THE MARCIA, MARCIA, MARCIAS

Oh man, this girl was a *nerd*. Like, there were nerds and then there were *nerds*.

"Yeah, I *think*. It came out like three years ago?" Karan had to smile; he could see her physically restraining her own emotions to his deliberate nonchalance about her favorite book. She opened her mouth to respond when more banging started.

"Five-six-seven-eight."

Great, a new band was on. Saru rolled her eyes, and instead of yelling just picked her chair up to move it closer to the end of her table, gesturing for him to do the same. Karan shrugged and complied, moving closer to Saru, his chair lifting from the floor with the disconcerting sound of something that has spent too long on a tacky surface. At least this would pass the time.

"You are missing out; this series is amazing. It has everything: romance, comedy, drama, tragedy, clever plotting, all of it!" Was it just Karan, or were Saru's eyes actually shining? He shook his head; it had to be a trick of the light.

"It sounds like a Bollywood movie." He laughed. He was surprised when she didn't immediately snap at him but grinned back instead.

"You're not wrong; it's just missing the musical part. You have to buy the e-book for that."

It took him a second to realize she was joking.

"Oh, ha! Talk about a nightmare situation. That's all I need, is for my mom to discover singing e-books. Oh man." He shuddered at the thought of his mom introducing e-book songs into her antakshari repertoire.

"Gita—my sister—*loves* Bollywood music. And I get it, it's fun. I've just never had any interest in the dancing-and-music part of it. I like the stories, though."

Karan shrugged noncommittally before responding. He wasn't a musical guy, either, but he *really* wasn't a *"Rahul, naam to suna hoga"* kind of guy.

"I'm more into, like, the Criterion Collection."

"That feels kind of snobby, don't you think?" Saru's entire body had moved several inches backward at his admission. Hilariously enough, she was in time with the percussion of their current soundtrack.

"Okay, Miss 'YOU'VE NEVER HEARD OF SPACE CROWNS.'" She frowned. "Fair point."

This was starting to actually get enjoyable. Maybe Karan owed Jonah for being a blackmailing asshole. He was just about to ask her what else she was into when he was beaten to the punch by a conspicuously well-dressed older white dude who looked like he had literally run to Saru's table.

"Excuse me, are you Kareena?!"

THE MARCIA, MARCIA, MARCIAS, CONTINUED

Saru's head swiveled around to stare daggers at whoever had just asked her if she was that famous Indian-American pop star, which was definitely not irritating, and definitely had not happened four hundred other times over the course of Kareena's short career.

She took in the dude standing in front of her, from his expensively distressed jeans to his too-rich-to-really-be-that-torn-up button-down. Then she poured every ounce of ice that she could into her voice.

"No."

"You look *just* like her." He was so committed to his absurd idea that he didn't even notice when the back end of the crowd slammed up against him like the powers in the sky were telling him to cut it out.

"Wow, you've guessed it. I'm famous and I'm here, at a local battle of the bands . . . selling merchandise. Way to go. You solved it." Saru rolled her eyes and glanced over at Karan in the universal way brown folks did at the small packages of racism the world liked to Secret Santa into their laps.

The man flinched a little at her tone, but then his smile morphed into a slight sneer.

"Look, she's hot, it was a compliment."

He sidestepped over a few feet to the right to look at another table before she had a chance to respond.

Jerk. People did that all the time. She and that Kareena honestly didn't even look—

"No offense, but uh, you do *not* look like Kareena." Karan voiced her thought out loud before she could even get there herself. She threw him a dirty look.

"What's *that* supposed to mean?"

"That you don't look like the only other Indian girl that guy's probably ever seen?"

". . . Oh. Okay. Yeah. It happens all the time, and it's super annoying." Karan tipped his chair back and looked up at the ceiling.

"Yeah, people ask me if I'm Michael Singh *all* the time. But you know, maybe they're all, uh—"

"A little racist?" It felt good yelling that part over the din of the crowd and the music they were screaming along to.

"You said it." Karan raised an eyebrow and let out a puff of laughter. But there wasn't any joy in it. "Just once it'd be great if it could work out in my favor, like, 'Yes, I am Michael Singh. Please give me a free smart watch.'"

"There was one time that someone bought my food because they thought I was their friend from middle school."

That time his laugh was real.

THE MARCIA, MARCIA, MARCIAS, CONTINUED AGAIN

"So, I think we were talking about how you're a snob," the girl—Saru, Karan reminded himself—said with a grin. It made him feel good. He smiled back and shrugged, unsure of how to respond in a way that wouldn't make him sound like an *actual* snob. She shot him a small smile and shook her head before turning back to the music.

They listened to the band play onstage for a few minutes. Karan started getting nervous about the conversation dying. Maybe he should say something? Or maybe Saru had just been being nice and really was just waiting to get back to her book? He looked over at her and she was nodding in time to the music. Screw it. He looked around and saw the set list his friend had taped to the cash envelope sitting on the vinyl tabletop in front of him.

"There's a band here called Reckless Love!" he yelled.

"What?" she replied without looking at him.

"I SAID THERE'S A BAND HERE CALLED RECKLESS LOVE!" he yelled louder.

"I heard you. I just think it's a funny name."

Karan rubbed the back of his hair like he did when he was feeling awkward.

"Oh, sorry—what's so funny about it?"

"Isn't all love reckless?

Well, that's not where he thought this conversation was going to go. Saru had settled her chin in her hand, and her eyes had unfocused behind her lenses.

"Uhhhh . . ."

Then she shook her head and looked like she realized she'd said more than she'd meant to.

"I mean, that's from a book. This book." She lifted up her giant fantasy novel. "Yup. Just thinking about how I could be at a book party right now."

She sounded like she was lying, but Karan was not going to go down *that* road. Luckily, Saru changed the subject before he had to. She faced him again, not even flinching when a random body jostled her whole table.

"*Anyway*, we know why I'm here. Why are *you* here?"

Karan sighed. This was not going to make him look great.

"My friend Jonah blackmailed me into it."

Instead of laughing, Saru widened her eyes and turned her chair entirely toward him.

"That's incredible! What did he blackmail you with?"

"Incredible?"

"I mean, come on. Who blackmails in high school?" She scrunched her nose and flung her hand up in that universal gesture of *Are you kidding me?* And that was a fair point, actually. Who did blackmail in high school? "Is your friend super into *The Godfather*? Full disclosure: I haven't seen it, but I can't imagine there's not blackmail in *The Godfather*."

"Are you just free-associating right now?"

"Are you changing the subject because it wasn't a good blackmail story?"

The emcee's voice cut into their conversation. "All right, Battle of the Bands crew! Get ready because up next is Chump Two Point Ohhhhh!" Karan looked at the stage and watched Jonah fiddle with his bass, plucking a few notes just before the band launched into their first song.

CHUMP 2.0, THE GRANTS

Saru bit the inside of her cheek to keep from smiling. Karan still hadn't answered her, instead watching the latest band kick off their set and busying his hands straightening the small piles of merchandise still covering his table. A few more people came up and bought some of the buttons and snap bracelets he had for sale.

"Fine, if you won't tell me, I'm going to make assumptions." She tapped her chin in mock concentration. "I'm guessing you told your mom you were seeing a PG-13 movie, but really you were seeing a *rated-R movie.*"

"Okay, while that would absolutely be punishment-worthy in my household, my friends don't know that, so keep it on the DL? What else you got?"

"Maybe you lost the remote and your dad doesn't know who did it, but it was *you* all along and your buddy threatened to tell him."

Karan placed a hand over his heart and looked shocked.

"My dad would never get mad at me; he is the opposite of a scary uncle."

Saru narrowed her eyes. *Hmm.*

"You got a B on a test and changed it to an A."

"Haha. I am a straight-C student, thank-you-very-much." He sat up straight in his seat and adjusted a tie he wasn't wearing. "Grades are a failing instrument of a dying infrastructure." Karan dusted some invisible lint off his shoulder. "It's my way of sticking it to the status quo."

She couldn't help herself and let out a loud bark of a laugh. Karan looked startled for a second before cracking a grin of his own.

"Honestly, it's not that interesting. We cut school and went to the beach last week, but I'm pretty sure it was all a ploy so that he could blackmail me into doing this the whole time."

"Next time you should at least hold out on cutting class to do something really good."

Karan's smile took on a mischievous glint.

"Like a book party?"

"Like a book party."

BREAKFAST OF CHAMPIONS

"Oh! This is my sister's band."

A new band had gotten onstage and was tuning their instruments. In the back right-hand corner Karan could see another Indian girl who looked a little bit like Saru . . . if Saru had short, spiky bleach-blond hair and bright red lipstick. Then the girl onstage furrowed her brow in obvious annoyance and yelled something at the drummer, and Karan really saw the resemblance.

"Do you like their music?"

Saru grimaced and paused, clearly trying to find a diplomatic way to say *No, but I love my sister.*

"Gita's a great bassist, and she says they have a real shot at winning. Apparently, their lead singer is dating a judge?" She caught herself at the implication in those words. "Not that that's the reason they'll win, but it might give them an edge."

"My friend's band is not good, so that's fine."

"Oh man, I'm so sorry." She seemed to realize something. "Since they're already done, shouldn't they come by to let you leave? Can't they sell their own stuff?"

The thought actually hadn't occurred to Karan, and he felt both a little silly and just a touch relieved. He wasn't going to examine that relief just yet, though.

"What the hell, you're right." He pulled his phone out and texted Jonah to find out why the hell he hadn't come to let him go home. It wasn't like he was going to bail; he was having a good time, but Jonah deserved an all-caps text with several red-faced, expletive-censoring emojis.

"I'm gonna—uh, watch while you deal with . . ." Saru waved toward his phone, and he rolled his eyes but thanked her all the same. As she turned back to the stage, Karan hesitated just a second, looking at her profile in the low light of the auditorium.

BREAKFAST OF CHAMPIONS, CONTINUED

Saru heard Karan begin to furiously type into his phone a moment after training her eyes on the stage. She wasn't lying; Gita was a really good bassist. Her sister had started plucking at her bass, and the crowd was getting hyped.

The band's sound might not have been up her alley, but she couldn't deny that they had some serious stage presence. The drummer was actually drumming with *flair*, she could see the glint of the keyboardist's manicure pounding the keys from here, and in the spotlight the singer's cheekbones looked like they could cut glass. Not to mention Gita, who was folded over her bass, kicking her way across the stage to the beat of the song. It was mesmerizing. Saru was so entranced, she didn't even realize how quickly the first song went by, and then they were calling out the title of their second—and last—song. It was a fast, frenetic piece, and Saru recognized the bass line from listening to her sister practice in her room.

The last note rang through and there were no other words for it: she watched the crowd actually *go wild*. Warmth spread through her chest. She loved seeing her sister succeed, even if it did mean missing out on Prince Deverindara's adventures for one more day.

Then the singer shouted out, "Thanks, we're Breakfast of Champions—thanks for supporting the music! We've got T-shirts and a bunch of stuff for sale right back there sold by our bassist's kick-ass little sister! HEY, SAH-*ROO!*"

A hundred heads swiveled back to stare at her.

Oh God.

I WANT YOUR P.S.

Karan, admittedly, had stopped paying attention when Jonah had texted back that he and the band were, quote, busy, unquote, and so, quote, wouldn't be able to chill at the merch table, unquote, and were, not a quote, being huge dicks about all of it. He should just leave. It would serve his friend right. Except right as Karan was *barely* considering it, he heard the band onstage call out Saru's name. His first thought was *How do people keep mispronouncing names that are just two syllables?* His second was noticing that the girl herself had absolutely frozen next to him.

"Saru?"

He could see the muscles in her jaw working like her teeth were milling down into flat little lines while she ground them together. She spoke, and the words sounded like they were fighting their way out of her mouth.

"Karan, are all those people moving this way?"

He looked at the crowd. It was indeed shuffling its way toward them in a grotesque mimicry of an indie zombie movie cast entirely with scene kids in band tees. All thoughts of Jonah and leaving forgotten, Karan tried to reassure Saru.

"Look, it's okay, we can do this. I'll help. It's gonna be fine."

All of a sudden the crowd turned into one giant blob of arms stretched out toward the shirts and pins, random bills of cash tied into reaching fingers. It was hands down the most chaotic thing he'd ever had the misfortune to experience in his entire life.

SAFE & SOUND, SHIFTER FOCUS

Two bands later, he and Saru collapsed back into their chairs. She had three T-shirts, two buttons, and a handful of stickers left. Everything else was gone. Well, no, her book, too. The giant book was there.

His table was, of course, still full.

"That was terrifying. Band kids are *terrifying.*" Saru had taken off her glasses and was rubbing at her eyes. And maybe he noticed how long her lashes were.

"Those weren't band kids. Band kids are like—you know, hats?" He gestured like he was wearing a huge band hat. "And the gloves?"

"The pope?"

"What?"

"The hat, like the pope?"

"No, the hat like in band."

Saru put her glasses back on and shot him a quizzical look.

"None of these bands have worn hats."

He was about to respond with a word his mother *definitely* would have grounded him for using when he saw her lip twitch, just the slightest bit.

"You're screwing with me."

She let out her full-blown smile.

"I'm screwing with you. Which isn't very kind, but was pretty fun. I feel a little sorry, though, since you just helped me not become a walk-on part for *The Walking Dead*."

"I was *just* thinking they were like zombies!!!"

AMINA ABOUD

"So, what ended up happening with your friend?" Saru's eyes shot toward Karan's cell phone, still sitting on the table. He hadn't said anything or made a move to leave yet. She was waiting for Gita to return from backstage. Though if she was being honest with herself, there was a reason she hadn't sent an irritable text asking her sister where she was yet.

Karan groaned and rubbed the back of his head. It was the third or fourth time he'd done it that evening, and she was starting to realize it happened when he was uncomfortable.

"He's being a dick. Has to"—Karan brought his hands up and somehow used his fingers to make the most sarcastic air quotes she'd ever seen—"'network.'"

"Well . . . at least you have company?" She glanced away as she said it, no need to find out if he'd be able to tell she was blushing. When she looked back at him, he was giving her a strange look.

"That's true, I—" Before Karan could finish whatever he was going to say, a loud voice cut through the speaker.

RECKLESS LOVE

"Hey, everyone, we're Reckless Love!"

Karan and Saru stared at each other before screaming out in unison: "Reckless Love!"

And he didn't know why, but they stood up and cheered, and from behind their tables, they danced along with the crowd.

BIG TALK, MEGAN TALLEY

"I have *never* done that before!" Saru was sweating, and she didn't care because so was Karan.

"Me neither. And I know what you're thinking—we're Indian, we automatically have rhythm! Not true, Saru. Not true. So I hope you won't judge my dancing." She appreciated the way he said her name, with that *r* rolling just slightly up against the roof of his mouth.

"I can't promise there's no judgment, but I can promise I won't like you any less because of it."

Oh no, had she just said that out loud? Karan looked just a little shocked, or maybe grossed out? No, not grossed out. Maybe he was going to smile? What was his face doing?! Did he—

"Hey, Saru!" Gita's arms wound around her shoulders from behind. "Thank you, favorite sister in the world!"

Saru deliberately looked away from Karan and back toward her sister.

"I know! You were *great*, didi! Killed it. We sold almost everything." Gita eyed the table in appreciation.

"You really are the best, wow. I think if you left now, you might still be able to make it to the bookstore. I may have called in a favor with my buddy Molly who told me she's working that release thing you wanted to go to."

"WHAT?!" Everything else was out the door. Saru hugged Gita tight and rushed to shove her things into her bag. She reached for her book but found it already in someone else's hands. Karan was holding it out to her, wincing a little at what was probably still a really sticky back cover.

"So, you're gonna go to that book party?"

MEGAN TALLEY, CONTINUED

Saru had said she liked him, and maybe she meant as a friend, but also maybe she meant more than that? She was cute as hell! And funny! And now she looked horrified, and he was definitely going to say something to her, but her sister came over.

It all happened very quickly, and before he knew it, Karan had lifted the book up and immediately realized it was covered in *something* he already regretted touching. But it was totally worth it when she grazed his fingers to take it from him.

"You wanna come?"

He spared a small glance at his friend's merch table.

"I can watch it. I'm here for the night anyway." Saru's sister wasn't looking at him, and was instead shooting a series of very obvious looks at Saru, which she was studiously ignoring. He smiled.

"That'd be awesome. Let's go to a book party."

Saru smiled back. "Let's go, Deverindara."

"What?"

"Don't worry about it."

ALL THESE FRIENDS AND LOVERS

KATIE COTUGNO

Josh shows up to band practice on Thursday wearing tortoise-shell glasses, a dark green hoodie with a hole in the sleeve that he's had since seventh grade, and his *I have a brilliant idea* face.

"I have a brilliant idea," he announces, then pauses to make sure he has our full and undivided attention. "Yacht rock."

I blink. "Yacht rock?"

"Yeah." Josh plays a kicky little lick on his guitar, a late-'70s *wahh-wahh* kind of sound that somehow evokes sherbet Miami sunsets and mustachioed guys in wide-collared button-down shirts with tufts of visible chest hair poking out. "The Doobie Brothers, Hall and Oates, Christopher Cross!" He turns to Franco, clearly delighted with himself. "You used to play the saxophone, right?"

Franco peers back at him, expression dubious under his thick black eyebrows. "I mean, in fourth grade band, sure."

"Like riding a bike, man." Josh is already fussing with the arrangement of "In My Life," one of the songs we've been rehearsing for the

Battle, his curly brown hair falling down over his eyes. Franco and I exchange knowing looks. In the fourteen months since Josh started this band, it's been a ska outfit, a Dave Brubeck–style jazz quartet, and briefly a hip-hop ensemble until Franco and I convinced him that was culturally appropriative and also reminded him that none of us knew how to freestyle. Josh took the critique in stride; two days later he showed up to rehearsal with a washboard he'd ordered from Amazon Prime and tried to sell us all on hipster bluegrass. The constant shape-shifting should be annoying, and sometimes it is, but honestly that's kind of the whole beauty of Josh: when he's excited about something, it's basically impossible not to be excited, too.

"Yacht rock could be cool," I say now, shivering a little as I experiment with a couple of practice chords. The sun is going down, the late-afternoon air spring-chilly, and my legs are bare between the hem of my sundress and my beat-up Keds. We used to practice in the finished apartment above Franco's parents' garage, but then his grandma had a stroke over Christmas break and moved in there along with her mean cat and an entire army of bobbleheads made to look like Republican politicians, so now we have to rehearse outside in the backyard, snaking an industrial extension cord from an outlet in the basement out across the concrete to power Josh's amp. The whole operation takes half an hour to set up and always reminds me of the afternoons we'd spend constructing intricate Lego towers in Josh's room when we were in elementary school, Josh adjusting the details this way and that with his chubby little-kid fingers so that by the time we were ready to actually play with them, my mom had arrived to pick me up. "Classic Beatles by way of Toto's 'Africa'? I'm kind of into it, actually."

"Of course you are," Franco mutters, ignoring the death stare I immediately shoot his way. "You know who *does* play the saxophone?"

he continues, poking thoughtfully at a blemish on his chin; he's been on Accutane since spring break, but honestly it doesn't seem to be doing a ton for him. "Gi—"

"Don't say it," I snap, reaching out and nudging his hand away. Gigi quit the band three weeks ago with no warning whatsoever. Also, she quit being my best friend. "And don't pick your face."

Franco shrugs and turns back to his drum set. I reach for my water bottle, trying to swallow down the bad taste in my mouth.

We spend the next hour swapping out Lennon and McCartney for Seals and Crofts, turning up the synth on my keyboard, and cheerfully defiling the work of the greatest songwriting team of all time with a mellow smooth-jazz groove. "You really think it's a good idea?" Josh asks as we're breaking down the equipment, Franco looping the extension cord around his arm and bringing it back into the house, where his mom uses it to power her off-brand Peloton machine. "The yacht rock thing?"

"I think it's kind of brilliant," I promise, which is true, no matter what Franco suspects about my motives. I've had a thing for Josh pretty much forever: all through middle school, even though he was slow to start wearing deodorant; freshman year, when he experimented with a man bun and a multitude of leather chokers; the summer after tenth grade, when he dated not one but three different girls named Nicole, all of whom he met at the snack bar at our town pool. Gigi and I had a running joke about how there must be an endless supply of them in the freezer behind the counter, right in between the Chipwiches and SpongeBob ice cream novelties. "We might actually have a chance of winning this year."

Josh smiles, the corners of his hazel eyes crinkling up with the relief of having been reassured. Then he frowns. "Would be better with a saxophone," he says worriedly. Franco chokes back a laugh.

* * *

Ms. Saeed catches my eye just as the bell rings for the end of English the following morning. "Elisa," she calls, "can you stay for a minute?"

I head up to her desk as everyone else shuffles out into the hall-way, the thump of textbooks slamming shut and the mousy squeak of sneakers on linoleum. Ms. Saeed has been tutoring me after school twice a week since the beginning of the year, helping me pick out the themes in *Beloved* and *The Things They Carried* and proofreading my five-paragraph essays, never once blinking when I get caught up short by unfamiliar words.

"So, I don't know if you've noticed," she says now, gesturing down at what looks like the Earth itself shoved up underneath her sweater, "but I'm pregnant."

I laugh. "You know, I kind of figured something like that was going on, yeah."

"Friday's going to be my last day before I head out on maternity leave," she tells me, gathering her dark hair into a stubby tail at the back of her neck and fanning herself with a stack of file folders. "You guys are going to have a sub for the rest of the year, but I feel like you and I have been making some pretty good progress together, and I don't want us to lose that. Ms. Cherry runs a study group of her own after school a couple of times a week. I spoke to her and she's happy to have you join. She and I are teaching from the same syllabus, so the transition should be pretty easy."

"Oh," I say, "sure, that'd be great." I like Ms. Saeed, but I've had enough extra help in my academic career to know that one study group is basically the same as another. "Thanks a lot."

I say goodbye to Ms. Saeed and head toward the cafeteria, rounding the corner toward the hallway where the junior lockers are—and coming within centimeters of crashing right into Gigi. She's wearing overalls and a black-and-white-striped tank top, and in the moment before she rearranges her face into a mask of cool indifference I swear it looks like she might be about to burst into tears.

"Shit," I say, which feels like an understatement. Gigi doesn't say anything at all.

My mom is leaning against the kitchen counter in her scrubs when I get home from band practice that afternoon. "I picked up dinner," she says, nodding at a bag from the rotisserie chicken place near our apartment. "How was your day?"

"It was fine." I pop up on my tiptoes to peek inside, pulling out a tub of potato wedges and another of the maple carrots she knows are my favorite. "What about you?"

My phone vibrates in my pocket as she's telling me a story about a woman who nearly delivered triplets in the hospital's south elevator; I wait until she's done to fish it out, hoping in spite of myself for a text from Gigi. Instead it's just a link from Josh, a Spotify playlist of his own creation full of Steely Dan and Kenny Loggins. "Inspiration!" he's titled it, along with a string of boat emojis.

I frown. It's not that I don't like Josh's mixes—the opposite, in fact; there's a whole folder of them saved to my hard drive dating back to fifth grade—but there was a tiny part of me that thought our weird eye contact in the hallway this morning might mean something had finally jangled loose between Gigi and me. We haven't talked at all since the night of our gig at Franco's sister's thirteenth birthday, two dozen sweaty middle schoolers wobbling around the decaying roller rink on the edge of town. This was back when Josh was going for a new wave sound, all of us wearing matching sunglasses and dressed in itchy thrift-store sweaters. It wasn't my favorite of our musical incarnations by a long shot; still, I thought everything was going fine until Gigi walked off the stage halfway through the set and marched directly for the exit.

I startled, my hands hovering uselessly above my keyboard. Josh gaped. Only Franco kept on playing, oblivious, his eyes closed behind his shades as he banged cheerfully away on the drums.

By the time I made it outside, Gigi was nowhere. *Where'd you go???* I texted, standing in the rainy April parking lot. I was still wearing my silly plastic sunglasses. *Are you okay??*

Three dots appeared, disappeared, came back again. *I'm fine*, she told me finally. *I'll explain later.*

Only she didn't.

In the three weeks since then, I've tried everything I can think of to get her to talk to me: waiting at her locker; dropping by her after-school job as a checker at Stop & Shop; texting her the full lyrics to Celine Dion's "Where Does My Heart Beat Now," our favorite corny '90s ballad, one line at a time. I even messaged her on Instagram like she was some social media influencer I was pursuing for a brand partnership and not a person whose retainer was shoved into the glove compartment of my car at this very moment. The girl is a brick wall.

I have no idea what I did wrong.

Now my mom nudges me with one sneakered foot, eyeing me over her waxy cup of Diet Coke. "Everything okay?" she asks, and I nod like a reflex. My mom has raised me on her own since I was four, when my parents got divorced and my dad moved back to Michigan; she works twelve-hour shifts as a labor and delivery nurse and does home health care on her days off just to keep me in piano lessons and SAT prep. The last thing she needs is me whining at her over dinner because my friend is being mean to me. I'm seventeen, not seven.

I offer to do the dishes after dinner, and once they're all drying on the rack, I head into my room and lie down on my bed, scrolling idly through Josh's playlist. I tap the triangle to listen and close my eyes.

When Ms. Saeed said "study group," I was picturing half a dozen people, but when I walk into Ms. Cherry's classroom the following Tuesday after eighth period, it's actually just Hot Pete Gardello sitting with his notebook open at a desk in the front row.

"Hey, Elisa," he says, lifting a casual hand in greeting, and I blink at the sound of my name. Hot Pete Gardello and I do not run in the same circles by any stretch of the imagination. He's junior class president and co-captain of the baseball team, the star of an often talked-about talent show skit in which he gamely lampooned his own popularity like a famous actor hosting *Saturday Night Live*.

Also, as his name might suggest, he's hot.

"Um, hey," I say, taking a seat two rows over from him. He's wearing perfectly broken-in jeans and a heathery blue T-shirt that makes his eyes look Photoshop bright. I stare at his Adam's apple for a second before I realize I'm doing it, watching the muscles in his throat move as he swallows. Pete Gardello is the kind of person who makes you want to gaze.

Tutoring with Ms. Cherry is basically the same as working with Ms. Saeed, as predicted, although occasionally Ms. Saeed and I would talk about *The Bachelor* and Ms. Cherry does not strike me as someone who watches. We spend an hour on reading comp and this week's vocabulary unit before wrapping up at four-thirty; Hot Pete Gardello and I head down the hallway, not walking together so much as silently going to the same place side by side. I keep waiting for him to speed up, but he matches my stride until we get to the parking lot, when he throws another wave in my direction. "See you later, Elisa," he says.

Our cars are two of the only ones left by now, parked on opposite sides of the student lot. I'm just rolling my windows down—it's nice today, the rustle of summer coming up in the trees—when I hear the telltale scraping sound of a dying battery echoing across the concrete. I crane my neck to peer in the direction of his shiny black Jeep, and there it is again.

"Everything okay?" I call across the lot.

"Uh, yeah!" Hot Pete Gardello hollers back, waving an *all good here* hand out his driver-side window. Then, just as I'm about to turn the key in the engine: "I might have left my lights on this morning, I guess."

I meet my own eyes in the rearview mirror, barely able to keep from laughing at the absurdity of it. In the second before I remember I can't tell Gigi about this, I think she's going to die when she hears. "You need a jump?"

Hot Pete Gardello pokes his head out the window. "You know how to do that?"

I can't resist making a face. "Why, because I'm a girl?"

"No, because I don't."

"Oh." That surprises me: it feels like Hot Pete Gardello should have been born with all necessary life skills already preprogrammed into his brain, though I guess maybe part of being popular is that you never have to learn how to do certain things for yourself because someone will always want to help you. Case in point: "Well," I say, "I can show you if you want."

I pull into the empty spot beside him before climbing out of the driver's seat and opening the trunk, pushing aside a jack, some emergency flares, a first aid kit, a case of bottled water, and a box of thirty-six nut bars from Costco before fishing out a set of jumper cables. "Wow," Hot Pete Gardello says, getting out of the Jeep and peering over my shoulder.

I cringe. "We take emergency preparedness very seriously in my family."

"I see that."

I have him pop his hood and I clip the cables between his engine and mine; in the second before I push the thought from my mind, it occurs to me that it kind of looks like our cars are holding hands. I turn my key in the ignition, smiling reflexively as his engine rumbles to life; Hot Pete Gardello smiles back, a quick white grin that makes me feel very flustered. "Look at that," he says. "You're a magician."

"Hardly," I manage, feeling myself blush. "Anyway, I should go. I've got band practice."

"You guys doing the Battle?" he asks. "What's the name of your band?"

I can't help but wince. "Evelyn Nosebleed."

His eyebrows twitch. "That's . . . evocative."

"Yeah." I nod grimly. "My friend Josh read something online that said your ideal band name is your grandmother's name plus the last thing you went to the ER for."

"Your friend Josh went to the ER for a nosebleed?"

"He has a delicate system," I say automatically. "Anyway, it made more sense when we were punk."

"What are you now?"

That stops me for a moment. I think of Josh and his yacht rock playlist, of my long string of unreturned texts to Gigi. "You know," I say slowly, "that's a really good question."

Hot Pete Gardello nods. "Well," he says, "thanks again for the jump."

"Anytime," I tell him, then get into my car and pull out of the parking lot. When I glance in the rearview mirror, I see that he's still standing by his driver-side door, watching me go.

The rest of the week passes like that: Gigi avoids me in the hallway. My mom picks up butter chicken for dinner. I sneak glances at Josh during practice, watching as he chews his bottom lip while he tunes his guitar.

Thursday after school, there's a note on Ms. Cherry's door that says she left early to get an emergency root canal, so I head out to the parking lot and find Hot Pete Gardello standing against the retaining wall with what looks like a Juul hanging out of his mouth. "Hey, Elisa," he calls.

"Okay." I shake my head before I quite know I'm going to do it. "I have to ask. How do you know my name?"

Hot Pete Gardello looks at me a little strangely. "I mean, we have tutoring together," he points out. "And you jumped my car?"

"No, I know," I clarify, feeling more than a little foolish. "But, like, you knew it before that, too."

Hot Pete Gardello shrugs. "I know everybody's name," he says, like he's the vice principal of Raritan River High School or one of those local politicians who are always standing outside Stop & Shop passing out pamphlets. I guess he basically is.

"Fair enough," I concede grudgingly. Then, squinting at the Juul: "Are you *vaping*?"

"What? No." He takes it out of his mouth, and I realize it's the butt end of a candy cane, red and white stripes bright in the afternoon sun.

"You realize it's May."

"I do, yes." He smiles sheepishly, like I've caught him at something way more illicit than off-season sugar consumption. "I buy like twenty boxes every year when they go on sale after Christmas and ration them out until Thanksgiving."

Something about him spending all year hoarding such an obviously bad and useless candy makes me like him more. "Really?"

He nods. "I ripped through my stash this year, though. I'm almost out."

"Can't you get them online?"

"Of course you can," he says, "but that ruins the experience. You have to buy them in person at a store or they don't taste right." He crunches the end of the candy cane between his molars. "Are you hungry?" he asks.

"For candy canes?"

He shakes his head. "For pizza."

That stops me. "Seriously?"

"I never joke about pizza," he deadpans, and I have to admit, he doesn't seem to be. "And you've got tutoring time to kill, right?"

"Um," I say, tipping my head for the sound of the catch, hearing nothing. "Sure."

I follow him to the pizza place around the corner from school where the normally grouchy guys behind the counter greet him like he's the mayor, sliding two slices of pepperoni into the brick oven before he even orders. "Can I ask you something?" I say as we slip into a booth by the window. "What are you even doing in tutoring?"

Hot Pete Gardello smirks at me across the melamine table. "You're really blunt, huh?"

I feel myself blush. "Just with you, apparently." It's true; something about the absurdity of him talking to me at all makes me brave, like when halfway through a dream it suddenly occurs to you that nothing is real and you can do whatever you want. "I'm serious, though. I mean, I know why *I'm* in tutoring."

"Why are you in tutoring?" He raises his eyebrows.

"Dyslexia," I explain, folding my floppy slice of pizza in half and taking a bite. "Like, a lot of dyslexia."

That makes him laugh. "Great quantities of dyslexia?"

"Tons."

"Heaps."

"Scads," I say, "which is a vocabulary word I know on account of all my many years of tutoring." I shrug. "I think it's why I like music so much, actually. Like, I can't always read things right, but I can always hear them." I glance out the window for a moment, embarrassed at having said so much. "Anyway. You're smart, is what I'm saying."

"You're smart," he counters. "If it wasn't for you, I'd still be sitting in the lot at school with a dead battery."

I shake my head. "Somebody would have come along to bail you out like five minutes later," I predict. "I just got there first."

"Maybe," he admits, taking a sip of his soda. "I bombed my SATs."

I think he's exaggerating—it's hard to imagine anything bad happening to Hot Pete Gardello—but when he tells me his score, my eyes widen. "Don't you get that many points just for writing your name?" I can't help but ask.

"That's a myth, actually," he informs me. "Anyway, Ms. Cherry offered to help me out."

"Ms. Cherry offered to tutor you for your SATs?"

"She really likes baseball," he says with a shrug.

"Of course she does." I shake my head. "What happened?"

"With the SATs?" Hot Pete Gardello shrugs again. "I choked, I don't know." He leans his head back, a tiny nick visible on his throat where he must have cut himself shaving, then sits upright again. "This is going to make me sound like a total boner, but sometimes it's like people have all these expectations for me, you know? And I guess I just kind of cracked under them a little bit."

"You're right," I tell him, plucking a piece of pepperoni off my pizza and popping it into my mouth. "That does make you sound like a total boner."

Hot Pete Gardello grins.

Gigi is sitting on the front stoop of my apartment building when I get home that afternoon, the sun catching the pink streaks woven through her long black braid. Gigi was the only member of Evelyn Nosebleed who could conceivably be a rock star in this dimension without completely changing both her look and her personality. "We need to talk," she announces.

"Oh, *now* you want to talk to me?" I'm aiming for snotty, but it comes out strangled. Sometimes I feel like I've spent my entire life trying to be cool or aloof, but in the end I'm always about as subtle as a golden retriever, my feelings perpetually obvious in the wagging of my tail.

"Look, I'm sorry," she says, standing up and wiping her palms on the seat of her jeans—she's nervous, I realize, and it satisfies me in some small mean way. "I can explain."

"Can you?"

Gigi's dark eyes narrow. "I mean, if you'll let me talk, maybe."

"Why should I?" I ask, bristling—forgetting for a moment that this is all I've wanted since that day outside the roller rink. "You've been perfectly happy to shit all over me all this time, but now, suddenly—"

"That is *not* what I've been doing!" she bursts out. "Like, come on, Elisa. Do you really think I liked not talking to you for a month?"

"How should I know?" I counter, loudly enough that a man walking his dog glances over at us curiously. "Seriously, what conclusion should I have drawn when you just unilaterally decided to—"

"You're my best friend, Elisa!" Gigi makes a face like I'm being difficult on purpose. "You know that. I just . . . handled this badly, okay?"

Something about the way she says it has me standing very still. "Handled what badly?" I ask.

Gigi blows a breath out, sitting down on the stoop again and flopping forward, resting her forehead on her knees for a moment before finally looking back up at me. "So that night at Franco's sister's party," she begins, her voice so quiet I have to strain to hear her. "Remember how Josh asked me to help him carry a bunch of shit in from his car right before we went on?"

"Sure," I say slowly, though in truth I was only half paying attention; I'd been scrutinizing the girl who worked behind the skate rental counter, trying to figure out if Josh had been flirting with her as we'd been setting up. She'd had a lip ring, I remember. I'd wondered for a moment if maybe I should get one, too.

"Well," Gigi says, sounding miserable, "I went out there with him, and all of a sudden he started randomly saying all this stuff to me."

I frown. "What kind of stuff?"

She hesitates. "I mean . . . nice stuff," she says finally, shrugging a little; she isn't quite meeting my eye. "And he kissed me."

I can feel all the air whoosh out of me at once. "He *kissed* you?" I repeat.

"I had no idea he was going to do it," she clarifies quickly, holding both hands out like she's trying to physically shore me up. "I mean, obviously I would never have—"

"No, of course not," I say, visions of Harvey Weinstein and Woody Allen and that guy from the *Today* show filling my head. "I know you wouldn't." Holy crap, is Josh a sex pervert? Does he just go around, like, forcing himself on unsuspecting people? Do we need to tell an adult? "So you quit the band and totally ditched me because Josh kissed you and you didn't want him to?"

"I—" Gigi looks surprised. "No, Elisa." She shakes her head. "I quit the band and totally ditched you because Josh kissed me and I *did* want him to."

The summer after third grade, my mom and I went on vacation to Los Angeles to visit her college friend Christine and an earthquake happened while we were in the hotel room. I still remember the rumble of it under my feet, the whole building shaking violently: my mom grabbing me with one arm, still wearing her towel, our suitcases falling down off the luggage racks and spilling their contents across the carpet. Only the generic hotel art stayed where it was above the headboards, and it wasn't until way later that I realized it was nailed to the wall for exactly this eventuality: to remain fixed in place while everything around it shifted.

"Oh," I finally say.

"Nothing else happened," Gigi promises immediately. "I would never do that to you. I haven't even talked to him since then. I haven't talked to anybody since then, except Franco."

I whirl on her. "*Franco* knows?"

Gigi frowns. "Does it matter?"

"Of course it matters!" It makes me want to rip my own skin off, actually, the idea of all three of them having this information all this time and me walking around like a total joke thinking some random girl named Nicole or the roller skate rental clerk was all that was keeping Josh and me from eventually living happily ever after. That it was only a matter of time until he finally realized—until he finally *saw*—

"I've gotta go," I hear myself say, shaking my head and brushing past her, fumbling with my key.

"Elisa, wait."

"I can't talk about this right now. I have to learn how to make the Beatles sound like a band you would listen to while you did cocaine on a boat."

"What?" Gigi asks, but her voice barely carries. I'm already on the other side of the door.

"Okay, hear me out," Josh says when he strolls into Franco's backyard ten minutes late for practice, instead of *hello* or *how are you guys* or anything to suggest he isn't the center of the entire universe. "I'm thinking maybe we ought to go in a different direction."

Franco looks up from his drum kit, frowning warily. "Wait," he says. "*Now?* Dude, it's three days until the Battle."

"I know, I know," Josh says, that manic gleam in his eye. "But I just think that without a sax player we're not really committing to the aesthetic anyway, so maybe we should just go ahead and—"

"No," I hear myself say.

Josh blinks, looking over suddenly like he hadn't even realized I was here. "No?"

"No."

"What do you mean, no?" he asks slowly. He sounds so surprised that I laugh out loud. I realize all at once that in twelve years of friendship this might actually be the first time I've ever turned him down for anything; the thought of it fills me with a jagged, clanging anger, the sound of it louder and louder until finally it's all I can hear. I'm sick of going along with whatever harebrained whim he has in the moment that he has it. I'm sick of acting like he's some creative genius the rest of us have to tiptoe around. Most of all I'm sick of standing behind my keyboard waiting for him to notice me, like a song he knows so well it doesn't even register anymore. I'm sick of all of it. "I mean *no*, Josh. Franco's right: the Battle is in three days. This isn't the time to just—"

"You haven't even heard what I'm going to say."

"I don't need to," I snap. "I don't care if it's grunge or big band or Russian opera—"

"It's not any of those things, actually."

"I don't care! I'm saying it's a ridiculous idea, Josh, and you're ridiculous for having it, and if you want to do it so bad, you might as well just beg Gigi to come back and play for you instead because I'm done."

All at once Josh's eyes narrow. Behind the drums, Franco gets very still. "Is this *about* Gigi?" Josh asks, and his voice is so quiet.

"What? No!" I sound shrill even to myself, loud and panicky, a CD skipping in my mom's ancient car. I have to get out of here. I have to hit pause. "But she got one thing right, that's for sure." I yank the cord out of the back of my keyboard. "I quit."

The next day seeps by in a miserable blur. I've alienated every single one of my friends, so I spend lunch in the library, scrolling through my phone for something to listen to that doesn't remind me of anyone or anything. I'm useless in tutoring, the letters rearranging themselves in front of my eyes. "Sorry," I say finally, dropping my pen onto the desk with a clatter. "I'm stupid, I guess."

Once Ms. Cherry lets us go for the day, I all but run out of her classroom, but Hot Pete Gardello catches up with me in the parking lot. "Hey," he calls, footsteps quick on the concrete behind me. "You okay?"

"I'm fine," I assure him, cheeks burning as I dig my car keys out of my backpack. The last thing I want is to have a meltdown in front of Hot Pete Gardello, of all people. "Long day, that's all."

"Are you sure?" he asks. "I mean, you seem like you're . . . maybe not fine."

What Hot Pete Gardello knows or doesn't know about how I seem—or why he cares—is beyond me. "Okay, enough," I blurt. "Like, quite seriously, what do you think you're doing?"

He frowns. "What do you mean?"

"Why are you being so nice to me?" I demand. "Buying me pizza. Asking how I am. If it's because I fixed your busted car that day, we're, like, more than even at this point."

Hot Pete Gardello looks at me for a minute, an expression on his face I don't quite recognize. "It's not because you fixed my car," he finally says.

"Then why?"

His mouth does something that isn't a smile—a twitch, uncertain, there and gone again. "I thought it was pretty obvious."

I blink at him. "What?"

"Elisa," he murmurs, and it sounds like a sigh. "Come on."

Is he saying—?

I mean, it definitely *sounds* like—

Doesn't it?

I shake my head, trying to clear the sudden buzzing. It's like everything I thought I understood about the world has turned inside out on itself in the last twenty-four hours: Gigi. Josh. Hot Pete Gardello.

Nothing is actually what it looks like to me. It's like I have dyslexia about the entire world.

"I should go," I hear myself say.

Hot Pete Gardello shakes his head. "Elisa," he starts. "Can we just—"

"Um, not right now," I interrupt. There's a part of me that knows I can't keep on doing this, careening around with my hands clamped over my ears; still, I push past him and reach for the car door. "I'm sorry." I gun the engine and peel out of the parking lot, turning up the radio until it's all I can hear.

My mom picks up Thai food on her way home that night, the two of us standing in the kitchen over plastic tubs of noodles and green curry with rice. "Want to know something funny?" she asks, pouring me some iced tea from the plastic jug in the fridge and handing it over just before my eyes start to water. "Your teacher was one of my patients today."

"She was?" I ask once I've gulped half the glass. The truth is I haven't thought about Ms. Saeed since she went out on maternity leave, and it makes me feel a little bad now, although I can't imagine she's thought about me, either. "Was she okay?"

"I was her nurse, wasn't I?" My mom smiles. "She had a little girl."

I raise my eyebrows. "Isn't it a HIPAA violation for you to be telling me that?"

"Cute. She told me to say hello to you, actually. And to make sure you were going to tutoring."

"What? No, she didn't." I frown. "Really?"

My mom nods. "She said you've worked way too hard to give up now."

She says it so casually, catching an errant bean sprout between her chopsticks; I don't know why that, of everything that's happened recently, is what makes me burst into tears. "The noodles are spicy," I insist, even as my mom drops her dinner and wraps her arms around me, surrounding me with the freesia smell of her deodorant and the antibacterial soap they use at the hospital.

"I know," she murmurs softly, and hums a quiet tune into my hair.

I spend a long time in my room that night, plucking out idle chords on the keyboard and humming to myself under my breath. I think of Gigi trying to protect me from the way she was feeling. I think of Ms. Saeed and her baby asleep in the hospital across town. I think of Hot Pete Gardello at the pizza place, the way he handed me a napkin from the dispenser before taking one for himself, and finally I pick up my phone.

"I think I have a plan for the Battle," I tell Josh when he answers, because I know he'll hear the *I'm sorry* behind it. He picked up on the very first ring. "Meet you at Franco's after school tomorrow?"

"Always," he says, no hesitation in his voice at all. "I'll be there."

I nod even though he can't see me. "I might be a tiny bit later than usual," I warn him. "I just have to make one stop first."

We play second to last at the Battle, all of us lurking around the gym sizing up the other acts until it's finally our turn to go on. "You ready?" Josh asks me, reaching for my hand and squeezing as the lights go down.

I squeeze back, a dozen years of friendship tucked between our sweaty palms. "You bet."

We start out with a straightforward, slightly snoozy cover, making it all the way through the first verse before cutting off abruptly, Franco knocking his drumsticks together as we start again, way faster this time. I grin as the crowd starts to shift in their seats, nodding along as they realize what we're doing: switching up the arrangement at every break, careening from punk to jazz to bluegrass to, yes, yacht rock. "I love it," Josh said when I suggested playing the song in a bunch of different styles. "It's a gamble, but a smart one. It's weird, but it works."

It's mixed up, in a good way.

I spy Gigi in the crowd, the swirling lights bouncing off the pink in her hair; I catch her eye and smile in a way I hope will cut through all the noise. She raises both hands in response, reaching out across the auditorium in my direction. The drums thump, steady, deep in the base of my spine.

Once we're done, I hang out with Franco at the back of the auditorium for a while, watching the last band play. I spy Josh talking to Gigi, then take a deep breath and turn away. Out in the lobby I find Hot Pete Gardello with a cluster of his equally hot friends, their laughter loud and rowdy; I'm expecting him to ignore me, but instead he peels away. "Hey," he says to me, hands tucked deep into his pockets. "Nice job up there."

"Thanks," I tell him. Then, reaching into my backpack: "Did you know there's a Christmas-themed store up in Plainfield?" I ask.

Pete tilts his head to the side for a moment, reaching out and taking the candy cane from my outstretched hand. "I did not," he says.

He smiles then, slow and steady. It looks like my favorite song.

A SMALL LIGHT

JENNY TORRES SANCHEZ

Last summer, DeeDee and I went to the Commoners concert. It was outside, and it was hot as hell. Like a fucking sauna. Everybody was sweating and looking anxious and miserable. We stared at the stage—plain and industrial—knowing that soon, *soon*, it would be transformed into a little slice of heaven.

"This is gonna be cool as fuck!" DeeDee told me. Her eyes glimmered with excitement—and with her typical over-the-top eye makeup. DeeDee always looked like some kind of glam rock star from the '80s. Makeup like David Bowie, take-no-shit attitude like Joan Jett. She took a long drink from a beer and passed it to me.

I took a sip and handed it back to her. Dee liked to drink, but me, not so much.

"You happy, little brother?" she asked.

She'd sprung for the tickets by working a ton of overtime at Atomic Records. It was my birthday gift. She'd driven us there, and even though

I'd had to drive us home because Dee was drunk, it was the best night of my life.

Robert Patrick Riley played for four hours straight. No bullshit talking between songs. No tales of this or that. No fucking breaks. That guy played from one song right into the next seamlessly. The sound of his voice, that hypnotic guitar reverberating even in so much open space, moved through each one of us like something holy.

I always get lost in the music. But that night, it felt like I *was* the music. Like I was being born into the universe, note by note, floating freely everywhere.

Robert Patrick Riley stood center stage like some kind of mythical creature in the mist of so many smoke machines. I hardly noticed anything else. Except every once in a while, DeeDee and I would look over at each other at the exact same time and we'd laugh like neither of us could believe how fucking amazing this was.

Then came the last song, sad and beautiful, like a poem. The stage flared with a bunch of little fires that slowly, perfectly, fizzled into darkness and left the crowd breathless.

It was magical.

I remember thinking how lucky I was to have a sister like Dee who did shit like this. Who knew it was hard for me to interact with people, who beat up Sam Tillner when I was in sixth grade and she was in eighth for calling me a "poor brown weirdo freak!" Who basically made me not worry about making friends because she'd be my best friend, she'd do the talking, she'd make friends enough for both of us.

She'd be my bridge to the rest of the world.

That's my sister. Or at least that was my sister.

I never thought of that bridge collapsing.

Or how stranded I'd feel when it did.

*   *   *

The bell rings, and I'm headed out of English class when Ms. Cherry gestures for me to come over to her. She waits as I pull off my hoodie, take off my headphones.

"Where's your essay, Vinnie?" she asks as they slip down around my neck.

I shrug. "Forgot."

Ms. Cherry takes a deep breath. "Vinnie, you haven't turned in the last three assignments. Is everything okay?"

"Yeah . . . I'm just . . . slacking off, I guess," I say, forcing a small laugh. But both my excuse and my laugh sound fake and stupid to me.

Ms. Cherry stares at me, analyzing me the way she analyzes the books and poems and short stories we read in class. "Okay," she says finally. "But I want to see you get back on track." The bell rings and I look toward the door, but Ms. Cherry isn't done yet and another class doesn't trickle into her room.

"Listen, I don't like to see my students fail. I want to see you all succeed. So I'm going to give you another chance to write this essay, but it better be *good*."

"Thanks, Ms. Cherry," I tell her, relieved. I grab my headphones to put them back on, but Ms. Cherry stops me.

"Hold on. There's one more thing." She eyes my headphones. "You seem more far away lately. And I'd like to see you get out of yourself a little, Vinnie. Out of that little world you encapsulate yourself in."

I clear my throat and hold on to my headphones, sensing she might take them away right there and then. "I need my music, Ms. Cherry," I say.

"Oh, I know. Music is beautiful. It's really poetry." She smiles like she gets it. "I'm not telling you to forget about music. I'm just telling you to use it to find your people."

I suddenly feel a little pathetic and wish I could sink into my hoodie and disappear. Part of me wants to tell Ms. Cherry I *had* my people. DeeDee and her friends and all those people at the underground concerts DeeDee would take me to with free tickets courtesy of the record store *were* my people. Those bands were my people.

But I don't say anything.

Ms. Cherry points to a poster on the wall of her classroom.

I laugh, relieved that what she's suggesting is funny enough it prevents me from getting all emotional right there in front of Ms. Cherry.

"Battle of the Bands? Are you serious? Come on, Miss. I'm not in a band. I don't even play an instrument."

"I'm not saying you have to perform. I'm sure they already have their acts lined up. But I know for a fact they could use some help behind the scenes. I'll even throw in some extra credit."

I shake my head. "I don't know."

"Why?" she asks gently. "Do you have other activities? Younger siblings to take care of after school? Responsibilities when you get home?"

Ouch. Ms. Cherry really just called me out like that. I picture myself on my bed, listening to music. "Not exactly," I say, knowing that even if I tried to lie, Ms. Cherry would see right through it.

I stare at the poster. Battle of the Bands. Anxiousness tightens my chest.

"I mean, who do I even talk to . . . ?"

Ms. Cherry smiles. "Don't you worry about that! I've got all the information you need. A student of mine is mostly running this thing and she's pretty stressed out." Ms. Cherry chuckles. "She could use some help. So, is it a yes?"

"I guess."

She nods approvingly and scribbles something on a pass. "Perfect. So after school today, go to the theater and find a girl named Lilly. She's in my last class of the day, so I'll tell her to expect you." She hands me the pass. "This will be good for you, Vinnie. You'll see."

"Sure . . ." I say and slip my headphones back on, back into the heavy drums and guitar of the Commoners, the haunting voice and lyrics of Robert Patrick Riley. I walk the empty halls, both comforted and saddened by the solitude.

Later that day, my feet and stomach feel full of lead as I walk to the school theater. I turn up the volume on my phone and music blasts louder into my headphones, calming my anxiety for a minute. I stop and brace myself outside the doors of the theater before finally stepping inside.

Inside are a bunch of people I don't know scurrying around like ants. I watch as some guy yells at some other guy, as more people come in and out, as instruments in big black cases and amps are dragged in. I let the music in my ears calm the uneasiness I always feel around people.

The thing is, they *do* sort of seem like my people. Like the musicians at the clubs Dee was always taking me to see. I mean, it feels familiar. Sort of. Even if I don't really know anyone.

Maybe Ms. Cherry was right. Maybe I *could* do this somehow. Especially since DeeDee is doing her own thing now.

A girl with a clipboard rushes past me, looking stressed.

Something tells me that's Lilly.

I follow her and reluctantly pull off my headphones as I approach. The haunting music of the Commoners slips away and the real world crashes in.

"Don't touch the curtains!" the girl hollers at the top of her lungs. Two guys onstage laugh as they hang on to and swing from the black velvet curtains onstage.

"Lilly?" I ask. She whips around, irritation on her face that she covers up with a quick smile.

"How may I help you?" I can't tell if she's being genuine or sarcastic.

"I'm . . . uh . . . Vincent. Ms. Cherry said . . ."

"Ohhhhh!" she yells. "Yes! Okay, great, yes, yes, yes! She told me you were coming!" Now her smile is kinder and she's taking me by the shoulder. "As you can see, it's complete chaos at the moment and nobody is really doing what they should be doing. Just what they should *not* be doing." She glances toward the stage again as someone's equipment gets tangled up in the curtains and they pull and tug at it, trying to free their amp. Lilly looks like she's going to burst. Instead she closes her eyes and lets out a long breath before turning back to me and continuing.

"So, listen, I could use help with just trying to keep things in order."

"Okay, but I don't really know . . ."

"Don't worry about not knowing what order means. Just . . . ugh, help me keep them from hurting themselves. Or each other. Or me hurting them." She lets out a laugh.

"Right," I tell her. "Okay, I mean, I'll try."

She smiles. "Good! Yes, great!" She looks back at the stage. "SERIOUSLY! What is so hard about not touching the curtains!" She rushes to the stage to give hell to whoever is back there.

I stand there wondering what to do. If I bail, will that Lilly girl even notice? The F in Ms. Cherry's class flashes in my mind, reminding me I need the extra credit.

I creep up to the nearest group and ask them if they need any help. They look at me like I confuse them. I think how much easier things would be if Dee still went here. If she hadn't already graduated.

"Don't touch," some guy in super tight pants says as I reach to help with his guitar. He looks like he can barely move.

I move away and feel like some kind of weird lurker as I skulk up to other bands and ask them if they need any help. *Nope. No, thanks. Nope. Don't touch the instruments.* Suddenly some guy with a snake tattoo who is looking around like he owns the place gestures for me to come over to him.

"Hey, need any help?" I ask, relieved that someone finally notices I exist.

"Yeah, sure. Go get me a cheeseburger. I'm starving." He shoves five dollars in my hand and waves me away like a fly. I don't know what to say, so I just shove the money back at him, slip my headphones back on, and walk away before he can say anything else.

I wonder for the millionth time why it's so hard for me to interact normally with people. What is it about me that makes it so hard for people to treat me like everyone else? Or makes people say shit like that to me? Or makes it hard for me to know how to respond?

I want to get out of here, but I'm afraid Lilly will rat me out to Ms. Cherry. So I sit in one of the auditorium chairs and watch clips of an old movie I used to watch with DeeDee called *Dumb and Dumber* on my phone.

I haven't watched the whole movie in forever. When DeeDee still lived at home, we used to watch it all the time, cracking up and eating Hot Pockets while Mom worked.

Dee doesn't get mad at me a lot, but when she does, I can't stand it. I haven't texted since I stopped by her place a couple of days ago—a motel room that advertises hourly and weekly rates. She wasn't happy to see me. I can still see her face, irritated, tired, as she said, "Just go home, Vin."

Her shithead boyfriend, Duke, came outside and peered at us over the motel railing, like he was staring me down. Like he knew that I had this bad feeling about Dee being there, a bad feeling about him.

Duke had isolated her from everyone little by little. I felt like something bad was going to happen to her, now that he had her alone.

A fresh feeling of dread washes over me, and I text Dee.

Sorry for dropping by the other day like that. Come over? I'll make your fav hot pockets and we can watch Dumb and Dumber.

I look for the GIF we'd always send each other—the one of the two main characters in blue and orange tuxedos dancing—and hit send.

I stare at my phone, hoping but knowing a reply won't come.

I look around the theater and notice fewer people around. No sign of that girl Lilly, either. So I slink out.

I drown out my thoughts with music as I pedal to the motel. She'll be mad. But I have to check on her. I feel nauseated as I lean my bike against the motel wall and hurry up the stairs before I can change my mind. Maybe she'll be here alone.

I knock on the door.

"What the fuck?" Duke swings the door open and stands there shirtless, barefoot, in jeans.

From the doorway, I notice Dee on the bed, staring at the television. She looks over at me, her eyes half closed, trying to focus on me.

"Dee . . ." I call to her.

"Dude, what are you doing here?" Duke says, blocking the doorway.

"I just want to talk to her," I say, trying to get past him to her, but he doesn't move an inch.

"We told you to stay away."

"It's okay . . . leave him alone." DeeDee's words are slurred, and she struggles to stand up. Duke pushes me outside.

"Let me just talk to her a minute," I say to him.

"Damn, man. Don't you understand?" he says. "She needs some space."

"Hey," Dee calls from inside. I look up, and she's made her way to the doorway, but Duke is pushing me up against the balcony banister. It digs into my back as he pushes me harder and harder against it, and for a minute, I think he's about to toss me over it.

"Leave him alone," Dee says, stumbling out and reaching for Duke's arm. He shoves her off and she falls to the ground.

I shove him back with all my weight. But before I can get to her, I feel myself being pulled back. "Did you just push me, you little shit?"

"Come on, stop," my sister mumbles, trying to get up. But a hard thwack lands on the side of my head and I stumble to the ground, my ear ringing like I've just been hit with a baseball bat or something. I feel the spot, then look at my hand, expecting blood, but there's none.

"No!" Dee yells. She starts crying and Duke goes to her.

"It's okay. I'll take care of this. Come on, get inside," he whispers to her. I try to get up, but I feel dizzy. Duke helps her up and walks her slowly back inside. "You're just drunk, baby," I hear him tell her. "Don't worry, okay, I'll be nice to your baby brother."

A moment later, Duke comes back, stares down at me on the ground like I'm pathetic, like he feels sorry for me.

"Listen, man. I didn't want to do that, but you're making this hard. She needs to get away from you and your mom for a while. She told me how your mom is always working. How she's had to do everything since your dad left, including taking care of you. Dude, you leeched on to her. Let go for a while."

His voice is soft, but his words hit me as hard as the punch. Leech? Had I been a leech to Dee? My eyes sting with tears as he puts his hand on my shoulder.

"Oh my God, dude. Don't fucking cry. Come on, get up. *Man* up." He holds out a hand and pulls me up roughly. "Be cool, Vin. And stop worrying. I'm gonna take care of her. But you coming around here, that's no good for her. So if you do . . ." He shrugs like he won't be able to keep from punching me out again if I do.

I stand there trying to let it all register. Trying to understand. But none of it makes sense.

"Go home," he whispers, and heads back to the room, closes the door.

I stand there for I don't know how long, until the only thing I can think to do is go home.

I get on my bike and slowly pedal away. Then faster and faster. Headlights flash, making my head throb, as I turn down street after street. The wind dries the stupid stinging I feel in my eyes. I turn up the music.

Robert Patrick Riley's voice fills my ears again as I ride through the night, singing about sadness and loneliness, making it sound like something beautiful and noble. Maybe it is.

But mostly I've learned that loneliness is really fucking lonely.

I think of what a shitty brother I've been. A leech. Worrying only about my feelings, about me. Me, me, me. All this time Dee has been lonely in her own way. Lonely enough to run to someone like Duke.

And think someone like him is better than having no one at all.

All week, I try not to worry about her. But I do. Every minute. At night, no matter how much I try to drown out my thoughts with music, I can't. And the only thing that makes me tired enough to not think is riding all the way out there and lurking in the darkness and keeping watch for a little while. I sit in the parking lot, waiting, listening. Sometimes I want to run up those stairs and bang on the door and demand Dee come back home to our cramped apartment. To our exhausted mom and to me, her needful little brother.

But I don't.

All week I go in and out of my classes, wondering how you save people who push you away.

All week I go to Battle of the Band rehearsals and watch other people who aren't me laughing, living their lives. I watch lead singers announce their bands, all cool and effortlessly— *We are the Marcia, Marcia, Marcias. We are Breakfast of Champions. We are Reckless Love. We are Safe & Sound*—before ripping into their songs. I overhear conversations between the girls checking mics and cords, going on about some guy named Brenner they want to bone, and somehow, they all seem connected. They're all pieces of a giant puzzle that fit together. Except the piece that is me.

All week I text Dee pictures of the bands. Of the poster. But she doesn't reply.

All week I walk around the school halls surrounded by so many people but with only Robert Patrick Riley's voice in my head.

And now, tonight, people pour into the theater lobby, waiting for the doors to open for the Battle of the Bands.

Most of them have their tickets, but some get in line. I have my headphones on, even though there's no music so I can hear how many tickets people need. The noise canceling is on, but it doesn't really cancel noise. I can still hear the faint voices of people.

Suddenly the doors open and people begin trickling into the theater.

Little by little, the crowd noise goes with them.

Little by little, the lobby empties.

And I'm alone.

I have to stay here at least fifteen minutes into the show for any latecomers, so I sit there, in that glass booth, watching old videos of the Commoners. I think of the concert and wonder when they'll be on tour again. I think of how I'll get a job, buy tickets. Next time, I'll be the one who saves up, who does the saving.

I look through the pics of us last summer. Selfies with us all lit up in red and blue from stage lights. Laughing.

I send her that picture. And then the next one. And then the one after that. And then all of them, one after another after another. I text her more *Dumb and Dumber* GIFs. I text her pics of Atomic Records, where I stopped by looking for her a few days ago and Mr. Khatri told me she quit. I text her the funny, disastrous interview with Robert Patrick Riley where the interviewer obviously wasn't familiar with the music of the Commoners. A photo of me in this ticket booth, sitting out here as the show plays on inside.

I want to remind her she's not alone in the world. That even though we might feel lonely, it doesn't mean we are actually alone.

I'll check on her again tonight, I think to myself. *I'll knock on that door and take another punch, or however many Duke wants to issue out, whatever it takes.* I look around, needing to leave now but realizing I have no idea what to do with the money from ticket sales.

And that's when I see her coming into the lobby.

Dee looks at me sadly but smiles. "Hey, calm down," she says. "You look like you just saw fucking Santa."

I rush out of the booth and go to her, hug her. "You're here . . ."

She almost seems like herself. She almost looks like herself with her usual over-the-top makeup. But her left eye looks darker, the makeup the wrong shade of purple. I stare at it and she looks away, shifts her weight.

"Yeah, I mean, you know. I got your pics. *All* of them." She glances back at me. Her eyes are filling with tears. I try not to fall apart right then and there. "So, any of these guys the next Robert Patrick Riley?" She laughs. "Yeah, right. The guy's a fucking poet, you know . . ."

"What happened, Dee?"

"Their third album went platinum, but it's their second album that really takes risks. That has more artistic merit."

"Dee . . ."

"I was thinking, I'm gonna do it, Vin. I'm really gonna do it—you know, write like you told me I should, for *Rolling Stone* or some shit like that. I can do it."

"I know you can," I say softly. But now the tears are spilling over.

I don't make her say it. I don't make her tell me. And even though anger rages through me, makes me want to run out of that building and find him, beat the shit out of him even if it means he might kill me, my love for my sister is stronger than my hate for him.

"I'm so stupid," she whispers, crying harder. "So fucking stupid. I can't believe I didn't see it, Vin. Except, I did, you know, I just . . . pretended I didn't because . . . I wanted someone to love me—God, that sounds so pathetic . . ."

It breaks me, seeing my sister, my hero, come apart like this.

"You're not stupid," I tell her.

Her voice breaks. "Even when he . . . punched you, I told myself you just tripped. I told myself I was drunk and just imagined it. I pretended it was *you*, that he didn't mean it. But . . . you must think I'm the worst . . . you must . . . I'm sorry."

"No, it's okay. You're okay. He's one of these people, Dee. Gets in your head, makes you believe things that aren't true," I tell her, remembering how he talked to me after hitting me that night, like he was a friend issuing out some warped tough love or something.

"Don't tell Mom, okay?" she whispers. "It's over. I'm just . . . I feel like I should've known better."

The lobby door opens, and Dee wipes her face quickly as some guy runs in. "I'm late!" he yells. But then just stands there and stares at us with bulging eyes, his face frantic and sweaty.

"Are you . . . okay?" Dee asks.

"I'm late for an important date!" he yells, and suddenly starts laughing like he's just said the funniest thing. But then his laughter immediately turns to crying as he runs to the theater door, swings it open, and stumbles in. Music spills out into the lobby, loud and intense.

The heaviness of a few moments ago is broken, and Dee shakes her head, smiles softly. "I guess we're all a little fucked up."

"Guess so . . ." I say.

"What do you say, should we check out this shit?" She gestures to the theater, and I nod.

There are only a couple of bands left to play, but we head into the auditorium and sit down anyway. The latest band, Once Bright, is being called to the stage when I suddenly remember I left all the money unattended, the cash box wide open in the unlocked ticket booth.

"Holy shit, I forgot something I have to do," I whisper to DeeDee. "I'll be right back."

I rush to the ticket booth and breathe a sigh of relief when I see the cash box is still there, then another as I count the money and it all seems to be there, too.

Lilly rushes to the booth suddenly and I think she's going to ask me where the hell I was, but she just stands there looking at me funny.

"Uh . . . do you want a ticket?" I ask even though I know she doesn't need one.

"What? No. This is *my*—never mind. Listen—" She starts talking fast, the way she does. Talking about how no one sees her. How she's invisible and voiceless. How there are all these people around her that should be listening to her but don't.

I stare at her, not sure exactly why she's telling me all this. And then, suddenly, I realize it's because she thinks I'll understand. Because loner me who wears headphones all the time to avoid interacting with or talking to people, who people ask to get a *cheeseburger* for them, of course would understand.

The thing is, she's right. I do.

"I want to do something," she says. "Something beautiful and wild."

I stare at Lilly, who in this moment seems lonely. Like me. Like Dee.

I feel something like destiny in my heart. Something like hope. Like even though life can be full of so much darkness, in that darkness there's *music* and *light*.

Without even knowing what it is I'm agreeing to, I nod. "Let's do it," I tell Lilly.

Because sometimes, even a small light matters.

SET THE WORLD ON FIRE

LAUREN GIBALDI

You. Don't. Touch. The. Curtains. I silently seethe, watching yet another floppy-haired boy walk past me, clutching his guitar as if it's both a delicate baby and something he wants to smash. Musicians are like that, it seems—full of contradictions.

It's not like I'm against floppy-haired boys, or musicians in general—let's be honest, there are some really cute ones in the orchestra (like the ukulele player who, okay, we were all in love with during *The Addams Family*)—just those who come into the theater acting like they *own* the place, when, in fact, they're barely renting it for their five minutes of Battle of the Bands fame.

And it's not like I'm *that* particular or anything, just practical. Because every year it's the same: a group of bands descends on the stage, full of demands and ignorance. Every year they come with their guitars and amps and drums and zero regard for the sets and props and *history* around the backstage area. How many backdrops have to be mended? How many couches, reserved for shows, are jumped on and crushed? How many props are casually thrown around by people who will probably never set foot back in the theater for an *actual show*? It's as if *their* music matters and nothing else.

I'm not *bitter*, just annoyed. Okay, okay, maybe both. Because despite everything, I come back every year to handle this. Because who else will? No one else wants to deal with it. And I'd really rather my second home not succumb to the treachery of floppy-haired boys— especially since none of them ever look at me. Not one.

But this year will be different because Steven is here.

I look around again, hoping to catch a glance, but I haven't seen him since sound check, when he showed me his guitar and I showed him my clipboard.

So here I am again, watching yet another band leave the stage and touch the black velvet curtains. I sigh into my headset.

"How's it going down there, Lil?" Hailey asks from the light booth.

"Oh, you know," I say. At least I have her and Sarah and Katrina, the other tech girls. At least they understand. The show usually runs fairly smoothly, but tonight has been intense. This drummer Beckett is in half the bands, which means *those* bands have to be spaced out so she has a second to breathe. The Greatest Place disappeared; then Mina asked to take their place *last minute*. Dane, one of the judges, disappeared and then reappeared. There was a fight, and I'm pretty sure the couple in Reckless Love—the band currently performing—broke up. In theater, we know to leave the drama for later, not for when we're supposed to be 100 percent concentrating on what's happening onstage. But apparently that's not a thing with musicians—they dump out their emotions everywhere. "Why are they all like this?" I grumble.

"Hey, can you not—" I ask the guy running his hands over the curtains, but he doesn't even turn his head. I sigh and look back at my clipboard.

"Big Talk, you're on," I say to the band waiting (thankfully) on my left. They don't even look at me, just back and forth at one another, and *come on*. Are they . . . nervous? I know who they are; they've performed before. They're good. And their lead singer is . . . Wait, where's their lead singer? No. No, no, no, this isn't happening.

They talk among themselves, and I can feel the heat rising in my face. You have one job—literally, you just need to perform. Why can't bands get this right? Why is it so freaking hard?

"You're. On," I say again, louder, hoping they see how serious this is. Because the next band isn't lined up yet, and I don't want to have to stall *again* because someone decided to be dramatic and not show up. COME ON.

"Okay," they say and walk onstage—with Jess, the lead singer's girlfriend, but no lead singer—and oh my God, why is this happening? Just as I feel my face near exploding, they start playing with Jess at the mic, and I let my shoulders relax a bit. They're . . . not great, but they're playing, and at least I don't have to rearrange the lineup. They're making it happen, which I respect.

Maybe that's the big secret of success—going out there and just making it happen.

I look around to see if Steven is here—if he's witnessing this, too—but there's still no sign of him. He's up soon. Thankfully, the next act, Megan Talley, is waiting in the wings. I allow myself a second to breathe.

There's a screech of the microphone, and I whip my head around, only to see the (former?) lead singer of Big Talk onstage trying to sing. He and Jess grabble for the microphone, and then, in the blink of an eye, he's nearly on top of the judges' table. Did he . . . fall off the stage?

I look back up in time to catch the final chord hit and see Jess and the bassist making out.

WHAT IS GOING ON TONIGHT?

"Lil, are you seeing this?" Hailey asks into the headset.

"WHAT IS HAPPENING?" I answer. "Did they just kick out their lead singer and then start making out?"

"So badass."

I silence my headset and seethe. Please, no more surprises tonight. Please.

"I have to follow that?"

I turn around, and Megan is applauding with the rest of the crowd.

I clear my throat and say, "You'll be great." Because she will be. She's always great. She's Megan Talley of get-every-lead-role fame.

"I hope," she says, then adds with a smile, "Hey, you're doing awesome. Thanks for taking care of our home."

She's also Megan Talley of incredibly-nice fame.

Big Talk walks offstage, and Jess and the bassist are holding hands, looking like they could fly away with happiness. God, I want that.

"Thanks," I say. "And you're on. Break a leg."

Megan gives me a smile and walks onstage with this presence that asks for lights to shine on her. And I know she's going to win. If not first, a runner-up. Because as jealous as I can be of her, she's just that good.

She's also a theater girl, so I can take a second to calm down. I know she won't make this a nightmare for me.

An arm goes around my shoulders, and I stiffen, then jump when I realize it's Steven.

"How's it going?" he asks.

I almost cry when I see him; all the pent-up stress and anticipation and frustration with *everything*, it all feels like it wants to spill out. The very first time we talked, I was upset I didn't get a role in *The Sound of Music*. It's like he knew, because he just came up to me and started talking about our teacher's shoes, of all things. Mr. Zagajewski's bright green shoes. And I don't know, after that, I felt like he knew how to make things better without even realizing he was helping.

"I'm alive," I say, settling into my smile.

He pulls his arm away and says, "So, when you said you worked on the show, I didn't realize you were practically in charge. You gotta brag about it."

"I don't do much . . ." I start, then say, "Okay, yeah, I'm basically in charge."

He smiles, and I remember when he told me he'd signed up for the Battle. I knew I was stage-managing it from that moment. I really wanted to hear him play, and he never mentioned any gigs. He was always so closed off about it, but . . . I just knew he'd be good. His long fingers, his soft voice . . .

The Megans of the world always get the guys they want, but that hasn't really happened to me. The guys I like always, well, fall for the Megans. But maybe . . . maybe tonight could be different. Maybe him being here, seeing me like this—basically running things while rocking my best backstage black shirt—maybe it's finally my turn.

"I . . ." I start, but his eyes flick away toward the stage. His face drops, frozen; he looks like he's seen someone come back from the dead, like he can't believe what's unfolding. I turn around, and it's still Megan onstage, playing some radio hit. I turn back to him, but he's no longer looking at me; his eyes are glued to the stage.

And just like that, I'm ignored again.

His face gets ashy, pale, and I ask, "Are you okay?" But nothing. At all. His bandmate, Ken, comes up, and they talk in hushed tones, so I take a few steps back. They're mumbling and arguing and something is going on, something I want to fix because that's my job as stage manager, and maybe I want to help him a little bit more. But I don't think I can do anything here. Just wait.

When Megan's done, I will myself to walk up to them.

"You're up now," I say, but they're not paying attention to me at all. It's like I'm not even here. After a beat, they both walk to the stage, determined. And my heart drops because, well, that was that.

Onstage he holds his guitar and . . . nothing. At all. Whatever's going on in his head isn't leaving because he's just standing there and the crowd starts to boo. My heart starts racing because *what do I do?* Is this another situation where I need to stall? Bring in backup again? I want to hug him, I want to be there for him, but I can't just run onto the stage.

Just as I'm about to call Hailey, Megan, from front row center, gets the audience to start chanting. Megan makes him smile.

And so he plays. He plays so soulfully. Like the music is part of him and he's slowly revealing it to us. It's so perfectly him, quiet and earnest. His eyes are closed. He's uncomfortable, scrunching his face and a bit jittery, but it only adds to how cute he looks up there. And with each note, his face relaxes, his shoulders fall, like this—like playing—is helping him get past something. I wish I knew what it was. But instead I signal the next band, Evelyn Nosebleed. I breathe deep. I wait.

As he plays, I think of Big Talk and how Jess sang with them and was *so freaking brave.* When was the last time I did something like that? When was the last time I was *bold*?

Never.

I play by the rules. I go onstage at the right time. I make sure everyone else does as well. I don't complain when I don't get the role I want.

I don't touch the curtains.

So as Steven finishes, I feel myself being pushed toward him, wanting to touch him and tell him how well he played. Wanting to tell him how much he means to me, how much our talks mean to me. He waves to the audience. He's going to come to me. I'm going to tell him I like him. I will do it. I will be bold.

But he turns. He exits the other side of the stage, and I can feel him leaving me. Because as I hold my breath, I see him there, talking to Megan.

Screw this.

I put my headset down on my stool. I walk past the guys from Raging Mice, who are definitely tossing around a lamp from *Spring Awakening*, and seriously, why would they think that's okay? But I let it go. I keep walking until I'm off the backstage, down the hall, and out into the main lobby. I'm shaking, maybe from frustration or jealousy, or maybe from *this*. From leaving. This whole year, my whole past school life, is illuminated in front of me, sharply in focus. I obey the rules, never stepping a toe out of line. I follow through; I'm the leader. I hear the comments said behind my back, I see the eye rolls, I know the teacher's-pet nicknames. But I never let it affect me. I'm dependable and ready . . . but for what? For this? For sitting around? For no reward, for life to just keep on going?

I want to jump on the stage, too.

The lobby is empty, save for Vincent in the ticket booth. He's still there, for some reason; it's not like anyone is still getting tickets. He seems about as dedicated to his job as I am, which is weird because he's never helped out before. He's usually walking around alone, with his headphones on. Why is he even here?

"HEY," I practically yell into the ticket booth, jumping at the sound of my own voice in the desolate room.

"Uh . . . do you want a ticket?" he asks, looking at me curiously. "Show's almost over. You can just go in."

"What? No. This is *my*—never mind. Listen. I've been working backstage all night, and no one sees me. It's like I'm invisible. No one listens to me, and I'm supposed to be in charge. And I'm . . . like . . . tired of it. So I want to do something. I want to do something beautiful and wild."

I feel like we're at a precipice and everything relies on what he says. The night will split into two multiverses right now: one in which I do something wild, and one in which I don't. The question is, which multiverse will *this* me be in?

"Let's do it."

"Okay," I breathe out, readying myself for . . . what? "Okay, let's close up shop and go." I reach inside the booth and flip the OPEN sign to CLOSED, and he eyes me dubiously. "What? I run this place."

He shrugs and walks out. He's hunched over in a hoodie, so I can't really tell how much taller than me he is. An inch? A foot? He won't look me in the eye but keeps looking back into the theater, as if someone is waiting for him.

"What's your plan, anyway?" he asks, stuffing his hands into his pockets.

"I . . ." I start and then stop because . . . what *is* my plan? I haven't thought past this moment and start feeling nervous from the pressure of dragging him into this. Evelyn Nosebleed's music explodes in the theater.

Explode.

"Fireworks," I say.

His head jerks up. "What did you say?"

"Fireworks. Last year this guy in drama lit fireworks onstage. Not big ones—like, small sparklers or whatever—but he lit them onstage for the end of a scene and it was A Thing because our director didn't know about it, and, you know, he could have set the stage on fire."

"So you wanna do that?" he slowly asks.

"I was the one who said it was irresponsible, that someone could have gotten hurt. Even though . . ."

"Even though you thought it was hella cool."

"Yeah. Exactly," I say quietly, remembering how horrible I felt vilifying Ben for something everyone thought was awesome—even me. But I had created my image, and my image said to follow the rules. And fireworks? Not part of the rules. It's a tough box to be in, and I can feel it opening. "He was suspended."

"Where's he now?"

"Graduated," I say. "My teacher confiscated the rest of the fireworks. And they're still in her desk drawer."

"And you know this how?"

I grin. Maybe this is my way of undoing what I said. "Sometimes being teacher's pet pays off."

"You and I are very different people."

"Yeah." I shrug. "We are. Is that okay?"

He cocks his head to the side and looks at me for the first time. "Yeah. But, hey, before we go, give me a second."

He runs back in the theater and a minute later he's back. "Sorry, my, uh, sister is here. I wanted to . . . She's with a friend now, so that's cool. This girl who used to go to shows with us. I guess her sister is performing tonight." It isn't much, but how he says it—how *relieved* he seems when he mentions her having a friend to be with—something is there.

"Do you want to go back to her?" I ask tentatively.

He takes a second, then says, "No. No, let's do it."

"Then let's go." I grab his arm, run back through the lobby, down the hall, and backstage.

"I've, uh, never been back here," he whispers, and I want to be like, *Yeah, duh*, but I don't say that. The show's still going; Sarah's wearing my headset now. They have to be wondering where I went; they're definitely pissed. You don't mess with the tech girls. I feel that pang in my stomach, pulling me back. But . . . I don't want to go. Because everything looks fine. The bands are playing, the show is going on. They don't need me right now.

I lead Vincent around the backstage, through old set pieces and the pulleys for the rig system, past the flight of stairs that leads to the prop closet, and over to the stagecraft room. Once inside, we walk past all the paint-splattered wooden tables and paint cans to another door that leads to the drama teacher's office. I pull out my key.

"You have a *key*?" he asks.

"Of course I do." I know Ms. Weisman won't miss the fireworks; she probably doesn't even remember having them. She asked me to clean out the office last week; who knows, I might have thrown them away back then. But why *didn't* I throw them away back then? Well, because. I wanted to preserve the memory.

Inside the office, Vincent looks around while I go straight to the desk and pull out the handful of sparklers and fireworks.

"Voilà!" I say proudly.

"Okay, wow, you weren't kidding."

"Cool, right?"

"Extremely," he says, taking one and examining it. "I'm still kind of thrown that you're doing this."

"So am I. I'm just . . ."

"Tired?"

"Exhausted," I agree.

"Yeah, me too," he says, scuffing his shoes on the floor. "I thought I'd do this—you know, selling tickets—to be part of something. And impress my sister. But, uh . . ."

"You sequestered yourself inside a ticket booth."

"Yep."

"But . . . I guess it worked, right? I mean, your sister came . . ."

"Yeah," he says with a smile. And I feel it.

"I originally did theater to have a voice. I was really shy and thought if I forced myself to be someone else in front of people, I'd open up."

"Did it work?"

"Kind of. I guess I'm not as shy anymore—obviously—but I think I keep playing roles instead of playing myself."

"So who are you right now?"

"I don't know? Probably not me, but far from what I have been, and that's cool. Maybe doing the two extremes will make me find the happy medium."

"So your happy medium is a thief who keeps people in check."

"What every girl aspires to be."

He laughs and I smile and we stand like that, looking at each other, realizing that we really have no clue who the other is.

"Okay," I say. "I guess let's do this."

"Let's do this," he says.

We walk through the classroom and return backstage.

"Where are we . . . doing this anyway? What's the plan?" Vincent whispers.

"I have no clue," I admit. We're standing in the shadows, only visible if you really look, and of course no one is. There's a lot of noise backstage and in the audience, but there's no one onstage. I look at my phone and realize the time—it's the end of the show. Everyone is waiting to see who won.

I look up and a glimmer of gold catches my eye. Fairy dust.

I walk behind Vincent and slowly untie the rope knotted around a hook on the wall. "Last year we did *Peter Pan*. We made Peter fly by using our fly system. Toward the end, when you have to clap to make Tinker Bell live, we released fairy dust onto the stage and it was, you know, exciting. It was rigged onto the fly system. We can tie the sparklers onto the fly system, then lower them during the announcement of the winner."

"Cool," he says.

I take the sparklers out of my pocket and grab the duct tape in the corner that's always there for emergencies. I tie the twenty sparklers onto the hook and make sure they're as tight as possible. (I want to make a statement, not burn the place to the ground.) I look across the stage and see Sarah. She can probably see me if she looks hard enough, or knows to look, but she doesn't. Probably still cursing me out.

The lights turn on and Mr. Bolivar goes onstage, beaming at the audience. The judges walk up to join him.

"All right, ladies and gentlemen, let's give it up for all of the competitors! Wasn't it an amazing show?"

Applause, whistles, shouts. I want to pay attention, but I can't. The rope in my hands feels heavy, and my heart is racing. Now that the stage lights are fully on, if we take a step, we'll be illuminated. We crowd around the pole, arms touching, trying to be—ironically—as small and invisible as possible.

"In third place we have . . . Breakfast of Champions!" Leon, Gita, Sophia, and Beckett run onstage and holler. Leon does a rather suggestive pose, and Gita waves to someone in the audience.

"In second place we have . . . Megan Talley!" Knew it. Megan runs onstage and bows. She grins at someone in the audience. Probably Steven. I try to shake the feeling away.

"And in first place in this year's Battle of the Bands we have . . ."

"Now," I whisper. "Light them." Vincent gets out a lighter and lights each sparkler in one swift movement. Without another thought, I pull on the rope so the group of sparklers flies high over the stage. A trail of smoke and dots of light float behind the ball of bursting sparkles. It lights up the stage just as Safe & Sound is announced the winner.

I look up and laugh, feeling a weight leave my chest. I feel . . . free . . . like my thoughts and worries and blocks I put on myself are all escaping. I'm glimmering. The world is glimmering. Rodney and Raven from Safe & Sound hug in wild excitement, celebrating their moment just as I celebrate mine.

Mr. Bolivar looks up and freezes, clearly not knowing what to do. Does he interrupt their moment? Does he find the culprits? He smiles, nervously, and shakes more hands. Then he sees me. His eyes lock on mine. I look across the stage and see Sarah gaping at me, shaking her head. She's disappointed, and angry I'm busted. But I'll take it.

As Safe & Sound walk offstage to properly celebrate their win, and as the crowd starts to leave, I find myself walking onstage. To my stage. The one I'm always behind, and never on. Just as quickly as the stage lit up, it dies down, the sparklers fizzing out. I turn around and look at the dwindling audience. Instinctively I look for Steven, but I don't see him. He's probably celebrating with Megan. But honestly, that doesn't matter. Because here I am.

Vincent, too, is onstage with me, looking straight into the audience at a girl staring back at him. His sister? They smile at each other.

I give him a second, and then say, "Let's go." I lead the way out— back through the stagecraft room, past the office, and through the drama room's door, out into the night. It's dark out, and despite it being dark backstage, my eyes still take a second to adjust. There are some kids running from across the way and I swear they're howling.

"That was pretty cool. You're going to get in trouble, aren't you?" Vincent asks.

"Yeah, definitely. I don't know. It's okay."

And it is. So many emotions bubble inside me, I don't know what to do or say. I did something amazing, something completely outrageous. *I did it.* I just want to scream, but instead I hug Vincent and let out a loud "Ha."

"What're you doing next weekend?" I ask.

"I dunno," he says, giving me a smile I hadn't seen all night.

In the background I can hear it—music. But who? No bands are left. Still, with the music playing fast and hard behind us, life feels a little perfect.

Music can set the world on fire.

And tonight, for a brief moment, so did I.

THE SISTERHOOD OF LIGHT AND SOUND

JEFF ZENTNER

An unspoken rule of the Sisterhood of Light and Sound (SOLAS) was that all chitchat during setup for a show was to be as arbitrary and unconnected to the task at hand as possible, a sort of conversational *Look, Ma, no hands*, to signal blasé confidence. They adhered to this convention while prepping the stage for the Raritan River High School Battle of the Bands.

"Wait, you thought he was Laura Linney's *husband*?" Hailey asked, her incredulity momentarily halting her mic-cord winding.

Katrina fiddled with a malcontent mic stand. "This cockeyed turd has erectile dysfunction," she muttered to herself. Then back to Hailey: "*He is her husband.* That's why she doesn't cheat with Karl even though his abs look like a wooden muffin tin."

Hailey gave Katrina a skeptical look.

Katrina returned the look. "You think Laura Linney was afraid to cheat on *her brother*?"

"Why are you assuming that cheating has anything to do with anything? Sometimes people just change their mind about boning."

"By the way, do you love that they landed on the name Karl for the sexiest dude in the movie?"

"'This was the hunkiest name we could imagine. Karl.'"

"Instead of, like, Jaxby or Falkyn."

They both laughed.

Hailey was about to say *Chadward*, but stopped short as Sarah strode purposefully up the aisle toward the stage, clipboard under one arm. The roll of gaffer's tape and holster with multitool festooning her belt slapped at her sides, making a sound like the head of staff in an English manor house clapping crisply for everyone to come to attention.

Katrina and Hailey did just that.

"What's with that cord?" Sarah asked.

"It's fritzing out," Hailey said.

"That's drum mic three." Sarah clutched her clipboard to her chest and beat a tattoo on it with her fingers, as though to remind Hailey what a drum was. Sarah *really* loved her clipboard. It wasn't a normal clipboard made out of that sort of vague cardboard with a creaky, tarnished guillotine-like clip. It was clear plexiglass—sleek and modern—its gleaming silver bar clip with an ergonomic little swoop in the middle for ease of gripping. An Apple sticker adorned the top left corner. In the top right corner, a sticker of her father's band: Arthur Crow and the Condemned.

Sarah was rightfully proud of them, even though their iconic '80s post-punk goth-rock status brought her little social cachet at their Post Malone– and Lizzo-fixated school. Her father was one of the most famous people in New Brunswick, New Jersey—a far cry from his relatively lesser celebrity in Los Angeles, where they'd lived until a couple years prior, when Sarah's stepmother, a native New Brunswickian, decided she needed to be near her ailing parents.

"I know." Hailey pointed at the tape tag with DRUM MIC 3 written in Sarah's architectural handwriting.

"It was *vocal* mic three that was janky."

"Oops. I rock." Hailey made sure to say *I rock* instead of *I'm sorry*, which Sarah mandated because young women were expected to apologize too much.

"Put that one back, get a new cord from the navy blue bin—*not* the cerulean bin—label it, pull the janky cord, toss it in my solder pile."

Katrina made a final adjustment to the mic stand. "Speaking of which, Brenner has a bum jack on his guitar. It was cutting out during sound check."

Sarah opened her mouth to speak.

Katrina headed her off. "Yes, I checked it with another cord. Two, actually."

Sarah came as close to smiling as she ever did during preshow. She loved profound competence above all else. "Hey, you two might just pull this off without me next year. Tell Brenner to see me in the sound booth in twenty minutes. I gotta heat up my soldering iron. Did I tell you my dad got me a new one for tour?"

Katrina and Hailey swapped a quick *Uh oh, now we have to feign excitement over a soldering iron* glance.

"What kind?" Hailey asked.

"Hexacon Therm-O-Trac," Sarah said, with casual humility.

"Wow," Katrina and Hailey said simultaneously. Sarah was often lacking at reading sarcasm, but they still strived for as much earnestness as possible.

"Hey, in *Love Actually*, is the guy who Laura Linney visits in the care facility her husband or her brother?" Katrina asked.

Sarah was already back to studying her clipboard with furrowed brow, but she didn't hesitate or look up. "Brother. Obviously. Hey, when Rock Your Mouth is on, will one of you slyly turn the volume down on the guitar amp and I'll goose the guitar in the monitor so he won't notice? His stage volume is a pain in the ovaries."

"I'll handle it," Katrina said. "No, but listen. He moved to England with her. She calls him 'darling.'"

"Siblings move together," Sarah said. "When my dad first moved to the US from Australia, his brother came with."

"And you can call your brother 'darling,'" Hailey said. "Beckett and I call each other 'loverpants.'" Mentioning her and her twin sister's mutual pet name gave Hailey a twinge in the solar plexus. It always feels wrong to refer to one of the private rituals you share with someone you love when you're on the outs with them.

"Then why won't she bone Karl?!" Katrina practically shouted, turning a few heads in the bustling auditorium. "If Beck was going bonkers and you had a chance to bone a cool hunk named Karl—"

"Never use the phrase 'a cool hunk named Karl' ever again; it stresses me out," Hailey said. "And it depends on when. If Beck were freaking out right now, I'd let her and still bone Karl."

"Twin drama?" Sarah asked.

Hailey sighed. "Not speaking at the moment."

"You okay?" Katrina asked.

"Fine."

Hailey wasn't, though. She wasn't lying when she said that she and Beckett weren't speaking at the moment. But what she left unsaid (because saying it felt like peeling off a scab) was that she and Beckett hadn't been speaking for a *lot* of moments. In fact, they hadn't talked much all year, since their grinding and agonizing drift apart upon arriving at their new school and finding themselves on unequal social footing. At this point, Hailey couldn't remember if the wedge between her and Beckett was the not-talking or whether the not-talking was because of the distancing.

It didn't really matter. The reasons for an estrangement never matter as much as the end result, which is a lot of pain. The slow alienations hurt most of all because you can't trace them back to a single, possibly reparable mistake. Instead, they seem like something inevitable— a larger failure.

And it heaped insult on injury when Beckett started joining bands late in the school year without so much as hinting that Miss Somewhere, their band, should play the Battle of the Bands. If she had, Hailey would have instantly swallowed her pride and met her halfway by explicitly suggesting it. But no olive branch of a hint? No pride swallowing.

The auditorium began filling with a trickle of groups of two to four people.

Sarah checked her phone. "Okay, showtime in twenty-five. Should we go do the Ritual?"

"This'll be SOLAS's final Ritual together," Hailey said, with the mournful air of someone thinking about yet another way their life was shrinking.

"I'm just gonna go tell Brenner to meet us in the sound booth in, like, ten. See you guys up there," Katrina said. She strode away.

Once Katrina had left earshot, Hailey extended an open palm to Sarah. "Pay up."

Sarah folded her arms. "What?"

"You know what."

"I said she'd be chill and you said zero chill?"

"I remember well."

"So."

"So pay up," Hailey said.

"Dude, she was chill."

"In what universe was that chill behavior?"

Sarah repositioned a mic in front of one of the amps approximately one millimeter. "She was like, 'Brenner has a bad jack, I'll tell him to meet us in the sound booth.' That's reasonably chill behavior, especially for her."

"That's just it: I'm not at *all* sure he really has a bum jack," Hailey said.

"And also the Earth is flat and vaccines cause autism, right?"

"You notice *any* cutting out during sound check?"

"No, but—"

"Me neither. She's planting evidence."

"*But.* I was going to say that I was distracted resetting drum levels because Beckett is like a different human being with every band," Sarah said.

"It's what makes her a great drummer."

"She kicks ass. It's just, if you're gonna have the same drummer in four bands, consistency would be nice."

Hailey knelt and positioned a piece of gaffer's tape over a mic cord on the floor. "What would have been nice is if she'd made time in her busy schedule for her own sister, but whatevs. We need to revisit why you owe me ten bucks."

"Oh, *do* tell."

"So Katrina invents a problem with Brenner's guitar—"

"Says you."

"*So Katrina invents a problem with Brenner's guitar.* And then who oh-so-casually offers to go fetch BrenBren to sort the fake issue?"

"Well, here's where your argument falls apart because I literally told Katrina to go fetch Bren Muffin."

"No, here's where I've gained the upper hand because Katrina *knew* that you couldn't be bothered to fetch Kylie Brenner yourself, so the most logical person to delegate to would be *the person standing right in front of you.* Who was Katrina, thus allowing her to maintain her paper-thin facade of chillness."

"No, here's where I've bested you—" Sarah said.

"*Bested* me?"

"Yes, bested you, because you posit a world that Katrina Garza moves through like a chess grandmaster, thinking thirty moves ahead, all in the service of bagging Brenmo."

Hailey looked at Sarah.

"Brenmo, like Venmo," Sarah said.

"Yes."

"You were staring at me blankly."

"I was giving you my *You're pretending not to know the truth, but you're gradually putting things together* look," Hailey said.

"That's a lot to hang on a single, frankly pretty inexpressive look."

"Ten bucks."

Sarah checked the time. "We better go do the Ritual."

Brenner's back was turned, and he was noodling on his guitar, the unamplified Strat sounding pale and thin—rather like him. Katrina thought he resembled David Bowie. He did inasmuch as both he and

David Bowie were terrestrial, bipedal, bilaterally symmetric, carbon-based, mammalian life-forms. At any lesser level of abstraction, the comparison crumbled.

"Hey," Katrina said after taking a deep breath and smoothing her midnight-blue hair.

Brenner spun, narrowly missing the bridge of her nose with his headstock. "Hey."

Katrina affected a schoolmarmish voice and wagged her finger. "Now, careful with that contraption, mister; you'll put someone's eye out, so. *A Christmas Story*? No? It's fine. Anyway. What?" *I'm referencing yet another Christmas movie within a fifteen-minute span?*

"I didn't say anything . . . just, 'Hey.' Also, I heard it was a BB gun in *Christmas Story*."

"Have you not seen it?!"

"Nope."

Be cool, don't go too big. Stick the landing. "Well . . . you . . . big old . . . piece of shit."

Brenner looked at Katrina like she just sneezed in his mouth. "Wow."

". . . is what my friends and I call each other . . . as a term of endearment," Katrina quickly added, her face incandescing a baboon's-ass vermillion. Her laugh sounded like a vibrating cell phone chittering across a glass coffee table.

"Oh."

"So. Nervous to play?"

Brenner shrugged. "Sorta."

"I'm not saying you should be." *Don't do weird voices. Don't do weird voices. Don't do—* "But," Katrina began, in what might generously be called a British accent, "I'm also not saying you *shouldn't* be. Just be the right level of nervous. Or, actually, don't be anything. Just . . . *be*. Live, laugh, love."

Brenner stared. "What's—"

"I don't know."

"Is that from something?"

"No. It's just a thing moms who like boxed wine say."

"I thought it was from another movie I hadn't seen."

"No."

"Don't wanna look like a big old piece of shit again."

Katrina laughed. This time it sounded like a spoon caught in a garbage disposal. "Yeah, no. No. No no no. No."

"You're running sound, right?"

"And lights."

"I thought I saw you setting up for sound check."

He noticed me! British accent again: "That's little old me, innit. I'm just a little sound-checking bird, innit, mate."

"Are you, like, a drama kid? You seem like one."

"Uh."

"I meant it as a compliment."

Since humankind's adoption of symbolic language, there has not been a more devastating compliment than being told you seem like a drama kid.

"Oh. Thanks? But no. I'm on crew."

"Cool. So, did you want to tell me something?" Brenner asked.

I'm busted. He knows. I don't know how, but he knows. "Like . . . what?" Katrina asked.

Brenner eyed her strangely. "Like . . . do you need me to sound-check again or something?"

"Oh!" *Whew!* "Yeah, you had a short in your jack." She pointed at his guitar.

"I didn't notice—"

"Yeah. Short in the jack. I heard it while you were sound-checking." *Don't. Don't do it.* "Guess it's better than having a jack in your shorts, am I right?"

Brenner's forehead wrinkled.

Katrina's face grew hot(ter). "Like masturb—"

"You think I would crank off in my shorts at a *battle of the bands*?"

"*No.* Lord, no! I don't think you'd ever crank off in your shorts at such an inappropriate time. Only at an appropriate time . . . for cranking off in your shorts. Not that I've thought about it at all, because I haven't. Ever. Gross."

"I was also joking."

"Oh." Katrina laughed louder than was strictly necessary. "Jokes! Love them."

"I didn't even hear a short in my jack."

"Yeah, it's there. So if you wanna drop by the sound booth in ten minutes or so, we can get that fixed. The short in your jack. Not the jack in your shorts. Joke. Joking. Okay, bye."

"If Katrina starts doing jokes and voices, it's over," Sarah said, positioning a wooden incense holder, threading a stick of nag champa into it, and setting a cigarette lighter beside it.

"Her jokes always come in about thirty percent hotter than they should," Hailey agreed.

Someone knocked at the sound booth door. Sarah and Hailey quickly hushed, even though Katrina wouldn't have felt the need to knock. Hailey answered. It was Beckett.

Hailey's heart surged. Before Beckett could say anything, Hailey had already envisioned Beckett's apology for the distance between them that year—accepting full blame and absolving her. She imagined her own magnanimous acceptance of said apology in which, as a gesture of reconciliation, she'd accept some of the responsibility. She'd say something like *We both could have done more.* She'd say—

Beckett stared at Hailey for a second with an unreadable expression, looking like she was seeking words but fumbling them.

Hailey stared back. "What? We're getting ready for the show." It came out sharper than she'd intended, but she wanted to hustle along Beckett's apology so she could accept it and they could be *them* again.

Beckett looked taken aback, her mouth slightly open, but still said nothing.

"Did you need to tell me something?" Again, Hailey said this with a smidgen more of an edge than she'd hoped, but Beckett was trying her patience.

"I need to talk to Sarah," Beckett finally said.

Hailey deflated and suddenly felt like crying. "She's busy." She tempered her tone with none of the magnanimity she'd laid in reserve to accept Beckett's nonforthcoming apology.

"I literally see her right over your shoulder."

"She's *busy* right over my shoulder. What do you want?"

Hailey could hear Sarah behind her, still puttering away as if to say, *Sorry, not getting involved.*

Beckett's voice was clenched. "Tell Sarah I wanted to use a different snare with the Marcia, Marcia, Marcias."

Hailey folded her arms because she didn't know what to do with her hands. "Sarah told me to tell you that we're back-lining the drum kit and we're not doing a new drum mix just so you can sound point-zero-four percent better with one of your nineteen bands."

"Hailey."

"Beck."

"Come on."

"I'm actually also super busy right now, so . . ."

"Can we talk for literally one second?"

"We've just been talking for literally one second about your sixty-third band, and now, *oops*, I'm all out of seconds." Hailey said.

"Hay—" Beckett started to say, but Hailey shut the door in her face before she could finish.

"Harsh," Sarah said.

Hailey didn't reply but busied herself answering a text. Her heart ached.

"You aren't in uniform, by the way." Sarah nodded down at Hailey's white-toed Chucks. Sarah required the wearing of all black, with all-black Chucks.

Hailey rolled her eyes and flounced over to a duffel bag in the corner, from which she removed a pair of black-toed Chucks, and sat on the floor to switch shoes.

Sarah's face tensed. "Oh, *now* you're giving me attitude? We're going to let things fall apart in our last show together?"

Hailey exhaled loudly through her nose. "Things aren't gonna *fall apart* if I have the wrong color rubber on my Chucks." This was all Hailey needed—to get into it with Sarah at the exact same moment that she had newly reopened her festering wound with Beckett.

Sarah turned to the soundboard, but then back to Hailey. "We've never talked about this, have we."

"About what?"

"You want to work in music, right?"

"Yeah."

"So, the couple of times I've worked my dad's shows before this upcoming tour, I got treated like dogshit. Dudes explaining to me the difference between an XLR input and a quarter-inch input. Guys who had been on my dad's crew for like a week giving me their coffee orders. And I'm not even sure they *didn't* know who I was. My point is that women in music have basically zero margin for error. We have to be five times as good as the men at everything just to be taken seriously. That's why I and everyone who works with me have to be five times better. Front to back, head to toe. Everything matters. Always."

Hailey's and Sarah's eyes met for a moment, and Hailey suddenly felt profound regret that this would likely be the last time they would ever work together. Sarah could be a real pain in the ass with her perfectionism. But she was on to something. And there's something bizarrely comforting about people who care not what you think of them. It means you have no reason to question it when they show you love.

Katrina burst in. "Hey, Sarah, I passed Beckett coming here and she asked—"

"No," Hailey said curtly.

"All righty," Katrina said. "Glad we were able to hash that out."

"We talked. The answer is nope."

"Okay," Katrina said slowly.

"Ladies, the hour is upon us," Sarah said. She picked up the lighter next to the incense holder and lit the stick of incense.

Sarah had picked up the tradition from her dad's former sound guy Curly, who kept a steady stream of nag champa burning during shows. Said it centered him, which allowed him to hear the mix better. To be sure, Curly also famously believed that holding in farts could cause liver damage, which may have been the true reason for the incense. Anyway.

Sarah placed the incense holder on the floor. The three encircled it and joined hands as the aromatic smoke wafted upward.

"O Great and Mysterious Goddess," Sarah intoned in a solemn voice, "she who has given us gaffer's tape and the SM57, let this Battle of the Bands not be a complete shit show."

"*Amen*," Hailey and Katrina murmured.

"Grant unto us patience in the face of requests for more vocals in the monitors," Hailey said.

"*Amen*."

"Guide our hands in stopping feedback," Katrina said. "Both the sonic kind and the kind where people wanna tell you what you could improve."

"*Amen*."

"Give us the grace not to cut the mics during ukulele covers of rap songs," Sarah said.

"*Amen*."

"Deliver us from acoustic guitarists who want to plug directly into the PA," Hailey said.

"*Amen*."

Sarah paused for several moments. When she spoke, it was with greater soberness than usual for the Ritual. "Thank you, Goddess, for the Sisterhood of Light and Sound. All the good times we've had together. May our group text be undying."

Katrina and Hailey were unaccustomed to such emotional nudity from Sarah.

They always went until they had nothing more to say, and then they finished out the Ritual by watching a YouTube montage of Nicolas Cage freakouts, followed by a video of "Hey Ya!" by Outkast where the song speeds up every time they say "uh" or "all right."

This time, though, after they ran dry of things to say, they stood there quietly, holding hands in a circle. One last time.

Brenner knocked on the sound booth door at about five minutes before showtime. Sarah pretended at annoyance, but truthfully, she was glad to employ her new soldering iron. Maybe three minutes had elapsed when she sent Brenner on his way with his Squier Strat in hand, nary a short in his jack or a jack in his shorts to be found.

With the air of a beneficent potentate, Sarah instructed Katrina to accompany Brenner to test his guitar and bring it back if there were any problems. Sarah knew there wouldn't be. Katrina knew Sarah knew. And Katrina was grateful.

The show began.

"So. You excited for tour?" Hailey asked Sarah, over the music.

"Yeah," Sarah said. The ambivalent timbre in her voice was unmistakable even through the cacophony. In forty-eight hours, she would be behind the soundboard at the Bowery Ballroom, watching her father hold a midsize crowd of mostly forty- and fifty-somethings in his thrall.

"Yeah?"

"It'll be one of the longest stretches I've gotten to see my dad in, like, my life."

"That's cool. Spending time with family is important," Hailey said wistfully.

Katrina reentered, trailing a rosy, giddy energy behind her like the sillage of a fine perfume.

The three watched the band onstage. What the musicians lacked in technique, they made up for in ebullient golden-retriever-esque enthusiasm.

Sarah nudged one of the sliders on the board approximately three atoms' length. "I always felt like . . . my dad wasn't mine. As if he belonged to everyone in the world more than me. There are some people who, when I tell them who my dad is, act like they want to ask me to name my top three favorite Arthur Crow and the Condemned albums, like he's more theirs than mine because they're bigger fans. And don't even get me started on the goth weirdos sliding into my Insta DMs trying to get to my dad through me."

As the Grants—a favorite of SOLAS because of their Joan Jett–esque vibe—started to play, Sarah, Katrina, and Hailey swapped glances.

"Am I hearing that lyric right?" Katrina asked.

Hailey cupped a hand to her ear. "I'm getting *heart shitter.*"

Katrina closed her eyes and listened intently. "Could it be *hard shitter?*"

"What's a hard shitter?"

"I dunno. Like not enough dietary fiber? What's a heart shitter?"

"Whichever it is, it's *shitter* that's really the operative part." Hailey turned to Sarah. "Didn't Bolivar lay down some no-cussing policy? Aren't we supposed to cut their mics?"

Sarah leaned against the mixing board (careful not to nudge any of the sliders) and folded her arms. "Sorry, what? I didn't hear any profanity because I was too busy." She studied her pinky nail and nibbled at a corner.

"Aha, yes . . . I was also too busy to hear any lyrics about heart shitting," Hailey said with a broad wink.

"Or possibly hard shitting, it's kinda tough to tell," Katrina said, also with an exaggerated wink.

Suddenly, the sound died. The auditorium erupted in boos and shouts of "Let them play."

Sarah spun around. "*Bolivar!* So help me God, if he touched the snake . . ." she muttered as she barreled past Katrina and Hailey, out the sound booth door.

Katrina and Hailey were both abundantly aware that "snake" referred to the bundle of mic cables running from the stage to the sound booth, but Sarah had instilled in them an indelible sense of duty, and so they felt duty-bound to snicker at "if he touched the snake."

They laughed, too, because it might be their final chance to enjoy Sarah's offering a tossed-off double entendre while charging into action—something that had traditionally occurred with some frequency. Katrina and Hailey could never be sure if it was intentional on Sarah's part—she played things arrow-straight—but they appreciated the ribald superhero-ness of it nonetheless.

Sarah returned, huffing and ruddy with the bright heat of recent confrontation, as the next band prepared to take the stage. She quickly consulted her mix notes and made adjustments to the board.

The show continued.

Breakfast of Champions.

I Want Your P.S.

Safe & Sound.

Shifter Focus.

Amina Aboud.

SOLAS was in the zone—each band sounded amazing. Well, that is to say: SOLAS ensured each band sounded as amazing as the musicians' abilities permitted. But each band, regardless of musical acumen, bathed in Katrina's artful lighting, glowed as if composed of some rare element under fluorescence.

Hailey looked out at the stage and saw Lilly, the stage manager, in the wings looking harried. Someone must have touched the curtains—the unpardonable sin in Lil's credo. "How's it going down there, Lil?" Hailey asked into her headset, over the din of Reckless Love.

Lil sounded at wit's end. "Why are they all like this?"

Hailey turned to Sarah. "Why are all musicians like this?"

"Like what?" Sarah studied the soundboard.

"Annoying in a way that makes Lil ask why they're all annoying."

"You're a musician. You tell me."

"I thought growing up with a famous musician would give you some insight."

Big Talk started up sans their normal lead singer. Sarah feigned annoyance at having to mix in a new vocalist on the fly, but she wasn't fooling anyone—she loved the challenge. She dialed their sound in and turned back to Hailey and Katrina. "Anyway. Famous," Sarah said, picking their conversation back up with a sad laugh. "My dad was just big enough that we had all the downsides of celebrity—like people posting pics of him looking like shit, making fun of him for moving to New Brunswick, and creepy stalkers—but none of the upsides, like him making enough money to retire from constant touring and be at his daughter's birthday parties. Very cool level of fame."

This was the most Sarah had ever opened up to Katrina and Hailey about anything. Katrina and Hailey had never been to her house for more than a few minutes. They'd never met her father even though both were secretly dying to.

"You know what's funny?" Sarah continued. "I never dreamed of running sound. I got into it as a way to get my dad to take me on tour with him. I worked *so* hard to get good enough at it that he'd consider me. Working shitty outdoor shows and running sound at bar mitzvahs and apprenticing with sound guys who didn't want me around. And now?" Sarah laughed ruefully. "I wish I could spend summer with my friends like a normal person and still somehow see my dad regularly. Guess we always want what we can't have."

A commotion from the auditorium drew their attention back to the performance. They looked in time to see Aaron, the front man of Big Talk, being pushed from the stage. Then April, their bassist, and Jess, who wasn't even in Big Talk, started making out onstage like they were fighting for possession of a single tongue.

"Lil, are you seeing this?" Hailey said into her headset.

"What is happening?" Lilly responded. "Did they just kick out their lead singer and then start making out?"

"So badass."

The final four bands queued up backstage. Sarah, Katrina, and Hailey, knowing that they were on the downslope of their time together, kicked their reminiscing into high gear.

They remembered the time that they were running lights and sound for the school's production of *Rent*, and they caught Katrina softly singing *"Six thousand twenty-two hundred four thousand minutes, four hundred fifty-two thousand moments so dear"* quite earnestly to herself as she broke down the stage. "They're just singing numbers, right?" Katrina had asked. "No, in fact, the song literally says many times that the number they're singing is the number of minutes in a year," Sarah explained. They laughed until they hiccuped. Hailey tried to get them to try a "surefire" cure, which was to count their hiccups until they got to ten, but after counting a couple of hiccups sequentially, they started going *"Seven thousand forty-two thousand six million hiccups,"* and so forth until they were worse off than before.

They remembered working an orchestra concert, during which they were so bored that Hailey suggested they try to do impressions of themselves—as in Hailey would try to do an impression of Hailey, Katrina would try to do an impression of Katrina. It turned out that it was exceedingly difficult to impersonate one's self—an enterprise doomed to hilarious failure. They later learned that they were heard chortling in the sound booth during a particularly quiet portion of a requiem. It was the rarest lapse of professionalism for Sarah, who took a dim view of their hijinks ever encroaching upon their work. But this one she shrugged off. "It was either that or fall asleep," she'd said.

The more they talked, the more they realized how little time they'd had together and how few memories they'd gotten the chance to make. It seemed like many, many more until they laid them out on the table. It wasn't nearly enough.

They were reliving the time when they were running lights and sound for an assembly and the principal got mad at the constant buzz of talking. In a huff, he'd tried to say, *Hey, folks, I have people to see and things to do*, but he got flustered and instead said, "Hey, folks, I have things to see and people to do," which sent the crowd into paroxysms of glee. Sarah's antennae visibly went up as Katrina finished her recounting of the story, tears of laughter streaming down her face.

"What?" Hailey asked.

"Where's Lil?" Sarah craned, scanning around.

"Dunno. Why?" Hailey asked.

"Haven't seen her for a while," Sarah murmured.

"Want me to text her?" Katrina asked.

But Sarah was already out the door. "Gonna be a shit show without someone shepherding," she called over her shoulder as she sprinted down toward the backstage area. She was never happy about being pulled away from Hailey and Katrina in the sound booth under the best of circumstances. And being pulled away for a second time during the final show of the Sisterhood of Light and Sound was far from the best of circumstances. But saving the day and keeping things running was what Sarah did.

The Battle of the Bands wrapped. As the winners were being announced, a mass of sputtering, blazing sparklers floated over the stage on wires, like a flaming sprite, trailing smoke and sparks behind it. The crowd gasped at the ardent spectacle.

Hailey and Katrina were no less awestruck.

"Holy shit," Katrina said, eyes shimmering like a child's. "That rules."

"Is *that* where Lil went?" Hailey murmured.

"Gotta be. She knows the wire suspension system. Plus, nobody else is getting away with horseplay like that with Lil on the prowl."

"She asked me once if we ever get tired of nobody seeing the work we do. Looks like Lil decided to get herself seen for once."

"Respect."

"Sarah's gonna shit like ninety-three bricks over fire code."

"Lil would have, too, before Lil maybe perpetrated this."

"Out with a bang."

Safe & Sound was crowned winner, wreathed in the last remnants of the smoke from Lilly's final hurrah.

Sarah, Hailey, and Katrina waited in the wings for the crowd to disperse before going quietly to work, a collective leaden sadness having enveloped them as they prepared to tear down the stage and thereby lay to rest the Sisterhood of Light and Sound, committing it to golden memory.

As Katrina was carefully winding a mic cord (*Nice big loops; the cord has a soul. Listen to it tell you how it wants to be wound,* Sarah taught), she spied Brenner approaching. Her heart buzzed against her ribs like a junebug against a screen door, her melancholy notwithstanding.

"Hey," he said.

"You guys kicked ass," Katrina said in her normal voice, without even being tempted to add a sweaty joke. Being in a somber mood was serving her well in terms of comporting herself with relative dignity.

"My jack worked fine. My guitar jack, I mean."

Katrina summoned a smile.

"So, my band and I were gonna grab Taco Bell after this, if you wanna come."

Katrina looked at Hailey and Sarah.

"It's cool," Sarah said. "Hailey and I got this."

A couple of moments passed. Katrina turned back to Brenner. "I'm gonna stay and help tear down, and then I think Sarah and Hailey and I were going to hang. But I'd love to get together another time."

"Shoot me your number." Brenner got out his phone and entered Katrina's number. "Everything okay?" he asked. "You seem different than before."

Katrina didn't answer for a second but looked wistfully at Sarah and Hailey. They were kneeling, disconnecting mic cables from the snake, laughing about something. "I'm good."

"Cool. Text me?"

"I will." She was not lying.

As Brenner turned to leave, he almost ran headlong into Beckett, who was ascending the stage steps, tapping her drumsticks nervously against her thighs. Hailey put an SM57 in the mic case and stood to face her sister.

They looked at each other without speaking, the weight of what they'd weathered in the last year—moving, changing schools, growing apart, their most recent fight, their catalogue of heartbreaks, late-night songwriting sessions—heavy on them. If there was one lesson Hailey had taken from this evening, it was that it's a terrible thing to be apart from someone you love. If there was another, it's that family—both the kind joined by a compact of blood and the kind bound by a shared history of shoddy mic cables, unreasonable demands for more vocals in the monitors, strictly mandated black Chuck Taylors, and impassioned movie arguments—matters above all else.

"You rocked tonight," Hailey said quietly. "With your various and sundry bands."

"I'm really sorry, Hay."

"Me too. About this week. About tonight. Bailing on our Halloween costume. About all the shit this year, really."

"I've missed you," Beckett said.

"Same, loverpants," Hailey said.

They smiled at each other, more warmly than they had in a long time. There was more to say and to work through. But it looked like the ice on the path there was thawing.

Beckett spun her drumsticks. "You got a Miss Somewhere song in you?"

"Now?"

"There's an amp, and the drum kit is still set up," Sarah said.

"Play us out," Katrina said. "Give us some teardown music."

Sarah pulled an SM58 from the mic case, walked over to one of the collapsed mic stands, set it up, put the mic in the clip, then deftly ran a mic cable to the snake. She sprinted in the direction of the sound booth, calling behind her shoulder, "You like a pretty wet reverb on your vocals, right?" Sarah knew the answer already, so Hailey didn't bother responding.

"I'm kinda guitarless," Hailey said. "I wasn't planning on playing tonight."

"Be right back—" Beckett said, walking backstage. She returned holding Hailey's Fender Jazzmaster by the neck. "Hey, look. Last time you put away your guitar, it must have fallen off the stand and rolled a couple miles here."

Hailey smiled and took her guitar from her twin. She slung it on, plugged it into the amp, and dialed in her sound, playing a couple of chords. She walked up to the mic. Beckett took a seat behind the drum kit and thumped the kick a few times.

Sarah called down from the sound booth, "You're live and ready to go."

And go they did. Hailey didn't check the mic. No need with Sarah behind the board. Beck counted them in, and Miss Somewhere started into one of their originals like a wave slowly breaking onshore. They sounded like Mazzy Star meets Beach House, and they had the sort of effortless chemistry that only people who once shared a womb can have. They had a sense of each other the way you have a sense of yourself, how you can perfectly touch the tip of your nose without looking.

Sarah and Katrina, who had never before heard them, stopped work to watch in wonder.

"They'd have won," Katrina said to Sarah.

"No question. Good job with Brenner, by the way."

Katrina beamed. "My jokes worked."

"Please consider that it wasn't your jokes specifically but rather your winning personality more generally that sealed the deal."

They watched quietly for a long time. Katrina couldn't be sure, but she thought she saw Sarah discreetly wipe away a tear or two. And that was surprising. Sarah wasn't the moved-to-tears sort. But she also didn't do the whole make-lots-of-friends thing. Which probably made it hard to leave behind the ones she had. So maybe it wasn't altogether shocking.

It soon became clear that Beckett and Hailey had no intention of stopping anytime soon. They played like they were trying to stitch up a wound that would start bleeding again if they stopped.

But both Katrina and Sarah knew well the keening wish that all good things lasted forever. And so they were in no rush to leave.

They went back to work.

ABOUT THE CONTRIBUTORS

BRITTANY CAVALLARO is the *New York Times* best-selling author of the Charlotte Holmes novels from HarperCollins/Katherine Tegen Books, as well as *Hello Girls* and *Muse*. In high school, she wrote a lot of short stories inspired by Something Corporate songs. Every year Spotify reminds her that Jimmy Eat World is her most-played artist.

PREETI CHHIBBER is an author, speaker, and freelancer. Her screamo claim to fame is that she once held Nate Barcalow's hand so that he wouldn't fall off the railing at a Finch show. She has several books and anthology appearances on the way, but for now you can find her co-hosting the podcast *Desi Geek Girls*. Learn more at PreetiChhibber.com.

JAY COLES is the author of *Tyler Johnson Was Here* and *Things We Couldn't Say*, a composer with the American Society of Composers, Authors, and Publishers, and a professional musician residing in Muncie, Indiana. He is a graduate of Vincennes University and Ball State University and holds degrees in English and liberal arts. Currently, he enjoys playing drums and piano in his free time.

KATIE COTUGNO is the *New York Times* best-selling author of six messy, complicated feminist YA love stories: *99 Days, How to Love, Fireworks, Top Ten, 9 Days & 9 Nights,* and *You Say It First.* She is also the co-author, with Candace Bushnell, of *Rules for Being a Girl.* Her books have been honored by the Junior Library Guild, the Bank Street Children's Book Committee, and the Kentucky Association of School Librarians, among others, and translated into more than fifteen languages. Katie is a Pushcart Prize nominee whose work has appeared in the *Iowa Review,* the *Mississippi Review,* and *Argestes,* as well as many other literary magazines. She studied writing, literature, and publishing at Emerson College and received her MFA in fiction at Lesley University. She lives in Boston with her family and has a knack for accidentally getting stuck behind tall people at concerts.

LAUREN GIBALDI is a public librarian and the author of *The Night We Said Yes, Autofocus,* and *This Tiny Perfect World.* She lives in Orlando, Florida, with her husband and daughters. She drummed for a band that only had one gig—her high school's battle of the bands.

SHAUN DAVID HUTCHINSON is the author of numerous books for young adults, including *We Are the Ants, The Past and Other Things That Should Stay Buried,* and *A Complicated Love Story Set in Space,* as well as the young adult memoir *Brave Face,* chronicling his struggles with depression and coming out. When he's not writing, he's probably baking or playing video games. He currently lives in Seattle. Find Shaun online at shaundavidhutchinson.com.

JUSTIN COURTNEY PIERRE is the lead singer/guitarist of Motion City Soundtrack and has never written a book, best-selling or otherwise.

He did, however, play in multiple high school bands and therefore is an expert on the subject matter contained within this book. Unfortunately, he chose to write about drugs instead. He currently lives in Minneapolis, Minnesota, with his wife and daughter and works far too hard at trying to understand things most people seem to know innately.

ASHLEY POSTON grew up on a heavy dose of rock and roll, but it wasn't until high school that she found her true music calling—punk rock (and she made everyone in marching band listen to her clarinet rendition of "MakeDamnSure" to prove it). Since then, she's retired the clarinet and taken up another hobby—writing. Her set list includes the geeky Once Upon a Con series, the Heart of Iron duology, and *Among the Beasts and Briars*.

JENNY TORRES SANCHEZ is a full-time writer and author of five novels for young adults. She was born in Brooklyn but has lived on the border of two worlds her whole life. She grew up listening to a lot of angsty music and trying to tune out the world around her. She currently lives in Orlando, Florida, with her husband and children. Visit her online at jennytorressanchez.com and follow her on Twitter at @jetchez.

SARAH NICOLE SMETANA is the author of *The Midnights*. Growing up in Orange, CA, she taught herself to play guitar and listened to a steady stream of emo bands, like Saves the Day and the Get Up Kids. In high school, she was often found gallivanting around Southern California's many awesome music venues (sometimes even playing at them) or filling notebooks full of lyrics. She currently lives and writes in Brooklyn. You can visit her online at www.sarahnicolesmetana.com.

ERIC SMITH is an author and literary agent who was once booed at a high school talent show while playing Third Eye Blind on the guitar. Badly. He is the author of *The Geek's Guide to Dating, The Girl and the Grove, Don't Read the Comments,* and *You Can Go Your Own Way.* He lives in Philadelphia with his wife and son.

SARVENAZ TAGHAVIAN is the author of *The Geek's Guide to Unrequited Love* (an Amazon Best Book of the Year and a YALSA Top Ten Quick Pick for Reluctant YA Readers), *Virtually Yours, Three Day Summer,* and more. She was born in Tehran, Iran, and grew up on Long Island, New York. She received her BFA in film and television from NYU's Tisch School of the Arts, which means she got to spend most of college running around making movies (it was a lot of fun). She also spent much of high school relegated to the ensemble of various musicals, which gave her plenty of time to hone her completely useless skill of composing parody lyrics to show tunes. She currently lives in Brooklyn with her husband and two young sons.

JENN MARIE THORNE was lead singer of LA band Punch Buggy Blue for like three weeks and never even played a gig but still acts like she's some rock star. She's now the UK-based author of YA novels *The Wrong Side of Right, Night Music,* and more, as well as books for adults and wee tots.

JASMINE WARGA is the *New York Times* best-selling author of *Other Words for Home, Here We Are Now,* and *My Heart and Other Black Holes.* Her book *Other Words for Home* received a Newbery Honor. She has never been in a band but spent tons of time during high school at the local music venue—Bogarts—listening to emotive indie rock.

ASHLEY WOODFOLK went to Warped Tour multiple times just hoping to get close to the drummer from Yellowcard. When she finally did, she dropped her open water bottle and soaked her Chuck Taylors. Now she frequents emo nights at dive bars in NYC, and though she's always avoided mosh pits, she writes about music like it's her job. She is the author of *The Beauty That Remains*, *When You Were Everything*, and the Flyy Girls series, and is a co-author of *Blackout*. She lives and writes in Brooklyn with her very cute family.

JEFF ZENTNER is the award-winning author of *The Serpent King* and *In the Wild Light*. Before becoming a writer, he was a musician who recorded several albums and appeared on recordings with Iggy Pop, Debbie Harry, Thurston Moore, and Nick Cave.